Prologue

Imagine what lingers on the black bottom of a lake. Debris, rivered in or tossed from boats, grows shaggy and soft. Pouty fish swim their strange lives, far from the hook, in inseparable breath and motion. Imagine patches of lake weed dancing like lithe, unobserved women. Stand on the edge of a lake, the low waves gulping at your shoes, and imagine how close you are to a world as silent and alien as the moon, out of reach of light and heat and sound.

My home is at the bottom of a lake. Our farm lies there, mud bound, its remnants indistinguishable from boat wreckage. Sleek trout troll the remains of my bedroom and the parlor where we sat as a family on Sundays. Barns and troughs rot. Tangled barbed wire rusts. The once fertile land marinates in idleness.

A history-book version of the creation of Blue Mesa Reservoir might portray the project as heroic, part of the grand vision to carry precious water from the Colorado River's tributaries to the arid

Southwest. Good intentions may have plugged the once wild Gunnison River and forced it to be a lake, but I know another story.

I used to stand knee-deep in this section of the Gunnison when it still rushed fast and frothy through the valley of my birth, the vast and lonely Big Blue wilderness rising above it. I knew the town of Iola when it woke each morning to fragrant breakfasts and bustling farms and ranches, how the sunrise illuminated the east side of Main then inched uptown, across the train tracks and schoolyard, to ignite the tiny church's one round red-and-blue stained-glass window. I timed my life by the hollow whistle of the 9:22, the 2:05, the 5:47. I knew all the shortcuts and townsfolk and the oldest gnarled tree consistently producing the sweetest peaches in my family's orchard. And I knew, perhaps more than most, the sadness of this place.

Good intentions relocated the Iola graveyard high on a hill— each of my family's headstones hopefully matched with their appropriate remains—where it still sits behind a white iron fence, bent and twisted from the weight of snow. Good intentions otherwise drowned the entirety of Iola, Colorado.

Imagine a town silent, forgotten, decomposing at the bottom of a lake that once was a river. If this makes you wonder whether the joys and pain of a place wash away as the floodwaters rise and swallow, I can tell you they do not. The landscapes of our youths create us, and we carry them within us, storied by all they gave and stole, in who we become.

PART I

1948-1949

One

1948

H e wasn't much to look at.
       Not at first, anyway.

"Pardon," the young man said, a grimy thumb and forefinger tugging at the brim of his tattered red ball cap. "This the way to the flop?"

As simple as that. This ordinary question from a filthy stranger walking up Main Street just as I arrived at the intersection with North Laura.

His overalls and hands were blackened with coal, which I assumed was axle grease or layers of dirt from the fields, though it was too dark for either. His cheeks were smudged. Tan skin shone through trickled sweat. Straight black hair jutted from beneath his cap.

The autumn day had begun as ordinary as the porridge and fried eggs I had served the men for breakfast. I noticed nothing uncommon as I went on to tend the house and the docile animals in their pens, picked two baskets of late-season peaches in the cool morning air, and made my daily deliveries pulling the rickety wagon behind my bicycle, then returned home to cook lunch. But I've come to understand how the exceptional lurks beneath the ordinary, like the deep and mysterious world beneath the surface of the sea.

"The way to everything," I replied.

I was not trying to be witty or catch his notice, but the angle of his pause and slight twist of smile showed that my response amused him. He made my insides leap, looking at me that way.

"Real small town, I mean." I tried to set things straight, to clarify that I was not the type of girl that boys noticed or paused to smirk at on a street corner.

The stranger's eyes were as dark and shiny as a raven's wing. And kind—that is what I remember most about those eyes from that first glimpse until the final gaze—a gentleness that seemed to fountain from his center and spill out like an overflowing well. He studied me a moment, still grinning, then pulled again at his cap brim and continued walking toward Dunlap's boarding house near the end of Main.

It was true that this one crumbling sidewalk led to everything. Along with Dunlap's, we had the Iola Hotel for fancy folks and the tavern tacked on the back for drinking folks; Jernigan's Standard station, hardware, and post; the café that always smelled of coffee and bacon; and Chapman's Big Little Store, with groceries and a deli counter and too much gossip. At the west end of it all stood the tall flagpole between the schoolhouse I once attended and the white clapboard church where our family used to sit, polished and proper, every Sunday when Mother was alive. Beyond that, Main Street dove abruptly into the hillside like a period after a short sentence.

I was heading in the same direction as the stranger—to drag my brother out of the poker cabin behind Jernigan's—but I wasn't about to walk right on this boy's heels. I paused there at the corner and shielded my eyes from the afternoon sun to study him as he continued on. He strolled slowly, casually, like his only destination was his next step, his arms swinging at his sides, his head seemingly a tad behind the pace. His dingy white T-shirt stretched tightly beneath the straps of his overalls. He was slim, with the muscular shoulders of a workhand.

As if he felt my gaze, he suddenly turned and flashed a smile, dazzling against his soiled face. I gasped at being caught eyeing him. A rush of heat tickled up my neck. He tugged his cap as he had before, turned, and strolled on. Though I couldn't see his face, I was pretty sure he was still grinning.

It was a fateful moment, I know in retrospect. For I could have turned and headed back down North Laura, toward home and fixing supper, could have let Seth stumble to the farm on his own accord, stagger in the door right in front of Daddy and Uncle Og with his own hell to pay. I could have at least crossed over to the other side of Main, put the occasional car and a row of yellowing cottonwood trees between our two sidewalks. But I didn't, and this made all the difference in the world.

Instead, I took one slow step forward and then another, intuitively feeling the significance in each choice to lift, extend, then lower a foot.

No one had ever spoken to me about matters of attraction. I was too young when my mother died to have learned those secrets from her, and I can't imagine she would have shared them with me anyway. She had been a quiet, proper woman, extremely obedient to

God and expectation. From what I remember, she loved my brother and me, but her affection surfaced only within strict parameters, governing us with a grave fear of how we'd all perform on Judgment Day. I had occasionally glimpsed her carefully concealed passion unleash on our backsides with the black rubber flyswatter, or in the subtle stains of quickly swept tears when she stood after prayer, but I never saw her kiss my father or even once take him in her arms. Though my parents ran the family and the farm as efficient and dependable partners, I didn't witness between them the presence of love particular to a man and a woman. For me, this mysterious territory had no map.

Except for this: I was looking out the parlor window on that gloomy autumn twilight just after I turned twelve years old when Sheriff Lyle pulled up the wet gravel drive in his long black-and-white automobile and hesitantly approached my father in the yard. Through the steam of my breath on the glass I saw Daddy slowly collapse to his knees right there in the rain-fresh mud. I had been watching for my mother, my cousin Calamus, and my Aunt Vivian to return, hours late from making their peach delivery across the pass to Canyon City. My father had been watching too, so antsy about their absence he spent the whole evening raking the soggy leaves he'd normally allow to compost on the grass over winter. When Daddy buckled under the weight of Lyle's words, my young heart comprehended two immense truths: my missing family members would not be coming home, and my father loved my mother. They had never demonstrated or spoken to me of romance, but I realized then that in fact they had known it, in their own quiet way. I learned from their subtle relations—and in the dry, matter-of-fact eyes with which my father later walked into the house and somberly shared the news of my mother's death with Seth and me—that love is a private matter, to be nurtured, and even mourned, between two beings alone. It belongs to them and no one else, like a secret treasure, like a private poem.

Beyond that, I knew nothing, especially not of love's beginnings, of that inexplicable draw to another, why some boys could pass you by without notice but the next has a pull on you as undeniable as gravity, and from that moment forward, longing is all you know.

There was merely a half block between this boy and me as we walked the same narrow sidewalk at the same moment in this same little nowhere Colorado town. I trailed him, thinking that from wherever he had come, from whatever place and experience, he and I had lived our seventeen years—perhaps a bit longer for him, perhaps a bit less—wholly unaware of the other's existence on this earth. Now, at this moment, for some reason our lives were intersecting as sure as North Laura and Main.

My heart quickened when the distance between us crept from three houses to two, then one, and I realized he was ever so gradually slowing down.

I had no idea what to do. If I also slowed, he'd know I was pacing myself off him, paying too close attention to a stranger. But if I carried on steadily, I would quickly catch up to him, and what then? Or worse yet, I'd pass him and feel the sear of his gaze on my own back. He'd surely notice my gangly walk, my bare legs and worn leather shoes, the outgrown fit of my old maroon school dress, the ordinariness of my straight brown hair not washed since Sunday bath.

So I slowed. As if attached by some invisible string, he slowed as well. I slowed again, and he slowed, barely moving. Then he stopped dead still. I had no choice but to do the same, and there we were, like two fool statues right there on Main Street.

He didn't move out of playfulness, I sensed. I stood frozen out of fear and indecision and the disorienting first rumbles of desire. I had known of this boy for mere minutes and less than a town block, yet already he had my insides tumbling like pebbles in a stream.

I didn't hear the doctor's plump wife or the steel wheels of her baby carriage coming up behind me. When Mrs. Bernette and her toddler suddenly appeared at my side, trying to maneuver a pass, I spooked like a squirrel.

Mrs. Bernette smiled suspiciously, her thinly plucked brows raised to indicate an unspoken question as she snipped a terse, "Torie."

I barely managed to nod politely, couldn't even remember the baby's name or reach out with a friendly tousle to his blond hair.

The stranger took one sly sideways step so Mrs. Bernette could pass. She looked him up and down curiously and smiled feebly when he tipped his cap and said, "Ma'am." She looked back at me with a frown, as if struggling to figure out a riddle, then turned and continued to waddle uptown.

We actually were a riddle, this boy and I. The riddle went like this: What, once tied together, have bound destinies? The answer: Puppets on the same string.

"Victoria," he said with casual familiarity, as he finally turned and faced me squarely. "You following me?" It was apparently his turn to be clever, and he grinned with equal amusement at his own wit as with what he'd mistook for mine.

I stammered like a child caught stealing a nickel before managing a curt, "No."

He crossed his tan arms and said nothing. I couldn't tell if he was pondering his question or me, or perhaps the happenstance of the moment.

When I could no longer stand my own discomfort in the quiet, I straightened in faux composure and asked, "How do you know my name?"

"I pay attention," he said. He was blunt yet somehow modest. "Victoria," he said again, slowly, seemingly for the pure pleasure of the syllables rolling in his mouth. "A name fit for a queen."

Charm belied his disheveled appearance and, despite my best attempts at aloofness, he could tell I thought so. His dark eyes extended the invitation before he spoke it, and then he said, "Care to walk with me? I mean right here," he pointed by his side, "in a proper way?"

I stalled, because, yes, I wanted to walk beside him, and yet either propriety or genuine teenage awkwardness held me back. Or perhaps it was premonition. "No, thank you," I said, "I couldn't . . . I mean . . . I don't even know your . . . ."

"It's Wil," he interjected before I could ask. "Wilson Moon." He let his full name hang in my ears for a moment; then he moved toward me with an extended hand. "Pleasure to make your acquaintance, Miss Victoria." Suddenly very earnest, he waited for me to step into the space between us and place my hand in his.

I hesitated uneasily, and then I curtsied. I don't know which of us was more surprised. I hadn't curtsied since I was a little girl in Sunday school, but the gesture rushed through my mind as the only thing to do, so afraid was I to touch his hand. I immediately felt foolish and expected him to laugh, but he didn't. His grin spread to a full smile, bright, immense, genuine, but not the least bit mocking.

He nodded knowingly, lowered his hand, let it slide into the pocket of his dirty overalls, and stood still before me.

I couldn't fathom it then, standing there suspended by his gaze, but I would come to learn that Wilson Moon didn't experience time the way most people do, or few other things for that matter. He never rushed or fiddled nervously or found a length of silence between two people an awkward vessel to fill with chatter. He rarely looked to the future, and to the past even less, but gathered up the current moment in both hands to admire its particulars, with no apology and no sense it should be otherwise. I couldn't know any of this as I stood stock-still on Main Street, but I would come to learn the wisdom of his ways and, in time, apply that wisdom when I needed it most.

So, yes, I changed my answer and accepted the invitation to stroll side by side down Main Street that October afternoon with a boy called Wilson Moon, who was no longer a stranger.

Though the conversation was mere pleasantries and the walk short, by the time we reached Dunlap's and scaled the worn steps to the porch, neither of us wanted to part. I lingered with him in the splintered doorway, my heart racing.

Wil didn't offer much about himself. Even when I asked if Wil short for Wilson was spelled with one *l* or two, he just shrugged and replied, "As you like." One thing I did learn about Wilson Moon that day was that he had been working in the coal mines in Dolores, and he had run away.

"I just up and had enough of that place," he said. "'Go,' I heard a voice inside me say, 'Go now.'" The coal cars heading to the Durango-Silverton line were filled and ready to be hauled, he said, and when the train's whistle blew, it sounded like it was calling for him, long and shrill and insistent. All he knew was that those cars were going somewhere other than where he was. As the train started its slow grind forward, he scurried up one car's rusty ladder and hopped atop a warm black bed of coal. The boss caught sight of him and chased the train a spell, hollering and cursing and furiously waving his hat. Soon the foreman and the mines were minute in the distance, and Wilson Moon turned his face to the wind.

"You didn't even know where you were heading? Where you'd end up?" I asked.

"Doesn't much matter," he replied, "One place is about as good as another, ain't it?"

The only place I had ever known was Iola and the surrounding land along a wide, straight section of the Gunnison River. The small town huddled against the foothills of the Big Blue wilderness on the south side and the towering Elk Mountains to the west and north. A patchwork of farms and ranches unfurled like a long tail along the river's edge to the east. My brother and I had been born in the farmhouse my daddy inherited from his daddy, in the tall iron bed that took up half the pale-yellow room tacked onto the back of the house, the room that was just for birthing and visitors until Uncle Og came to live with us after the accident. Our farm was nothing special, nor was it very big, just forty-seven acres, including the barns and the house and a gravel driveway as long as a wolf's howl. But from the barn to the back fence line our land produced the only peach grove in all Gunnison County, where the fruit grew fat and rosy and sweet. The curvy banks of Willow Creek carved the east border of our property, its icy water fresh from the mountain snow and eager to spill onto our trees and modest rows of potatoes and onions. At night, the creek sang a lullaby outside my bedroom window, hushing me to rest in the spindle bed where I had slept nearly every night of my life. The sunrise over distant Tenderfoot Mountain and the long whistle of three trains per day pulling through the depot on the town's edge served as my most reliable clocks. I knew just how the afternoon sun slanted into the small kitchen window and across the long pine table on winter mornings. I knew crocuses and purple larkspurs would be the first wildflowers to emerge across the farm each spring, and fireweeds and goldenrods would be the last. I knew that a dozen cliff swallows descended on the river with every mayfly hatch and that this would be the exact moment a rainbow trout would rise to Daddy's cast. And I knew that the fiercest storms, dark and ominous as the devil, nearly always blew in over the northwestern peaks and that every songbird and raven and magpie would silence just before the sky unleashed.

So, no, one place was not just like another in my mind, and I wondered why this boy didn't seem to know a thing about home.

"And your belongings?" I asked, intrigued by the life of a drifter.

"Same," he said with a shrug and a grin, like he knew something about belongings that I did not, which proved to be correct in the end. He would teach me how true a life emptied of all but its essentials could feel and that, when you got down to it, not much mattered outside the determination to go on living. If he had told me this then, I wouldn't have had the ability to believe him. But time pulls our strings.

I couldn't think of an excuse to follow him into Dunlap's. Even if I hadn't been in the company of a strange boy, a girl didn't go into the flophouse without a proper reason and a trusted escort. It was also getting on about supper time, and I still had the foul task of dragging Seth out of the poker shack and getting him home before Daddy came in from bailing the last of Mr. Mitchell's hay.

I suggested it was time to part by sighing, "Well . . . ," but I didn't actually begin to walk away. I expected him to take the cue, make the next move, but, again, he maintained a relaxed stillness, smiling at me, occasionally looking skyward as if reading something in the wispy early evening clouds.

"I guess I better be moving on," I finally said. "Supper to get and all."

Wil glanced at the sky again, then asked if I'd meet him the next day, show him around, share a piece of pie or some such.

"After all," he added, "you're the only person I know in this little cracker of a town."

"Well, you don't know me," I said. "Not much, anyway."

"Sure, I do." He winked. "You're Miss Victoria, queen of Iola." He bent and twirled his hand in a mock bow as if to royalty, and I laughed. Then he stood and eyed me so long I thought I'd melt like chocolate in the last rays of sun reaching low across the porch. He said nothing, but I felt as if he knew impossible things about me. He moved closer. I took my first deep smell of him, musky and sharp and strangely inviting, and stared for an instant into his bottomless dark eyes.

How does one live for seventeen years without ever considering whether she is known? The idea had not previously occurred to me, that someone could see into the heart of things and there you'd be. I stood on the dusty flophouse steps feeling transparent, held up to the light in a way I never imagined before meeting Wilson Moon.

Shyly, I stepped back; then I agreed to meet him the next day. I wanted more of him, like a craving for sunshine hidden too long behind the clouds. But before we could share a plan—choose a time, a place, a reason—a familiar voice hurled at me from the middle of Main Street and hit me like a rock.

"Torie!"

There stood my brother, Seth, swaying in the middle of Main, his left hand gripping the neck of a brown beer bottle.

"Torie, get away from that filthy son of a bitch!" he slurred, pointing at Wil with the bottle, spilling beer in dark splotches onto the dirt road.

"My brother. Drunk," I sighed to Wil, turning quickly. I trotted down Dunlap's steps, throwing back an exasperated, "I've got to go," and rushed to Seth's side before he could cause trouble.

"Who is that bastard?" Seth grunted through the Lucky Strike dangling from his lips, aiming the question more at Wil than at me.

"He's nobody," I said, pushing Seth down the street from behind, one hand on each of his shoulders as if holding the reins of a reluctant mule, steering him back toward the intersection of North Laura and Main. Though over a year younger, Seth passed me in height near his fifteenth birthday and had grown at least two inches in the six months since. I was not a tall girl, however, and, compared to other boys his age, Seth was still short and sturdy, built like a boxer in body and temper. I struggled to get him out of Wil's sight and away from the other onlookers and get us on home.

"Some boy asking directions is all," I lied, though not fifteen minutes earlier this had been true. "Just passing through."

"Brown son of a bitch . . . ."

"You stink, Seth," I cut him off. "Worse than that hog pen you'd better be tending when Daddy gets in."

"Screw Daddy," he slurred with drunken courage, taking a deep draw on his cigarette, then tossing it to the road.

"Just do as you're told for once and save us all a lot of fuss," I said, stamping out the Lucky Strike, then glancing over my shoulder to glimpse Wil still standing on Dunlap's porch, reading me like a mystery tale.

"Those pigs will fly from that crap-filled stall before I take orders from you, girl. Don't you reckon you can . . . ."

"Shut up, Seth," I sighed. "Just shut the hell up." I couldn't listen to another word. I hated him right then, even more than I ever had before. My loathing already had something to do with Wil. It had long had something to do with Daddy and Uncle Og and the mother and cousin and aunt I was starting to forget. But mostly my abhorrence for Seth was raw and ragged as a thistle, having grown a little sharper each day of our lives.

I started pushing him from behind with all my force. He took a blow, stumbled forward, then took another blow, cursing and whining and swigging beer the whole way but never fighting me. Maybe he was too drunk to care, or maybe he knew as well as I did that he had to be in the hog pen by the time the sun dipped behind the ridge.

We turned down North Laura. At its dead end, a thin trampled trail to our farm snaked through the weeds, past the tip of crazy Ruby-Alice Akers's pine-covered patch of land and across a wide, grassy field. It was the quickest route between the farm and town, and Seth and I had walked it a thousand times together. When we were children, our mother made it Seth's job to watch out for me when we walked that trail, coming or going, even though he was younger and far less responsible, simply because he was a boy. As we aged, I watched out for him, not because anyone told me to but because I had to, for my sake as much as his, for Daddy's sake too. But try as I might, I couldn't save Seth from his own mischief, and I was damn sick of trying.

I hurried him along the path, me pushing, him stumbling and cursing. Then he dropped the beer bottle from his hand. Before my mind could register that the bottle was in the path, I stepped square on it and toppled forward, pushing Seth to the ground and falling hard in the dirt on my right hip and elbow. Small things: a drunken boy's loose grip, a dropped bottle, a sprained ankle, a torn dress sleeve. But it is often the small fateful twist that alters our lives most profoundly—the beckoning cry of a coal train whistle, a question from a stranger at an intersection, a brown bottle lying in the dirt. Try as we might to convince ourselves otherwise, the moments of our becoming cannot be carefully plucked like the ripest and most satisfying peach from the bough. In the endless stumble toward ourselves, we harvest the crop we are given.

I lay in the dirt for a disorienting moment. Seth laughed weakly then silenced. Pain radiated through my lower leg. As I gingerly raised my chest from the dirt, Wil's arms suddenly slid beneath me with the sureness of a bridegroom scooping up his bride. And though there was no threshold—just the field of wilted goldenrods and tall brittle grasses—I remember that moment as our entry. I did not startle at his touch, did not protest his gentle embrace as he lifted with ease and cradled me against his coal-smudged chest, did not foolishly try to walk on the already bulging ankle.

"You followed me," I said flatly.

"Yep," was all he replied, looking down at Seth, who lay on his side at the edge of the path, passed out. "What do we do about him?" Wil asked.

"Not a damn thing," I replied to Wil's amusement. *Not a damn thing*, I repeated in my head, shocked at my rebellion in both language and deed. I would leave my brother sleeping in the dirt. I would ride in this stranger's arms.

I trembled. Whether it was from pain or anger or love's first sparks, I don't know—perhaps all these—but my body shook as if Wil had plucked me from a frozen pond. My arms clung to his sinewy neck as he walked. His head bobbed slightly at the pull, as if nodding agreement. I felt light as a child in his arms, trusting as a child too. It was not like me to so readily accept aid and protection, to have such little suspicion of a strange boy's intentions. And yet, this girl in his arms was me. We traveled on the path I had walked my entire life in a way I never before knew, feeling everything around me subtly transformed. My father was perhaps waiting at the farm by now, and Uncle Og was most likely sitting in his wheelchair next to the window or on the front porch as he did most days—each a potential witness to this stranger carrying me through the field. But after years of fearing my father's judgment and Uncle Og's rage, I did not care what they might think or how they might react. In comparison to the immensity of Wil's arms around me, Daddy and Og and authority and decorum all shrank. Even the surrounding mountains, even consequence, seemed insignificantly small.

I had left the farmhouse that morning an ordinary girl on an ordinary day. I could not yet identify what new map had unfolded within me, but I knew I was returning home uncommon. I felt as the explorers I had once studied in school must have when they glimpsed a far and mysterious shore from their seemingly eternal sea. Suddenly the Magellan of my own interior, I knew not what I had discovered. I lay my head on Wil's broad shoulder and wondered where and who he'd come from, and how long a drifter ever stayed in one place.

Two

The white farmhouse came into view, then the dilapidated chicken coops, the hog pen, and the patched gray barn that held equipment and bushel baskets and our gelding, Abel. No structures or fences had been painted since the summer before the accident. In fact, little on the farm had been cared for properly since then, and now, five years later, without my cousin Calamus to do the maintenance work and Mother to dictate it, the farm had become like a burlap potato sack to its former white linen. The transformation had occurred so gradually, I hadn't fully realized it until that moment, trying to perceive the scene as Wil might. My whole life was in that farm, and as he glimpsed it for the first time, I felt shabby and worn.

I wanted to say, "This isn't really who we are . . . or not who I am . . . it's just, there was an accident and . . . ." And yet, the evidence stood before us like a final proclamation of my family's fall.

Added to the dilapidated buildings was a drunken brother lying behind us in the dirt and, now, my father's rusty truck grumbling up the long driveway. As Daddy climbed out the driver's door and began walking toward us with fury in his step, I saw Uncle Og wheel his chair out onto the peeling front porch to get a closer look at what he no doubt hoped would be a scuffle. I hung there in Wil's arms, unable to wash clean any of what he was seeing or to run with him around back to our peach orchard, the one last beautiful thing. I closed my eyes, anticipating in Daddy's approach the full collision of my life with Wil's.

Surprisingly, it came from behind.

Seth had come to. He had silently stalked us until his tight coil of anger unwound in the powerful lunge that landed him on Wil's back. The fight that ensued is surreal to me now, my memory a slow-motion and hazy version of what actually occurred. I recall details I still can't explain, like how Wil managed to float me gently to the ground, out of harm's way, and how the boys spun above me like a small tornado, Wil dancing birdlike on the air to avoid Seth's furious punches. I clearly recall the one solid blow from Wil that landed Seth on the ground, bloody-nosed and swearing, and my father's arrival, gasping for breath, pulling Seth to his feet, then standing between the two boys with arms outstretched like a referee.

Seth panted and pushed his chest against Daddy's palm, cursing Wil and trying to get at him. Wil backed up calmly, eyeing Seth like a wolf confidently staring down its prey.

"Who in tarnation are you, boy?" Daddy hollered at Wil; then he barked a warning at Seth to quiet down, gripping his son's shirt collar in his fist.

"Wilson Moon, sir," replied Wil composedly, keeping his eyes on Seth, tipping the cap that had managed to stay on his head.

"That don't mean a damn thing to me," Daddy said.

"Just passin' through, sir."

"Passin' through with my daughter in your arms and my son on your back?" Daddy asked gruffly, suspicious and puzzled.

"Yes, sir," answered Wil with no attempt at explanation other than adding, "Picked up the one, tried to ride out the other."

Daddy glanced down at the ground where I sat, surveying my swollen ankle and torn dress, never going so far as to look for evidence in my eyes, then asked, "Did this boy hurt you?"

"No, Daddy," I replied. "It was Seth's fault. The boy found me hurt and was just helping me home is all."

"That ain't true!" Seth snarled. "That son of a bitch followed us from town to get his filthy hands on her." Pushing against my father with renewed furor, Seth punched the air toward Wil, shouting, "I'll kill you, spic bastard!"

Daddy gripped Seth tighter and looked with knit brows from me to Wil to me again. He ordered Seth to shut up, then asked me solemnly, "That true?"

"No, Daddy," I repeated. "Seth's drunk is all."

"That's plain," Daddy said, glancing wearily at his son, who, finally succumbing to Daddy's grip, hung from my father's fist and sullenly kicked at the dirt like a furious child.

Daddy surveyed Wil again, then fanned at him with his free hand, saying, "Get yourself on outta here, boy, and I don't want to see you near my land or my kin again. You got that clear?"

"Yes, sir. Clear as rain," Wil said, tugging his cap.

Wil turned without looking at me and strolled steadily through the yellow field back toward town. The lavender horizon seemed to sip at him until his form grew minute and disappeared. I wondered if he was heading back to the rails. If one place was as good as another to him, a different place on the line might now do him better than the town where Seth lived. It never occurred to me that he was pondering the opposite as he grew tiny in the distance, that Iola had become for him a place above all others, a place not to flee because of Seth but to remain because of me.

"The whole time I was walking away," he later told me, as we lay tucked together in the blankets of his bed, "I was figuring out how to get back to you."

I often wish he had kept on walking, hopped the next train to someplace else.

Daddy pushed my brother away in disgust, and Seth stumbled in the direction of the hog pen without protest. Daddy bent down, lifted me with great effort, and carried me toward the farmhouse. He felt bony and unhinged compared to Wil, less burdened by my weight than by the years of struggle since my mother died. I didn't dare wrap my arms around his neck as I had with Wil for fear I might drag him to the ground. Like the farm, my father had withered a little bit each day, and now riding in his once strong arms felt like being carried by a feeble old mule. I wanted to tell him to put me down, that I could hobble, but I knew he wouldn't oblige, and Daddy didn't like unnecessary words.

Uncle Ogden let out a high, long whistle as Daddy carried me up the weathered porch steps and past Og's wheelchair to the front door. Og's sinister grin let me know he had enjoyed the show, couldn't care less about my injury, and held high hopes for more trouble, which, sadly, would come. Daddy ignored him and brought me inside, where he placed me lengthwise on the sofa, then went to the kitchen to call Doctor Bernette. I arranged my leg on the muslin pillows hand-sewn by my mother, and I waited.

Mother had called this room the parlor. We were allowed to use it only on Sunday afternoons when the boys and I were clean and subdued after church. I'd played endless hours of checkers with Seth and Cal on the wooden board, our lanky bodies splayed atop the braided parlor rug while my mother studied her Bible in the corner rocking chair and my father read the newspaper and dozed on the gold wool sofa. Oftentimes Aunt Vivian visited from her boarding room in town. She tried to sit quietly and stitch but paused frequently to tell us a story she had read in *Collier's* or seen in a newsreel before a picture show at the theater in Montrose. Had it not been for her, I would not have known about a place called Hollywood or the lilting names of its stars—Errol Flynn, Basil Rathbone, Greer Garson, and my favorite, for its smooth, round syllables, Olivia de Havilland, a woman I could only imagine to be as beautiful as her name. Mother called it all nonsense, which made every tidbit Aunt Viv shared all the more delicious. Occasionally, Viv convinced Mother to let us listen to a Laurel and Hardy skit on the radio. The boys and I would roll with laughter, until the silliness unleashed Seth so thoroughly he couldn't resist punching or wrestling with Cal, and Mother would order the radio turned off and all children out of the parlor. I'd leave reluctantly but obediently, accustomed to being guilty by association, and Viv would shoot me a knowing, apologetic glance.

As I sat in the quiet twilight with those ghosts, waiting for the doctor to arrive and examine my ankle, I decided that if Mother were watching me from some celestial viewpoint, even now, she would scold me for having my leg up on the sofa. On the wall across from me hung the white shelf where Mother kept her porcelain cross collection. Beneath that hung one of her expertly embroidered Bible verses, a variety of which she had crafted and hung throughout the house as both inspiration and admonition. This one depicted two hands towered in prayer and encircled in psalm: "He must increase, but I must decrease. John 3:30." I noticed with a bite of shame the dust layering its dark wood frame. On the opposite wall hung another embroidery, bordered with a ribbon of blue flowers: "I will not forget thee. Behold, I have thee carved in the palm of my hand. Isaiah 49:16." I vaguely recalled a church sermon on that psalm and Mother reaching out to me as I sat properly beside her in the pew, giving my thigh a slight squeeze before reclasping her hands properly in her lap.

Through the sheer parlor draperies, I could see the side of Uncle Og's head and one fat shoulder spilling out of the wheelchair's tall wooden back. He stuffed a wad of chewing tobacco into his cheek, then stared off the porch in the direction Wil had departed as if still stalking his silhouette. Every few minutes he lifted a red coffee can to his lips to spit, followed by a swig from his silver flask.

Ogden had courted Aunt Viv in this same parlor, though he was so different back then that I could hardly connect the charming young college boy who once came to call to the broken man wasting on the porch. He and Viv had met in 1941 at a Spring Fling dance at the state college Og attended in Gunnison. Vivian had gone to the dance uninvited with two girlfriends, all seeking romance, all successfully luring a college boy who would eventually get down on one knee and propose. According to Vivian's report, when she showed up in our kitchen for breakfast the morning after the dance, giddy as a guinea hen, her college boy was the best catch of the lot.

I didn't disagree when she brought Ogden to our house for Saturday dinner the next week. Viv had told me he was not handsome in a Clark Gable *It Happened One Night* kind of way but irresistible in a Fred Astaire *Swing Time* kind of way. I had never seen a picture show, so I wasn't sure what she meant until I saw Og bound from his red Pontiac and up our walkway so light on his feet it seemed his brown-and-white wing tips barely touched the ground. Viv let out a squeal as she rushed to greet him, the brunette pin curls she had fidgeted with all afternoon too shellacked to her head to bounce. Og shook Daddy's hand at the front door and presented a bouquet of flowers to my mother. Wearing a red bow tie and a giggling Viv on his arm, he sprang into our farmhouse like a dolled-up jackrabbit.

He spoke animatedly all evening, delighting my family with tale after tale of his adventures. Even my mother, clearly taken aback by his zeal and surely concerned about his salvation, sniggered a time or two at his wit. I had never known anyone who had seen the sunrise over the Grand Canyon, climbed to fourteen thousand feet in the nearby San Juan range, ridden in a suspended metal chair and sailed down a snowy hillside with two boards strapped to his feet up north in Idaho. Ogden had done all this and then some with his brother Jimmy and seemed to relive the thrill of each escapade as he told his stories, even leaping from the dinner table to demonstrate his skiing form, his arms tucked in a tight *L*, imaginary poles in hand, knees bent, hips swinging. He made rhythmic swooshing noises and skied the slope of his memory while the rest of us sat with our utensils suspended in mid-bite and Vivian beamed.

The next Saturday, Og brought Jimmy with him to dinner and, much to my and the boys' amusement, the theatrics doubled. Jimmy was a couple years younger than Og, with the same agile build and an even greater tendency toward outburst. They worked off each other like Bergen and McCarthy and brought life and laughter to our house.

Og and Vivian married just before the harvest that year. We decorated the church with pale pink ribbons and the purple penstemons that Mother and I had cut from the orchard's edge. Jimmy stood beside Ogden as they awaited Viv's march down the aisle, both smirking as if at any moment they might launch into hysterics.

No one in the clapboard church that day could have predicted that within three months, politicians far across the world would decide to send bombs falling on a Hawaiian harbor that we had never heard of and the result would be the snatching away of Ogden and Jimmy to war.

When I was about five years old, news had spread like a stampede across town that the banker from Montrose, Mr. Massey, had stalled his shiny ivory Auburn Speedster on the Iola train tracks and it had been demolished by an oncoming engine. Folks told of Mr. Massey being crushed in the driver's seat, the car balled up around him like a cocoon; other rumors spread that he had been decapitated under the train's wheels or flung from the open convertible onto the engine's windshield to look the engineer square in the eye while drawing his final breath. Fact was, Mr. Massey leapt from the car before impact and escaped injury, but the story grew so outlandish that by day's end nearly everyone in town drove or rode a horse or a bicycle past the railyard to see the mangled Speedster for themselves. I was out on a peach delivery with Daddy and Cal, perched on an inverted bushel basket between their two seats, when Daddy turned the truck down a road we didn't frequent and took us past the depot and over the rails. The magnificent automobile—once so admired as it drove down Main, a link to another kind of life folks in Iola rarely even considered—had been transformed into a heap of debris, little more than an enormous crushed tin can.

The war did to Ogden just what that train had done to Mr. Massey's sleek automobile: taken something of unique beauty and promise and crushed it. One year later, the accident that stole Cal, Vivian, and my mother did the same to my family. I learned from a young age the tenacity of ruin. Through the parlor window, with every angry brown spit into his can, with every swig of whiskey, Og reminded me not to trust in appearances for clues to what might come.

When my father hollered from the kitchen that Dr. Bernette was on his way, then left to do his chores with a slam of the screen door, I had nearly forgotten about my injured ankle. I was thinking about Wil, weighing my desire to see him again against the stab of clarity that the wise thing to do would be to let all notions of him go while he was still beautiful and whole.

Three

My ankle wasn't broken. Dr. Bernette wrapped it with a wide white bandage and instructed me to keep off of it for a few days. His car wasn't even to the end of our long driveway before I disobeyed his orders by hobbling to the kitchen to cook. It was a good thing I did, for, injury or no, Daddy, Og, and Seth all showed up to the kitchen table hungry at seven o'clock like they did every night, expecting me to have a meal prepared. I had thrown the supper together hastily—cubed beef fried up with cabbage from the kitchen garden, a bowl of rolls left over from the previous night, four ears of buttered corn, the last slices of a two-day-old peach pie—but no one complained. The only sound through most of the meal was utensils clanging on plates and an occasional belch from Uncle Og. Seth kept his head low, trying to hide his bruised and swollen nose, and gulped his food in heaping bites. Either the fight had made him voracious or he just wanted to get away from the table as quickly as possible. He cleaned his plate in half the time as the rest of us and immediately stood.

"You ain't going out tonight, son," Daddy ruled before Seth had the chance to announce his plans.

"Why do you give a damn?" Seth retorted, squinting as if the kitchen lights were too bright. His disfigured nose made an alien of his face.

"Watch your mouth, boy," Daddy warned. He slathered butter on a roll and took a large bite, chewing slowly, staring down at the vacant stretch of table between him and Seth.

Seth shifted anxiously from foot to foot. Daddy swallowed and told him to sit down, adding, "Supper ain't over."

My mother had governed our family by the strictest rules of etiquette, Methodism, and practicality. In her mind, there was a proper and improper way to do just about everything, from table manners to speech to stitching, right down to the correct way to spread mayonnaise on a piece of sandwich bread, or beat the rugs, or talk the chickens into laying more eggs. We were not allowed to cross our legs in church, speak to an elder unless spoken to, or ride bareback, and I, as a girl, could not run in public other than in physical education class back when I was in school. After Mother died, Daddy tried keeping up her high standards and pervasive rules, but following them had never been his nature and enforcing them was even less so. Raising the children had been Mother's domain, and he never seemed to know what to do with us after she was gone. He laid down the law when he remembered to, more in homage to Mother or to express a foul mood than out of genuine concern for our behavior, and he applied the old rules so sporadically that Seth and I never knew what tenet we'd be held to or when. Most times,

Seth finished eating and left the table whenever he pleased. I was expected to do the dishes, that was clear, so I took my time and always finished eating last. That night, however, new rules applied.

"You're washing up tonight," Daddy told Seth before taking another bite of roll.

I don't know if Seth or I was more astonished by this matter-of-fact announcement. One principle that had been consistent in my family was that the women did all the domestic chores. My mother had done so without complaint. Whether Daddy's unusual demand was out of concern for my ankle or as punishment to Seth or both, he didn't say. Seth flung his head back and groaned. Uncle Og let out a wheezing, mocking chuckle.

Daddy finished his roll, wiped his lips with a muslin napkin, and said, "That Mexican boy is long gone by now. And if he ain't, going after him will just stir up trouble this family don't need."

Daddy's assumption that Wil was Mexican grabbed all our attentions.

"Mexican?" Og grunted with disdain, slapping his short stump of right leg, then berated, "You let a wetback get the best of you, Sara?"

"Maybe he wasn't," Seth bit back. "I don't know what the hell he was, other than a son of a bitch."

"That's enough," Daddy commanded. I didn't know whether it was the bigotry or nastiness or just the sounds of their voices he couldn't abide.

I wanted to stand and declare to them that they didn't know a damn thing about Wilson Moon. Already I felt I possessed Wil somehow, that the men at my table, though kin, meant less to me now than he did.

One rule my mother taught me by example was that a woman does herself a favor by saying very little. I often thought her aloof in conversation, especially with the workhands who ate at our table. But I came to understand that she, like I, like women throughout the ages, knew the value of employing silence as a guard dog to her truth. By showing on the surface only a small fraction of her interior, a woman gave men less to plunder. I feigned indifference to the subject of Wilson Moon, although my veins buzzed liked electrical cords at his mention. I finished my food. I drank my milk. I asked to be excused. As I stood, I noticed Seth scowling at me, furious about the role reversal, of course, but there was also something unreadable and frightening in his eyes. I hob-bled out of the kitchen and up the worn wooden stairs to the solace of my bedroom, my mind searching for a description of the emotion in Seth's glare. I couldn't name it. I didn't want it to be suspicion and, at that point in my life, I knew nothing about the untamable wildfire of revenge.

THAT NIGHT I LAY in bed and missed my mother.

It had been years since I'd longed for her in this way, and I was surprised that her memory came to me then, when I could have been distracting myself from my throbbing ankle by thinking about Wil, plotting our reunion or mentally reliving the exquisite feel of riding in his arms. It was not that I wasn't reminded of Mother often in the five years since she'd passed, but she had taught me to be sensible and efficient, and longing for something you cannot have employs neither of those virtues. I tried not to miss her as a way of honoring her practicality, which in my heart felt as absurd as it sounds. More honestly, wishing for her hurt too much.

After the accident, I first thought I missed Calamus the most. He had lived with us since I was a toddler, after his parents, my mother's older sister and her husband, were killed by a tornado that struck their Oklahoma turkey farm. Actual facts about their deaths were never discussed, so my child's imagination concocted the image of their entire house being swept into the sky, swirling amid hundreds of squawking turkeys celebrating the exquisite discovery of flight in their final moments, and little eight-year-old Cal left magically rooted to the ground, gazing up at the scene in wonder and resignation, waving goodbye. However he actually came to us, as far back as I could remember, good-natured Cal had been the confluence that merged the separate streams of our family into one river. He made Mother laugh sometimes, and his precise and willing labor seemed the only thing other than an exceptional peach crop that made Daddy proud. Cal could focus Seth's energy on useful things like fly-fishing and fixing motors and could even sometimes talk Seth's temper down. For me, Cal was often the only lap I could crawl onto when I needed a skinned knee kissed or just wanted a friend.

But after a while, as my memories of Cal faded, I came to understand what it meant to be a girl in this world with no mother. Surrounded by males, I was patternless. After Mother died, the men expected me to slip silently into her role—to cook their meals, clean their pee off the toilet, wash and hang their soiled clothes, and tend to every last thing in the house and the coops and the garden. My mother had taught me the basics of domesticity, but, at only twelve years old when it became my job, I didn't know if I was doing the chores correctly, and certainly not as well as she would have done. More than anything, I was unsure I wanted to do them at all or if I was allowed to say so. In time, I understood the answers.

Worse, within a few months after Mother's death, my body began to change. I was maturing faster than the few girls my age at school, and I had no way of knowing what was happening, no clue what to expect. I was too shy and I worked too much to be intimate friends with any of those girls anyway. My only hope was to avoid school-yard teasing by concealing myself. Not knowing where or how to buy a brassiere, I wore big sweaters and layered shirts. When that no longer was enough, I started wrapping my chest with an elastic bandage I special ordered from Mr. Jernigan after feeding him an overly elaborate lie about a sore knee.

My first period came not long after. I woke in a circle of blood and thought for sure I was dying. Modesty and intuition told me not to speak of it to my father. I stripped the sheets, horrified to see that the stain had seeped through to the mattress. With no time to prop-erly clean it up before I had to fix breakfast and walk to school, I wadded up the sheets and my stained underwear and nightgown, shoved them under my bed, and pulled my flowered quilt over the soiled mattress. Not knowing what else to do, I folded a stack of tissues and positioned them in my clean underwear to catch the blood. I pulled on a black skirt and, underneath, woolen stockings covered by a pair of summer knickers to try to hold it all in place.

"Why're you walking so goddamn slow?" Seth had complained as I followed him down the path to school.

"Mother doesn't want you using the Lord's name in vain," I replied.

"Yeah, well, Mother's dead, ain't she?" he replied, and he walked even faster until he was only a moving speck in the distance.

Never had my mother seemed more dead to me as when I walked to school that day, bleeding from my private place, fearing the tissues would slip, muscle cramps firing across my abdomen, certain I would collapse and die from this mysterious ailment before I reached the schoolhouse.

When I returned home, I discovered a bucket of soapy water and a scrub brush next to my bed. The sheets were no longer stashed but were lying in a pile next to the bucket, still bloodied but also filthy, as if they had been dragged through dirt. The soiled underwear was missing. I obediently started washing the sheets, scrubbing at the stains, wringing the water, then scrubbing again. Quiet tears trickled down the sides of my nose, pooled on the underside of my chin, and dripped into the bucket.

Daddy suddenly appeared in the doorway in his dirty overalls and frayed straw hat. He swirled his closed lips as if tasting the words he might speak. I wanted to tell him what was happening, the way I'd once reported the bloody wound I discovered when one of our best hogs took a bite out of another. I wanted him to make sense of it, like he had then—"territorial," he had said—and reassure me that bodies heal. He seemed to want to say something too, but instead he backed out the doorframe and turned to walk down the hall.

"Don't be leaving your private business where dogs can drag it into the yard," he mumbled from the hallway. His heavy steps followed, descending the staircase and passing through the kitchen. The screen door squealed open then slammed in his wake.

We had just one dog, a black-and-gray-speckled cattle hound we simply called Pup until he began regularly banking fish out of Willow Creek and earned the name Trout. He was just the sort of curious dog that would discover my soiled sheets, but Daddy had said *dogs*—plural—and though I know in retrospect that he had merely misspoken or I had misheard, at the time all my fears and innocence and ignorance compiled a vision of an entire vicious pack, enticed by this special kind of blood, stalking my family, waiting, perhaps, to attack me in the yard. I pulled the sheets to my face and wept into them, drenching my sweater and skirt. From that day on, I closed my bedroom door every morning when I left. I closed it at night when I slept. If I could have moved around the house and done my chores closed behind my own personal door, I would have. I was a girl alone in a house of men, quickly becoming a woman. It was like blossoming in a bank of snow.

Meeting Wil gathered the ghost of these old emotions and breathed in them renewed life. The feelings he ignited in me were my next step toward womanhood, and, just as I had five years prior, I needed another female nearby. Realistically, I would not have told my mother about Wil even if she had been in the next room. She would have been appalled at our Main Street breach of propriety and the boldness of him carrying me in his arms. It was not so much Mother's advice about love's blossoming that I yearned for. Rather, my wish that night as I slipped into sleep was for someone who would stand before the men in my house and argue for a woman's right to make her own decisions about love. I doubt that Mother would have helped me had she been alive. But the one benefit of having a dead mother is the ability to turn her into an unwavering ally, whether she would have been one or not.

That night, I dreamed of my mother, arms wide and sturdy, holding back a roiling flood while I escaped into Wil's embrace. Seth was fighting the waves behind her, desperate, furious, but unable to swim past her. His eyes, enormous and blazing, held the same eerie look that had that night followed me from the dinner table and up the creaking stairs.

Four

The thunderous growl of Seth's roadster engine rattled my windowpane the next morning, jolting me from a sound sleep. I leapt from bed, forgetting my injured ankle and collapsing to the pine floorboards the instant it bore weight.

Og's tirades had never before been of comfort to me, but hearing him ranting at Seth through his downstairs bedroom window meant I did not have to holler down at my brother through mine. It was 5:10 a.m., twenty minutes before my daily alarm moved me from bed toward the kitchen to start the coffee and breakfast and nearly an hour before the men in the house usually woke. Yet Seth was already in the yard in the dim dawn, working on the decrepit Chrysler he had never actually made drivable but liked revving to show off to his friends. I crawled to the window and rose on one leg. Through the panes, past the yellowing willow, I could see Seth's silhouette and the faint glow of his faded jeans and white T-shirt.

His head was bare; the crew cut that turned blond every summer
was already the pale brown of autumn. I had never known him to
rev the car without an audience, and certainly not at this absurd
hour, but nothing Seth did ever truly surprised me. He stood at the
raised hood and cussed back at Og, though from my vantage point
he seemed to be cursing the house itself, steam billowing from his
mouth as he ranted into the cold morning air.

"This is *my* house, you crippled son of a bitch!" Seth seethed.
"What do you ever do around here? Huh?! Don't you goddamn tell
me what to do!"

Seth called him a good-for-nothing, a leech, a lame dog, a lard
ass. Og hurled back that Seth was a loser, a pansy, a Sara. In a war
of hostilities, the two were equally matched.

I hobbled back to my bed, pulled the covers up against the chill
and hollering, and contemplated my brother, wondering what he
was up to now. I listened to him rage from the yard until Daddy
yelled at him to knock it off.

Seth was born with mischief as sure as bones and blood. Mother's stern restrictions bound his unruliness in forced obedience, but
his penchant for menace struggled just below the surface like a man
in a straitjacket. Her attention was nearly always on him, anticipating his next unsuitable move before he even thought of it, warning
against throwing a rock before he bent to pick it up, against pulling
a child's hair before he reached for it, against an outburst in church
before he parted his lips. She and Seth had developed a silent language spoken only with eyes, eyebrows, and one hand, a language
that, brief and simple though it was, held all the authority of God's
law. Well before Seth could hurl a peach like a baseball or leap into
a mud puddle, Mother would widen her eyes, raise her brows, and

make one quick chop in the air with her right hand, wordlessly saying, *Don't you even think about it. Don't you dare.* Seth, in reply, would narrow his eyes, pinch his brows, and chop his right hand in the air in frustration, the only mini-rebellion he was allowed.

Cal and I rarely "got the chop," as we called it, since we were so careful not to add to Mother's burden of Seth. I'll never know how much of my and Cal's consistent obedience to Mother's expectation came from our own virtuousness or from wanting to counterbalance the trials Seth caused, as if my family was on a precarious seesaw that had to be kept on center.

Mother's eyes couldn't always be on Seth, however, and, out of her suspicious gaze, he made plenty of trouble. I witnessed a lot of it, far more than a young girl should, and I imagined much more went on that no one ever knew. I saw him steal coins from the peach stand, kick Trout when the dog didn't listen and sometimes even when he did, sneak Daddy's truck away to who knows where when he was barely tall enough to see over the dashboard. He behaved even worse around his friends, especially at school, when he and boys like him turned the smallest disagreement into dusty fistfights or ganged up to swipe a sandwich from a younger child's lunch. Once, I came around the back of the barn to find Seth and the three Oakley boys from down the road pouring kerosene over bullfrogs and lighting them aflame, rolling with laughter as the poor creatures hopped about in terror. I ducked into the barn before they could see me and cried against our gelding Abel's soft muzzle.

The summer before the accident, whenever Cal got a break from mowing hay and all my chores were done, he and I worked on building ourselves a tree house in the biggest cottonwood overhanging the creek. We gathered scrap lumber from farms along our road, hauled it home a few pieces at a time on Abel's back, tied ropes, and hoisted each splintered board into the high branches. Cal did most of the work, but he gave me small jobs to make me feel like a partner. We asked Seth if he wanted to help, but he was into digging foxholes that summer with Holden Oakley, the oldest and rudest of the Oakley brothers. Mother had rolled her eyes and given them permission to dig pits on an unplanted corner of the farm where Daddy stored extra fencing and equipment. The boys fashioned branches into machine guns and rubbed coal bricks on their cheeks, and nearly every day they snuck up on Cal and me as we worked, ambushing us with spitty gunfire sounds from the ground below, yelling up at us about our ugly tree house, about our wasted time.

The day our project was finished—complete with a platform floor, four uneven but solid walls, a lean-to roof, and a rope ladder swinging to the ground through a square hole in the center—Cal and I hauled up a celebratory picnic, including perfectly tart lemonade we had squeezed ourselves. We sat side by side on an old blanket and ate our jelly sandwiches.

"Bet'cha a nickel Seth is gonna want to be part of this, now all the work is done," Cal said, leaning back on his elbows and admiring his handiwork.

"We best pull up the ladder," I said, more concerned about sharing my lemonade than anything else. Cal smiled at my idea, reached down, and lugged the ladder up to pile it on the tree house floor.

I felt the sweetness of being cut off from the world with only the safety and kindness of Cal about me, and I realized that not even the lemonade mattered so much. For the first time, I consciously considered the comfort of being where Seth could not be, and, in doing so, I realized far down inside my sister self, in a deep place I could not name, that I was frightened of my own little brother. I had listened to all the church preaching about darkness—about Satan and serpents and sinners—but at that age I knew nothing of the type of darkness Seth carried, the kind that perhaps some children are born with, those who spend their lives seeking to undo the rules others agree to live by. All I knew as I lay back on the blanket to listen to the sparrows twittering overhead and Cal's chewing and my own long exhales was a profound appreciation that Seth couldn't tear any of it down.

Cal and I fell asleep up there, like two birds in a nest after the exhausting work of its building, content and comfortable, high from the reach of cats.

We sat up in startled unison when the first rock hit the tree house wall and exploded our peace. It wasn't until the second rock hit moments later that either of us, groggy from sleep, could make sense of the disturbance.

"Seth," Cal sighed, and he clinched his jaw. Neither of us moved or spoke, not so much hiding as simply not wanting to respond, hoping he'd go away. Another rock hit the wall, then another. When the fifth rock split a board, Cal finally leapt up and hollered down at Seth to cut it out.

"Let me up!" Seth shouted back.

"No!" Cal refused.

"Let me up there now!" Seth repeated, followed by another rock striking the wall. Seth was short but muscular and known for his throwing arm. He struck out batter after batter in baseball games at the town field, knocked down all the bottles and won the bubble gum every year at the Gunnison County fair.

Cal refused again, and Seth began to fume at the base of the tree, calling Cal names my mother would have washed out of his mouth with lye soap had she heard. Though barely ten years old to Cal's eighteen, Seth didn't bow to Cal's elder status and never had. Certain from toddlerhood of his correct view of all things, poised on the perpetual defensive, Seth was determined not to look to his cousin for clues about boyhood or the workings of the world. He'd charge ahead of Cal in the yard, the fields, the orchard; he yanked tools from Cal's hand when he thought Cal was working too slowly and he could do the task better himself. And when Cal teased him or tackled him like an older brother, Seth unleashed a fury that erased the difference of size and years between them, forcing Cal to fight back or retreat. Cal learned early on not to cross Seth, a decision wholly responsible for whatever kinship existed between them.

I sat on the tree house floor, fiddling with a frayed edge of the picnic basket, unsure of what to do. It had been my idea to pull up the rope ladder and bar Seth access. I couldn't let Cal take the full force of the resulting collision.

"You said this tree house was stupid!" I yelled from where I sat, not knowing if my words would travel the distance down the trunk, partially hoping they would not. If there was one person in our family who crossed Seth even less than Cal, it was me.

As soon as I spoke, I knew I had made a mistake. Cal spun around to face me and sped a finger to his lips, as if by silencing his own mouth the words would stop pouring out of mine.

"Torie?! Is that you up there too, goddammit?" Seth demanded, surprised ire catapulting his voice right through the opening in the floor.

I thought he knew I was in the tree house with Cal. We had built it together, after all. It was my tree house too. But I suddenly felt guilty about being there, though I couldn't figure out why. As much as Seth refused to look to Cal for guidance, at eleven years old I looked to my older cousin for nearly my every move. If a thing agreed with Cal, it agreed with me too, for he was wise and good, and I loved the way his eyes arched into two little crescent moons when I did something pleasing or funny. He was a compass to be trusted.

"Don't say anything," Cal whispered, crouching down. "It will only make things worse."

"Why?" I questioned.

"He gets jealous is all," Cal said.

"Of a tree house he thinks is so dumb?" I asked.

"Of you and me," Cal whispered.

He sat down next to me on the blanket and arranged and re-arranged his legs a few times, as if to say, *Let's just wait this one out, let's get comfortable.* Seth was all the while yelling my name, pausing from time to time to beat the tree with a fallen bough or shoot at us with his imaginary machine gun, and, judging from the grunts and dull thuds from below, making futile attempts at shimmying up the wide, branchless trunk.

I had never before thought of myself as worthy of envy. Envy, as Mother and scripture had taught us, was akin to malice and even to murder in the eyes of God. "Envy rots the bones," says the proverb. "Envy put Jesus on the cross," preached Reverend Whitt. If I, mousey and unrefined as I was, could rouse envy, then surely anything could ignite its spark. I felt dangerously close to something sinister and was wholly unsure how I got there. All the while, Seth bayed for me from the base of the tree like a hound longing for its catch.

Cal and I sat up there an hour or more, silent, and Seth never gave up. As the sun started its slow summer descent along the western horizon, Daddy came looking for us to tend to the animals.

"What in the devil's goin' on out here?" Daddy hollered as he approached, causing Seth to finally quiet. Cal and I peeked out the bottom of the tree house to watch Seth get his due.

"Nothin'," Seth replied, looking at the ground, kicking at a stone. His sweaty hair was as spiked as sagebrush.

"Sounded like somethin'," Daddy said, his hands thrust deep into the pockets of his dirty overalls, the way he stood when he was looking for information.

"They ain't gonna let me up in that tree shack of theirs is all," Seth whined.

"How's that hog pen gonna get raked with you lollygaggin' in a kiddie house?" Daddy asked. "Git on now." Daddy watched as Seth, defeated, headed toward the hogs. I wasn't sure if he was pondering his son or just making sure Seth got to where he was told to go, but we waited a long time for Daddy to stop looking Seth's way and call us down from the tree.

The rope ladder swayed and spun with my trifling weight until Daddy held it taut at the bottom and I climbed to his waiting arms. I didn't often get a hug from Daddy, so I took the opportunity to embrace his neck, to bury my face in his shoulder and inhale him. I even wrapped my skinny legs around his waist until Cal scrambled to the ground carrying the blanket and picnic basket in one arm.

There was something in the way Daddy peeled me off his neck and put me down hard, and in the sharp tone he told us it wouldn't have killed us to let Seth up, that made me recall another of Mother's admonishments, from the book of John: "Whoever loves God must also love his brother." She frequently reminded us that we sin, we repent, not in isolation but in relation. From my youngest memories, I knew that Seth and I were eternally and mysteriously linked. I stood there as Daddy walked away, just a puzzled girl beneath the tree house that was now a little bit ruined, having no idea how far my brother and I would ultimately fall.

SETH REVVED THE ROADSTER one final time before I heard the kitchen door slam and Daddy's furious voice in the yard. The door slammed again, and once more a few minutes later, presumably as Daddy then Seth stormed inside. My alarm clock rang and I rose, dressed, and limped through the quiet, cold house to the kitchen. My ankle ached as I prepared breakfast, but I remained hopeful the injury was minor. If I could not walk, I could not attempt to locate Wil, to at least find evidence of his going or staying, of possibilities denied or still alive.

The men silently entered the lamp-lit kitchen one by one, allowing no eye contact with one another or me. Silverware clinked plates as ham was cut, fried eggs mashed, and all consumed. Seth exited first, then Og, then Daddy, and I was left at the table, relieved to finish my meal and clean up alone. The angrier they were at each other, the more I went unnoticed, which was exactly what I needed in order to find Wil.

As I was finishing the dishes, I heard Uncle Og's wheelchair creaking back down the hallway. The more weight he gained, the more the chair groaned, and the more sweat he worked up trying to move himself around the house. I expected the chair to someday split down the middle, dumping him cursing to the floor, each wheel fleeing as if finally freed from the displeasure of Og's constant company.

A teacher once told me that President Roosevelt had a wheelchair, presumably similar to Og's, with a wooden back and long planks ending in feet like two stiff legs of its own. Roosevelt never allowed himself to be photographed or publicly seen in the chair, my teacher said, a facade so well maintained that few people believed the rumor of his disability. He looked so presidential in newspaper photographs, and he spoke with power and eloquence on the radio. He even drove a fine automobile in parades and processions. I had never known anyone crippled until Og came back broken and mean from the war. The new Ogden bore no resemblance to the old, let alone to the only president I had ever known. It was not until long after both Roosevelt and Og had passed away and wheelchairs were no longer made of wood that I saw one of only two known photographs of the president in his chair, and I wondered how many war veterans, legless and miserable like Og, might have suffered a little bit less had the president not hidden his chair in shame.

As I stood on one leg drying dishes, I heard Og bang into the wall and curse. I turned to see him coming through the kitchen threshold carrying crutches in one hand and trying to advance the chair with the other. Our eyes met, and neither of us knew how to respond to this uncharacteristic act of civility.

"Here," he grunted, throwing the crutches to the floor; then he backed out the doorway and wheeled down the hall.

I had not seen these crutches since the day Uncle Og returned from the war a changed man.

I remembered driving to Montrose that day in our stiff Sunday clothes, the same summer of 1942 that Cal and I built the tree house. Eager to see my uncle again, I sat sweaty and fidgety between Cal and Seth in the back seat of the big sedan Daddy had borrowed from our neighbor, Mr. Mitchell. In the long front seat, Aunt Viv chattered nervously to Mother as Daddy drove, her carefully spun ringlets bouncing like springs. I imagined Ogden and his spry brother Jimmy stepping off the train in their handsome soldier's uniforms, looking up and down the platform until Og's clear blue eyes would light up at the sight of us, his new family, welcoming him home. I imagined Og grabbing Aunt Vivian around the waist and pulling her to his lips, kissing her the way I had seen him do in the orchard just days before he left for Europe to fight, her back arching gracefully like a willow.

We hadn't known Ogden long before the war so quickly took him after he and Viv married. But that didn't prevent us from looking like a *Saturday Evening Post* cover as we stood huddled together on the platform, ready to claim him and Jimmy as our own. As the black engine swelled into view, I needed no other reason than a vague notion of patriotism and popular magazine lore to adore him. He was a war hero, a movie star, a giant. I had worked myself up into such anticipation by the time the train ground to a slow, metallic halt in front of us that I could have been waiting for Roosevelt himself to burst from those steps.

The instant Ogden appeared at the train-car opening, I knew I had been tricked. My mind swam in an attempt to figure out by whom, but all I could come up with was by Ogden himself—this one-legged soldier, standing alone, arms wrapped tightly around yellowed wooden crutches, his dull eyes peering from beneath the capsized boat of his soldier's hat.

Vivian gasped at the sight of him and buried her face in Mother's shoulder. Mother shoved her off and hastily righted her, grabbing and maneuvering each shoulder as if steering a heavy plow. She whispered harshly into Vivian's ringlets, "You don't."

Cal and Daddy glanced at each other, then sprang to Og's assistance. He answered their outstretched hands with a swipe of one crutch, nearly hitting Cal square in the face and tipping himself sidelong into the doorframe, muttering, "Get your goddamn hands away from me."

Cal and Daddy stepped back, and we all stood motionless, dumbfounded, watching him clumsily descend the train steps and turn his back to us. I remember Aunt Viv's moaning and the hollow thud of those unexpected crutches on the wooden platform, over and over like a slow, ill heartbeat as he hobbled away. I looked at the sunken faces of the soldiers filing off the train. None of them was the Ogden I remembered. None of them was Jimmy.

We found Og staring at the pavement in front of the station. Daddy brought the car around, and my family slid inside. We waited for Og to join us—so long that Daddy turned off the engine and Aunt Viv's whimpering became the only sound—until Mother got out and somehow coaxed him into the front seat next to her. No one spoke the entire ride home. Vivian sat squeezed between me and Cal, staring in disbelief at the back of her husband's unmoving head. I placed my hand on her knee and she grasped it like a lifeline.

"It's God's will," my mother replied to Aunt Viv's tirade about her broken soldier when she burst through our kitchen door in tears the next morning. Viv lamented with uncensored volume why, if Og now hated life and everything to do with it, he didn't just die on the battlefield, didn't leave his body right there on the beach next to Jimmy's. Mother sat two coffee mugs on the table and told Viv to sit.

Whenever I heard Mother reference God's will—and I heard it plenty—I thought of it this way: God will or He won't. God will let a young soldier die in his older brother's arms. God will make war and bitterness and an alien of a man. God won't explain.

I limped across the kitchen and picked up the old crutches Og had tossed at me. I tucked them under my armpits and tested my stride.

God will pluck your mother, your cousin, your aunt from this earth like peaches pulled from the branch too soon.

I turned off the kitchen light without returning the clean dishes to the cupboards, pulled on my navy-blue wool coat hanging on the hook by the back door, splayed the laces of my shoe to accommodate my wrapped and swollen foot, and crutched out to feed the animals.

God will bring two strangers together on the corner of North Laura and Main and lead them toward love. God won't make it easy.

God will take a life, God will give a life, and God will make a life unrecognizable. God won't warn you what's coming next.

When the animals were cared for and the first arms of morning sun reached across the valley, I glanced around to be sure I was unnoticed. I climbed on my bicycle, positioned the crutches carefully across the handlebars, and, not pausing to wonder whether God will or God won't, I set out to find Wilson Moon.

Five

I expected obstacles in finding Wil, but I certainly didn't anticipate that Ruby-Alice Akers would be one of them.

Ruby-Alice lived in a faded brown farmhouse on a thickly wooded triangular plot of land down the road from my family. Though our nearest neighbor, she wore a sour expression and a constant black stocking cap over her colorless curls and lived with a menagerie of stray animals, and, thus, Mother found her too peculiar to warrant a good Christian's attention. We passed her place almost daily, but we never stopped for a visit or dropped off a neighborly pie. Mother instructed us not to look Ruby-Alice's way when we saw her riding about town on her rickety black bicycle with the frayed woven basket dangling from the handlebars. She was known to stare people down with her strange eyes and part her lips as if preparing to bark some rudeness but then never say a word. All Iola thought her crazy but harmless enough to just let her be.

One night at supper—back when Mother used to sit in the place at the table that Og later claimed—Seth's eyes lit up as he recounted pitching a series of rocks at the old woman as she ogled him from her bicycle out on our shared road.

"One clean hit her," he boasted, smirking through a half-chewed biscuit, "but that Mad Myrtle just kept pedaling as if she didn't feel a thing."

I expected Mother to scold Seth for violence against a neighbor, or at least for talking with his mouth full, but she continued to eat her ham in small, proper bites.

"She's the devil," Seth laughed. Daddy and Cal glanced expectantly at Mother, but she still said nothing. Seth's mouth ran with the unexpected freedom of a dog unleashed. "The devil in the flesh, living right there in them pines!"

He danced his index fingers above each ear like horns until Mother finally scolded, "There'll be no talk of Satan in this house."

Not long after, Ruby-Alice pedaled past Mother and me on Main. I couldn't help but look at her, wondering if she was indeed Satan in unlikely disguise, wondering if I could tell. She was ugly as the devil, that was clear. White matted curls stuck out from beneath the black cap. Her wrinkled skin was tinted a sickly blue. One eye was so deeply receded into its socket that it seemed to be missing. The other eye—ice blue, wild, and bulging—locked with mine for one alarming instant.

She stared me down and opened her thin lips as she sped past, but the only sound was her squeaking bicycle and the gravel popping beneath its wheels. A ragged little Chihuahua, black and pointy-eared as a bat, shivered in her wicker basket.

"Did you look at her?" Mother demanded, stopping to lift my chin and peer into my eyes.

"No, ma'am," I said, unsure why I was lying even as the words escaped my lips.

"Crazy as a cricket," Mother said, dropping my chin and grabbing my arm, continuing toward Chapman's grocery. "God help us."

My mother strode more quickly, as if escaping something menacing, even though Ruby-Alice had already disappeared with a slanting turn off Main. I struggled to keep up. I wondered, if Ruby-Alice Akers was the crazy one, why were *we* the ones in need of help from the Lord and not her?

I secretly started praying for Ruby-Alice. Every time she popped up, I ran the same brief, clandestine blessing through my mind, rapidly, like it was all one word, so as to get the trespass against my mother over with as quickly as possible: *GodHelpRubyAliceAkers-Amen*. I figured the phrase was efficient and to the point, covering lunacy and Satan and her blue skin and anything else that ailed her, and swift enough to be sent skyward without Mother catching on. It was strange to hide a prayer, something Mother couldn't get enough of from me and the boys, but, clearly, she had determined Ruby-Alice beyond salvation. Why I held the notion that I alone could return her to God's grace I cannot say, but I believed it with all my young heart. Even after she glared at me from behind a tree as I exited the church bleary-eyed and unsteady after my family's funeral, even at that moment when my mind felt mushy with grief, I thought, *God-HelpRubyAliceAkersAmen*. Reverend Whitt had his sons chase her off the church grounds. One of my few lucid moments from that dark day was watching her leap on her bicycle and speed away.

By the autumn when I was seventeen, I had long ago abandoned my childish prayers for Ruby-Alice's welfare and, though we were still neighbors, she rarely crossed my mind. I hadn't seen her since midsummer when she'd sped past our roadside peach stand, eyeing me in her peculiar way and sending Trout mad with barking. I had quieted the dog, apologized to the customers palming the early-crop peaches, and never thought about the old woman again.

When I set out to find Wilson Moon that morning—the crutches teetering across the handlebars of my bicycle as I maneuvered down our long driveway and onto the dirt road to town—there, like a sudden apparition in the pale light, stood Ruby-Alice Akers. She was without both black cap and bicycle. White hair spiraled rather desperately away from her pallid face. Her legs stuck like two pale toothpicks from worn leather boots. She wore a dingy muslin dress hemmed at her bony knees and layers of wool cardigans, all in shades of green so like the surrounding pines that her torso seemed to recede into background, amputating her into two colorless halves. Her sunken eye examined me as if I were a stranger, while her bulging eye struck out accusingly, like she had been waiting for me too long and now felt bitterness at my arrival.

I nearly fell off my bicycle trying to steer around her. She stood, glaring, unbudging. Her knobby eye surveyed the crutches and my bandaged ankle. She clucked her tongue and shook her head.

It never occurred to me to stop. The woman for whom I had harbored such concern as a child had become to me, as she was to everyone else, mere backdrop. At that moment, she was simply an obstacle, just as a cow or a piece of fallen timber on the road might have been.

I startled when she reached out, two snow-white palms with splayed, twisted fingers thrusting toward me as if to push me to the ground. I recoiled and sped away as best I could. As I did, I noticed her ramshackle black bicycle flung among the dead daises in the roadside ditch.

In retrospect, I am ashamed that I did not even pause to ask if she needed help. I was so focused on my search for Wilson Moon, or perhaps so conditioned to ignore Ruby-Alice as one might a stray dog, that it did not occur to me that she could be injured or disoriented. It certainly didn't cross my mind that she might be the one offering aid but had no clearer idea of how to approach me than I did her.

Downtown, Wil was nowhere to be found. Iola was quiet, just waking. A half dozen townsfolk walked to work or the café. Mr. Jernigan swept the walkway outside his hardware store. Two automobiles and a milk truck drove on Main. I rode my bicycle the length of downtown twice, as many times as I felt I could without drawing attention, hoping Wil would see me and appear in a doorway or window, grinning, beckoning. I imagined what he'd look like after he'd bathed at Dunlap's, perhaps found clean clothes, and my heart quickened. When there was no sign of him, I parked my bicycle outside the flophouse, positioned the crutches under my arms, took a deep breath, and hobbled up the wooden steps. The front door was propped open with a brown rock. I peered in, inhaling the smell of coffee and bacon and men but seeing only a long, wood-paneled mudroom lined with benches and cluttered with a half dozen hanging jackets and mud-encrusted boots. My mind raced for an excuse to enter.

A bearded man about Daddy's age but straighter and stronger strolled into the mudroom and sat on a bench. He reached for his boots and wedged one onto his right foot, whistling a quiet tune as he tied the laces. Reaching for his left boot, he glanced at the doorway and his whiskers spread into an unnerving grin. He let out a long high whistle through his corn-kernel teeth, looking me up and down and sniggering, "Well, well, look what we have here."

Every autumn Dunlap's filled with field hands seeking haying and harvest work, along with cattlemen hoping to get hired on to gather herds from the high meadows and drive them down valley before the first snowfall. The influx was helpful and welcomed, though some of the men, I knew, brought trouble. There was something about this one, with his yellow smile and eager eyes, that made me yearn for winter.

I stammered for a moment, gripping my crutches. I heard dishes clatter from inside and guessed that Mr. and Mrs. Dunlap were in the kitchen cleaning up after breakfast.

"I'm here to help the Dunlaps start the lunch fixin's," I lied with surprising ease.

"They're in the back, sugar," he replied, too cozily. I took another deep breath and crutched across the threshold and through the long room, feeling the man's eyes on me as I passed. "Ain't gonna be much help though, by the looks of it," he added with a nod and a smirk toward my bandaged ankle.

"I'll manage," I answered, emboldened by my quick lie and my first steps into the forbidden boarding house.

Inside, I expected to encounter more men, but, to my relief, they were apparently either in the washhouse or already gone to morning jobs. The sitting room was dark and dank with two worn leather sofas and a spattering of wooden chairs haphazardly arranged around a warm black potbellied wood stove. A stout brass bowl with a flared rim sat next to the brick hearth, and a board propped against it read "Please Use The Spittoon" in black, hand-painted letters. A six-point elk head hung on the wall and overlooked the scene with vacant black eyes. I followed the sound of the dishes.

I found Mrs. Dunlap drying the last of the breakfast plates with a red-checkered towel, lightly humming. Contrary to the dinginess of the sitting room, the kitchen had clean white walls and a high row of east-facing windows radiating morning sunlight. Mrs. Dunlap was a pale, tall, bell-shaped woman. She wore a plain white cotton dress covered by a denim apron tied loosely about her neck and waist. Her light brown hair was gathered in a navy handkerchief knotted on both sides of her forehead, the tied ends jutting out like an extra set of ears. She was so lost in thought and humming that she didn't notice me at the kitchen doorway until I deliberately cleared my throat.

"Oh! Torie, dear. I didn't see you there." Mrs. Dunlap patted her heart then greeted me with a warm smile, her small brown eyes arching kindly. She jumped with another start at first notice of my crutches, threw down her dish towel, and rushed to get a chair, saying, "What has happened to you? Here, get off your feet, hon."

I had forgotten what a genial woman Mrs. Dunlap was, having had only brief interactions with her since my mother died, but I remembered then the long, tight hugs she'd given me at my family's funeral and the many casseroles and pies she left on our front porch in the months that followed.

"I'm well, Mrs. Dunlap," I said, sitting and placing the crutches on the floorboards. "Just a twisted ankle. Those prairie dog holes, you know."

"Oh, I do," she commiserated. "I've done that myself. Vexing creatures. You poor dear." She pulled up a chair next to mine and settled in. "What can I do for you? And it's Millie, hon, just Millie."

The lies had flowed so easily since entering the flophouse that I opened my mouth and expected another to explain my visit. Nothing came. I fiddled with the wooden buttons on my coat. Millie leaned a bit closer and raised her brows.

Unable to invent a lie, and overly comforted by Millie's warmth, I stupidly told the truth.

"I was wondering if you have a boy named Wilson Moon staying here?" I asked shyly, my heart somersaulting at my first utterance of his name.

The change in Millie's expression instantly told me I had made a mistake.

"That Injun boy?" she asked with a grimace, pulling away as if from an awful smell. "Torie, honey, why on God's green earth would you be askin' about a filthy Injun?"

I was speechless. I had never seen an Indian before. All I knew was what I learned in school about their violence against my grandparents' generation as the whites tried to civilize the West, and how the government had long ago relocated them where they wouldn't cause more trouble. I remembered Daddy's and Seth's remarks the night before about Wil being Mexican. His being Indian would garner even more disdain. I simply couldn't believe it was true.

Millie waited for an answer, her demeanor turning to suspicion bordering on disgust.

"I . . . my . . . ," I stammered, "my daddy heard tell a boy by that name was looking for work. We have a lot of pickin' to be done these next two weeks. I don't know the boy, just the name I was told to fetch."

Millie relaxed. "Well, mark my word, your daddy don't want a thing to do with that boy. Why, I bet ol' Trout wouldn't let him get within a mile of your orchard." She smiled at her insinuation that Wil wasn't even worthy of a dog's approval. "We took one look at that redskin and threw him out of here last evening."

"Oh," I gasped, trying not to give myself away but unable to hide my alarm.

"Our boarders would be fit to be tied if we started allowing In-juns here, not to mention the disease they'd spread." She shud-dered, as if speaking of a rat infestation. "No, you tell your daddy we're happy to post a bill saying he needs a worker, but it's not going to be that boy. I imagine he's miles from here by now anyway. Well," she patted my leg with the assumption of alliance, "We sure hope he is, don't we?"

Her touch nauseated me. Fortunately, her husband entered the kitchen at the very moment I had run out of composure on the topic of Wilson Moon. Mr. Dunlap's arms overflowed with green ears of corn. Millie jumped to his aid.

"Morning, Torie. Good to see you," he said as casually as if I'd stopped in for a daily visit.

Millie interrupted before I could speak, clearly warding off men-tion of Wil, saying, "Mr. Nash is looking for a hand for the last of the peach harvest. I told Torie we'd let the men know." She winked at me.

"Happy to oblige," he said, pulling back the first long piece of husk and its underbelly of silky white threads. He was large and brawny, his veined forearms bulging with each sure tug. "A few of our boarders will be finishing up haying soon. I reckon someone'll be looking for more work."

I thanked him, then exchanged a few more pleasantries about the harvest and my ankle and the nice fall weather. As soon as politeness allowed, I gathered up my crutches, excused myself, and hobbled back through the flophouse. More cumbersome than my injury was my load of lies and the Dunlaps' rebuff of Wil—intolerance, I feared, he would receive from many others if he was in fact of Indian blood. As I reached the front porch, my coat felt suffocating in the morning sun. I flung the crutches against the railing and unbuttoned in near panic, wriggling out of the coat and dropping it to the porch floor, breathless and sweaty.

Far more concerning to me than the question of Wil's blood was the nearly undeniable fact that he had left town. With the Dunlaps' eviction and the hostility and threats he had received from my family, I couldn't imagine why he would want to remain in Iola. A girl as plain as me certainly couldn't keep him where he otherwise wasn't wanted. I took a deep breath, steeled myself with my mother's sensible practicality, and vowed to let go of all this nonsense. Wil was gone. I told myself my life was no different than it had been less than a day prior, before I had ever looked into his deep, dark eyes.

But as I crutched to my bicycle and headed home, I could only feign conviction. For in those eyes, I had seen not only an unexpected kind of man, but some new part of myself that I didn't want to let go.

Six

I woke the next morning with my mind whirling through the events of the previous two days. I needed the distraction of busy hands and convinced myself that my still-swollen ankle was surely well enough for me to get back to work.

Before limping into the kitchen to prepare breakfast, I returned Og's crutches. I leaned them against the wall outside his closed bedroom door and considered him in a new way: how it must feel to be Ogden, one leg lost to war, the other without foot or use after gangrene, a once agile body trapped in the confines of a chair. Since the day he'd returned from war, Og's fury was surely the lion concealing the lamb of his sorrow. Viv had made no secret of her discontent with her maimed warrior, despite my mother's cajoling for her to stop her wailing and embrace God's plan. When Viv died so suddenly, I resented Og for not being sad enough. But perhaps her absence was for him one less remnant of his former life that he could not rise to. If I was unable to tolerate a second day on those crutches, how did the former adventurer bear the whole barren reality of his postwar life?

I left the crutches and crept to the drop-leaf desk in the parlor. Inside, I found my mother's stationery. The plain lavender sheets sat in a neat pile, forbidden to me during her life, untouched since her death. I peeled off the top page, half expecting her scolding hand chop to appear before me. I pulled a still perfectly sharpened pencil from a silver tin and scrolled, "Thank you." I folded the note and placed it outside Og's door, never expecting, or receiving, a response.

Plenty kept me busy over the next several days. We had been picking and selling fine peaches since July, but it's the cold nights and warm days of early autumn on Colorado's western slope that sweetens the fruit sugar. Our customers most anticipated that precious final crop. Daddy's fall ritual was to wake several times per night to check the thermometer, knowing all too well the knife edge on which our success teetered. A sudden dip of just five degrees could transform a perfect and profitable late crop into hanging balls of mush suitable only for hogs and the garbage bin. The goal was to harvest slowly enough to keep our product fresh all autumn yet rapidly enough to clear the trees before the first hard frost. We had been lucky so far that fall, able to delay the final harvest a good two weeks past the norm, but Daddy wasn't one to believe in luck that holds, and I could tell he was nervous. Suspicious of a two-degree drop the morning Seth had stirred up such a racket with his roadster, and another degree lower the morning I quietly returned Og's crutches, Daddy gave the order to clear the rows as quickly as possible. Sore ankle or not, I was glad for the work.

I had picked peaches my entire life. It came as naturally to me as breath. I can't remember a time when I didn't know how to use smell and a gentle touch to determine the ideal ripeness, how to lightly lift and twist each peach from its stem so as not to gouge the fragile flesh, how to know which rosy fruit was ready for market, which for delivery, and which for eating off the tree. Unlike an apple or a pear, a meager span of days—three, perhaps four—determines the crucial moment to pick and eat a peach. My family had built our orchard's reputation not only on the perfect shape and taste of our peaches, but on our skill, handed down over three generations, in harvesting and selling them at the exact moment of ripeness.

With my orchard basket hanging from my left arm and golden banana-shaped leaves tickling my face and shoulders, I reached with my right hand to twist peach after peach from the boughs, frequently bringing the fruit to my nose to inhale the sweet aroma. Daddy was, of course, correct. The final batch, without exception, was ready to be plucked.

I chose to pick in solitude in the oldest block of trees at the far end of the orchard. Daddy picked in a newer block near the barn with Trout at his side. Seth picked in the rows along the creek. The Oakley brothers—Holden, Chet, and Ray—arrived midmorning to help. I couldn't imagine they did so out of the kindness of their ragged hearts. Sure enough, I later learned that their father had made an arrangement with Daddy to exchange his boys' labor for Daddy's and Seth's hand driving their cattle in two weeks' time. It would be a two-day commitment gathering the herd from the upper valleys and moving them down through Almont and Gunnison and onto their ranch outside Iola. Knowing the Oakley boys as he did,

Daddy told their father the deal only held if there was no mischief and no bruised fruit. I could smell their Lucky Strikes and hear them cussing and teasing within two minutes of joining Seth on the east boundary trees. They were either out of Daddy's earshot, or he was so eager for the help he let their antics go.

It went without saying that I'd pause from picking to have lunch on the table by noon. As the sun neared midline in the lapis blue sky, I gathered my full bushel baskets and placed them alongside the orchard road, where Daddy could most easily load them into the truck bed. I limped by Seth and the Oakleys—ignoring their muffled comments and sniggers as I passed—and on toward the house. As I neared, I could see Daddy talking to a stranger in the yard. The man was youngish and freckled, a head taller than Daddy yet seemingly half as wide, wearing soiled denim coveralls and a wide-brimmed straw hat. Well-worn work gloves hung from his back pocket. Trout wagged his tail in greeting, but the man seemed not to notice. When Daddy saw me approaching, he waved me over, and the man looked at me with a long, horselike face.

"Dunlaps sent him," Daddy said, pointing to the man without any introduction.

My heart sank. The long arms of my lies reached everywhere. I grasped for another deceit to explain why I had been in the forbidden flophouse, why I'd fabricated Daddy's request for a hand, but before I could utter a word, Daddy went on, saying, "Nice of 'em. We can use the help." He nodded toward the man and the man nodded back, sealing the deal. And then, to me, "Don't have much to pay, so give the boy a good meal."

I exhaled, smiled at the man, who did not smile back, and said, "Sure will."

When the men piled into the kitchen for lunch, their smells came with them. A pungent mix of sweat and tobacco and peach juice and autumn sunshine shoved out the aroma of the fixin's, even as I pulled the biscuits from the oven, even as I set the roasted chicken and potatoes in the center of their ravenous circle. Uncle Og rolled in, adding whiskey and chewing tobacco to the scent as he sullenly wheeled up to his usual place at the table.

I busied myself at the stove as they began eating, my back to the table, pouring roasting pan juices into a skillet and stirring up gravy for that night's supper. Daddy introduced the horse-faced man to the others at the table as Forrest Davis. Og grunted, and the young men said their hellos and then went on exchanging boisterous stories and insults. All ate heartily and no one noticed I didn't sit, which pleased me just fine.

I was stirring more flour into the gravy and paying little attention to the men when Davis, who had been silent until then, suddenly cleared his throat and said in a surprisingly deep voice, "Pert near had to bunk with an Injun at the flop. You all hear 'bout that?"

I halted, my back stiffening, my grip tightening on the whisk. My breath sat on the edge of stilled lungs as I listened.

"Bet that's the filthy son of a bitch you lit into, Seth," said one of the Oakleys through a full mouth—Holden, I guessed from his venomous tone.

"Heard he got tossed out of Dunlap's," Seth replied.

I wondered how he knew, who he had been asking and why.

"Did," said Davis, "But not before contaminatin' the washhouse. Snuck in, the skunk." Davis chewed, swallowed. "Dunlap caught him stealing clothes off the line. Run off with an armful."

The neglected gravy at my hand curdled and boiled over. Brown splatters leaped up and seared my thumb. I jerked backward, overturning the skillet with a clatter, spilling scorched goo across the stove top. The men behind me fell silent, looking at me no doubt, but my face was so flushed from the mention of Wilson Moon, I dared not turn around.

"Sorry," I said, grabbing a rag from the sink. "Butter fingers," I said with a phony chuckle as I wiped.

Conversation started up again. I lost track of who was saying what, just that one had heard that the boy had escaped from jail down south near one of the reservations; another had heard it was an Indian boarding school he had run from; another said he was a thief, a drifter who struck a town then moved on. They joked about his war paint, his moccasins, called him a godless savage, a prairie rat.

"Long gone by now, I'd reckon," said Davis.

"Better be," grumbled Uncle Og.

"Damn well," replied Seth. "I'll kill that redskin bastard if I ever see him again."

"That's enough," Daddy piped in for the first time. I heard him put his silverware on his plate and push his chair back from the table. "Let's get that fruit down, boys."

The men left the kitchen in a clattering mass, taking their cruel talk and sharp smell with them, leaving the table strewn with crumbs and dishes and a chicken carcass so clean picked it could have been devoured by vultures. My hands shook as I removed and scraped the plates. I had barely been able to conceive of the possibility that Wil was indeed an Indian or what that even meant to me, let alone believe he was a fugitive or a thief. The cruel talk about him seemed so wrong, yet what did I actually know about this boy other than that he had charm and mystery and the strength to lift and carry me as if I were weightless?

I filled the sink, standing on one foot to rest my ankle, and washed the dishes with absentminded strokes, recalling what it felt like to be in Wil's arms, to look into his kind, penetrating eyes. I remembered his tale about riding the coal train and wondered about truth and lies. I assumed the men were correct that Wil was long gone from Iola. And yet.

I dried and shelved the dishes, then headed back to my section of the orchard to pick for the afternoon. Above our farm, the arid earth was patchworked with pale-green sagebrush, red scrub oak, and raggedy pinyons. Scattered clumps of yellow aspen trees quaked like little celebrations across the otherwise solemn hillside. A few ponderosa pines rose above the rest and spread their wide, dark skirts. The sun beat down on it all as if uninformed that summer had ended. Standing in the shade of the orchard, where my heart was most settled and my senses acute, intuition told me, for better or for worse, that Wil was not far away. I don't know how I knew, but I felt him watching me as I reached and sniffed and twisted each soft, ripe peach from the bough. Later, he would tell me how the afternoon sun had reflected off the golden leaves and shimmered yellow upon my skin; how he'd watched me bite into a fat peach, juice dripping down my forearm and off my bare elbow; how my mouth glistened, as if inviting him to press his lips against mine. He said that this was the moment he realized he was falling in love with me, more deeply with each greedy bite and each unknowing glance toward him through the shaggy trees.

My hope that hard work would somehow thrust Wil from my mind proved entirely unfounded. On the contrary, throughout the long, quiet afternoon in the orchard, he alone occupied my mind. While I was lost in thought, the day waned quickly. As I filled my last basket before heading to the kitchen to prepare supper, I heard a sudden rustling to my left. I startled at the sound and tipped my basket, sending several peaches tumbling across the grass. The rustling grew closer, clearly the sound of branches being pushed away by someone traversing the orchard, not on the grassy aisles between the rows but crosswise through the trees themselves. My logical mind told me it was a deer approaching, but my heart begged for it to be Wil. I pictured him emerging from the foliage, one broad shoulder and then another until he stood silently before me, his knowing grin lighting his face, one palm extended as if asking for a peach to be placed in its center but, I'd know, actually wanting my hand.

Suddenly, Forrest Davis pushed his way through the neighboring row not twenty feet from me. His stride was purposeful, aggressive even, as if focused intently on some destination, though, had that been true, he would have been using one of the many paths to the farm road rather than shoving through line after line of trees. Davis paused to peer up the row opposite my direction. He wore his work gloves but carried no basket. Daddy normally didn't allow gloves for picking, believing touch to be as crucial as sight and scent for the harvest. I wondered if Daddy didn't take the time to specify, or if the new hand didn't take well to rules. Davis's big straw hat hung by a cord around his neck and lay across his thin upper back. His motions were quick and nervous. When he spun my way to peer down my row, his hatless forehead was immense, wide and protruding, accentuating the already horselike features of his freckled, high-boned cheeks and long, pointed jaw. I stayed stone still, foolishly hoping I'd go unnoticed. Of course he saw me, and he gave a jolt of surprise when he did. Our eyes locked for the briefest instant. He looked beyond me blankly, as if I were a mere rabbit. He craned his long neck from side to side, searching, then turned abruptly and, reaching his lanky limbs into the branchy space between two trees, disappeared. He continued on with a pause and a rustle, a pause and a rustle, until he traveled beyond my hearing.

Davis was looking for Wil. I was sure of it. I shivered, as much from the cooling afternoon breeze as from the brief but intent stare I'd received from the stranger.

It turned out that Davis was not the only one pursuing Wil. While helping Daddy and Seth make the town deliveries in the cool dawn the next morning, I discovered two notices posted outside Chapman's. There was no mention of name or specifics of the crime, but the two identical hand-lettered placards tacked to both sides of the entry were clearly meant to bring in Wil: "Thief Wanted, Brown Skin, Black Hair, Dangerous. $20 Reward. See Martindell."

Ezra Martindell was the closest thing we had to a law officer in Iola. His grandfather had built one of the first proper houses on Main nearly seventy years prior, and the whole Martindell family took it upon themselves to roost on their wide front porch and keep an eye on the town's doings. With no more qualification than that, Ezra's father, Albert, was deputized by the Gunnison County Sheriff's Department. After Albert died, Ezra took over the badge and the bossy swagger. Once telephone service was installed in Iola in 1942, Ezra's primary duty was to call Sheriff Lyle in Gunnison if anything seemed amiss and to keep order while the real officers made the thirty-minute drive. It infuriated me that the likes of Ezra Martindell could put a reward on Wil based only on lies and conjecture and perhaps a few missing clothes that might just as well have blown from the line.

What troubled me even more was the way Seth let out a bouncy whistle when he saw the notices, as if a challenge he was eager to meet had been set before him. Even worse was the knowing look he shot me as he put one grubby finger on the placard and tapped the word *Reward*.

"Damn straight," he said with a smirk. "I'm gonna win me that twenty bucks."

Seven

Daddy hadn't mentioned my limp that morning, but when we returned to the truck after the Chapman delivery, as I sat in the rear seat silently fuming at my brother's back, he said he wanted me working the roadside stand until lunch.

"If that Davis fella comes back, we should have enough hands," Daddy said. "Cora will be busy today."

Cora Mitchell, our neighbor's spinster daughter who lived in a rustic but tidy cabin on her parents' acreage, worked the stand for us most late-summer and autumn days in exchange for my daddy helping her daddy at their ranch most Mondays and Wednesdays. Our families had done it that way since well before I was born. Cora did a fine job talking weather and peaches and gossip with locals and making the strangers feel like kin. She had a way of charming a customer into buying a dozen peaches if he came for six, half a bushel if he came for twelve. She often sold out by early afternoon. There was no reason to put me at the stand with her other than the injury I was determined to ignore. But my anger at Seth and suspicions about Forrest Davis made me happy for a break from both.

"Suits me fine," I told Daddy.

Cora was waiting dutifully when we pulled up to the faded white clapboard fruit stand. As the lone peach grower in the area, we had the only permanent produce stall along Highway 50, just across the bridge on the Highway 149 cutoff to Iola. Some of the other area farmers occasionally set up tables there and sold their crops, mainly common vegetables and roots, but our stand had a proper tin roof and floorboards and a legal government permit. Legend had it that my grandfather framed that permit the day he picked it up in Gunnison and hung it on the parlor wall like it was art instead of tacking it up in the stand as he was told.

Daddy and Seth heaved the bushel baskets from the truck bed, each breath a puff of vapor in the cool morning air. Cora greeted us with her dimpled grin and immediately began arranging the new fruit on the angled display counter, quickly yet artfully designing precise rows, spinning the rosiest flesh up, tossing the occasional bruised fruit back into its basket. Cora Mitchell was a tall, rotund woman, perhaps the largest woman I had ever seen at that point in my life, and, though I had known her since birth, I was often surprised anew at her size. She wore an immense white blouse that tented across her great breasts and belly, the elastic ruffle digging into the doughy flesh above her elbow. Despite the chill, thin rivers of perspiration trickled from the edges of Cora's tight brunette curls as she worked. I took my place by her side, arranging fruit until the truck was unloaded and Daddy and Seth pulled away.

The morning started off slowly, with only a few local early risers visiting the stand for the first hour or so. Cora and I spoke pleasantries about the weather and our families and farms. She sat on the wide, well-worn stool her father had built for the stand long ago, and, though my ankle ached and another stool sat empty, I paced. In between customers, Cora busied her hands with knitting a green scarf, while I ran Martindell's placard over and over through my mind. I desperately wanted to tell Cora all I knew about the supposed thief, but my experience with Millie Dunlap kept my lips sealed.

By 9:00 a.m., cars lined the road and the stand thronged three customers deep. Cora chatted and flattered like a party hostess as she worked. She chuckled when they thanked us for being open so late in the season and told them to thank God Almighty for this fine fall weather. I hoped her gaiety would make up for my obvious distractedness. I tried to make cordial conversation, to correctly bag orders and count out change, but, more than once, Cora regarded me quizzically and teased me that my sore ankle had somehow infected my brain.

I couldn't reconcile my impression of Wil with the other version of him spreading through the town, that of a menace, a savage, a thief. I wondered how I could possibly discover the truth about him, to know him without the distortion of rumor, spite born of blind bigotry, or my own raw longing. Ruby-Alice Akers was the only outcast I had ever known. I was taught she was a crazy and wild and perilous thing, beyond respect and regard, not unlike Wil in the eyes of Seth, Millie Dunlap, Martindell, and others. I thought then about the morning two days prior when I'd discovered Ruby-Alice off her bicycle, standing alone in the road. Why hadn't I offered her my help?

During a lull between customers, I asked Cora if she had seen Ruby-Alice lately.

"More 'n usual, actually," she replied. The floorboards moaned as she moved from the cash bin to her stool. She sat and exhaled a few times through puckered lips as if blowing out invisible candles. "She's been out on our road this whole week, mostly just standin' there like she's awaitin' on someone. 'Spect you folks have seen her too most days, right where your drive in'ersects." Cora had a way of amputating words, as if some were too much of a mouthful to pronounce completely.

"Do you think there's something wrong with her?" I asked, not thinking through my phrasing.

"Well . . . ," Cora chuckled, meaning, *Where would the list begin? How can we even start?*

I tried again. "I mean, I saw her out on our road too. Seemed kind of odd, even for her. Do you reckon she's sick or something?"

"'Fraid I never thought to ask," Cora said. "Could be somethin'. Yesterday as Mama and I were drivin' to town, she stood smack in the center of the road, starin' in and lookin' 'round. We could barely pass."

I wasn't sure if I was comforted or disturbed that Cora and her mother had responded to the old woman with the same disregard as I had.

"Why's everyone so scared of her, anyway?" I asked. "Seth thinks she's the devil."

Cora laughed and replied, "Oh, I 'spect most folks aren't 'fraid of her so much as just naturally wary of peculiar. They've forgotten she wasn't always such 'n odd duck."

"No?" I asked.

"Naw." Cora shook her head. "From what I understand, she went funny after the flu swept in 'round here. Maybe from the fevers. Maybe from the grief."

"She lost kin?" I asked.

Cora nodded and raised her dark brows. "All of 'em."

"How many?" I asked in surprise.

Cora shrugged. "Can't say. I wasn't even out o' the cradle back then. I've just heard some talk. Naw, I grew up with the same Ruby-Alice as you. Wanderin' 'round on that ol' bicycle, starin' folks down with them wild eyes. Never sayin' a word. Takin' in all them stray critters for company. God help us."

"GodhelpRubyAliceAkers," I replied distractedly as I mulled Cora's words.

Cora nodded and picked up her knitting. In my mind I added, *Amen.*

When I was young, Cal and I would lie belly down on the bank of the orchard's small pond. He'd reach out his hand and sweep away the floating leaves, revealing a hidden world underneath. We'd loll there, side by side, patiently watching for whatever might swim past or bubble up, each minnow or worm or water bug a tiny miracle of discovery. My conversation with Cora felt like that, like pushing away the debris preventing me from seeing below the surface. Ruby-Alice was lonely and heart-shattered, not crazy or diabolical, just as Wil was simply a wanderer and a brown-skinned stranger in a town that saw few of either. Suddenly, I understood what I could not grasp before: the old woman had been waiting on the road day after day for me. The morning I sped away from her, she was reaching out, not to push me, but to alert me. Wil had stayed in Iola, hiding at Ruby-Alice's place. The old woman had given him refuge. I was sure of it.

"Cora, mind if I leave for a spell?" I asked, trying my best to sound casual though my heart hammered.

"Sure, hon, that's fine," she replied. "I know you'll be gettin' lunch on for the men soon."

Fixing lunch was the furthest thing from my mind, but Cora was right. I stepped out of the stand and checked the cloudless sky. I guessed I had a little over an hour to get food on the table. It took all my willpower not to run. I had no idea what would happen after I found Wil, but solving the riddle of his whereabouts emboldened me. I walked with speed and purpose and only a slight limp, so sure my theory was correct. I imagined various versions of our reunion, all of them ending with me in Wil's arms.

A girl of seventeen can be foolish, especially one who knows nothing of love's extraordinary power until it overtakes her like a flash flood. But in my intuition that Wil was near, in my certainty that I would find him, waiting for me, on the neighboring land where Ruby-Alice kept her strange creatures, I was utterly correct. I had only to traverse through the dark pines, unlatch a previously forbidden gate, and cross a yard full of free-roaming guinea hens and chickens and odd little dogs. I had only to knock on a petal-pink door I had never knocked on before.

I rapped my knuckles shyly, surely too quietly for anyone to hear. When no one came, I knocked again with more vigor. Then I stepped back, took a deep breath, and waited. It occurred to me at the last second to brush the hair off my face and right my dress, to square my shoulders and lift my chin. My appearance, which had always been an afterthought, suddenly seemed of great importance, but there was nothing much I could do about it as I saw the doorknob begin to turn.

The door opened with a metallic whine, and there stood Wilson Moon, smiling, radiant, a patient calm about him as if he had been expecting me all along. It struck me then, like jolting from a dream, that I had spent far more time with this boy in my imagination than in reality. We were hardly more than strangers, yet I had convinced myself he would receive me. Standing there before him, I blushed and fidgeted, not knowing what to say or do.

Luckily, he offered me his warm hand, and I took it. He led me into the house, and I followed.

THE MEN FILED INTO the kitchen one by one, again bringing with them their odors, appetites, and relentless exchange of insults. Once they settled in their seats, I delivered a plate of ham sandwiches and a heaping bowl of slaw, then returned with a jug of sweet tea. Hot and jittery from rushing, I kept my head low.

"You sick?" It was Seth who noticed my red cheeks and the sweaty edges of my hair. He gaped at me accusingly, as if I had no right to be ill or, worse, I was faking it. Davis lifted his horse face, studied me a few seconds, then stooped back to his plate.

"Had to rush here from the stand is all," I replied, turning back to the kitchen counter to slice tomatoes.

"Any business?" Daddy asked, pouring a tall glass of tea.

"Loads," I answered honestly.

"Any Injuns?" Seth taunted. He and the Oakley brothers erupted with laughter.

Uncle Og rolled in just then and took his place at the table, growling, "What's so all-fired funny?"

"Not a goddamn thing, cripple," Seth spit back.

"Enough," said Daddy, and the men ate.

Just one Indian, I wanted to gloat back at Seth. *Just my Indian*, I thought, still not entirely sure what that meant or if the label applied to Wil, but knowing I had found the man Seth and his cronies sought, and that I knew so much about him that they did not.

I knew Wil had been sleeping in an abandoned hunter's hut he'd found high in the hills of the Big Blue wilderness, that he'd been sneaking into town to do odd jobs for Ruby-Alice in exchange for food and blankets, and that he had been watching for me, even spying on me as I worked the orchard, confident we'd meet again. I knew the legal accusations against him were false the instant I saw he wore the same overalls and T-shirt, now clean, that he was wearing the day we met. Only his red ball cap was missing. I even knew the warmth of his palm against my cheek, the feel of his smooth skin, and, briefly, the salty sweet taste of his soft lips that left me craving more. I knew with utter certainty that he'd be waiting for me by the arched cottonwood at the end of the road just as soon as I could shoo the men from lunch. My secret tickled at my insides as if I had swallowed a spiraling feather. I cleared each man's plate out from under him before he could finish chewing his last bite and grinned with private delight as I stooped over the sink to wash.

When Daddy rose to exit, I told him I would be going back to the stand to help Cora shut down.

"Fine," he said with nary a glance my way, wholly unaware of the significance of my words, the first lie I ever told my father. It was a price I was willing to pay for my next embrace with Wilson Moon.

Eight

Wilson Moon became my lover. It began with the quick peck on the lips the morning I discovered him at Ruby-Alice Akers's and the long embraces when we met later that day, as planned, by the cottonwood tree that grew nearly parallel to the ground at the end of our road. Each new lie to Daddy came more easily than the last, and I managed to slip away from the farm to meet Wil nearly every afternoon once my picking was done. Sometimes we met under the cottonwood, sometimes by Willow Creek or the reedy shore of the Gunnison, sometimes at the lone blue spruce on the hill or at Ruby-Alice's place among the animal menagerie. Each time, Wil would be waiting right out in the open, as if his only care in the world was to welcome me and engulf me in his thick, sure arms. The musky smell of him soothed me as I buried my face in his chest and stilled. He'd pull away slightly, just enough to look at me with wonder, as if I were an apparition or a rumor newly discovered to be flesh and bone.

Some afternoons he'd see me coming and take off into the woods or tall grasses, so light and quick, and I'd follow. We'd fall together to the ground, to kiss, to laugh at nothing in particular. We'd roll onto our backs to watch the clouds transform or hawks circle or, once, a bald eagle speeding across the sky clutching a trout in its talons. Wil pointed and said it was a sign. I was too shy to ask him a sign of what, but the way he pulled me closer and kissed my forehead made me feel as if we'd been blessed. With neither of us much for talk, few words were spoken on those afternoon trysts. The silence felt just right, like a space carved out for our quiet delight. I once mentioned I had lost a lot of family and he said he had too. I later wished I had asked questions, but, at the time, the light rustling of the breeze through dry grasses and his shoulder pressed against mine seemed the kindest reply. He ate my peaches with wholehearted slurps and moans of appreciation, held my hand afterward so tightly that the residual peach juice nearly glued our palms together. He escaped category and convention and, sometimes, even logic, like when he knew just how to rub my sore ankle so that the final fluid drained away along with every last spark of pain.

I marvel in retrospect how our innocence steadily evaporated with each secret meeting and each caress, until, only two weeks after Wil first opened that pale pink door and received me, our passions drove us beyond all good judgment and into his bed, a two-hour trek to the secluded mountain hut high in the Big Blue.

Just after breakfast that morning, I watched Daddy and Seth slip on their heavy canvas jackets and weathered cowboy hats, then load the truck with saddles and long ropes looped in figure eights and the two canvas backpacks I had filled with canteens, jerky, canned beans, and mason jars of hardboiled eggs. They'd be gone two days gathering the Oakleys' cattle from the mountain pastures up north and herding them down valley to winter pasture.

As the old truck sputtered down the driveway, anticipation burned in my belly. I washed the breakfast dishes and tended the animals but thought only of Wil. Never before had I bathed on a Wednesday, but I filled the tub and took my sweet time, imagining Wil's touch as I smoothed soap across my skin, my insides stirring and opening and warming until I rose from the water, flushed and unsteady. I dried my hair in the autumn sun, then fed Uncle Og lunch along with a smooth lie about needing to stay the night with a seriously ill Cora Mitchell. His only concern was sufficient ham sandwiches and sweet tea in the refrigerator, so I hastily prepared plenty of both before slipping out the back door. By the time I reached Wil waiting for me at the rear edge of the harvested or-chard, I wanted to crawl straight through him. I followed him along the banks of Willow Creek, then up the long, steep trail above and beyond Iola. The landscape morphed from sage and rock and pinyons into grassy meadows sprinkled with yellow aspen trees as the trail trickled off and the air turned thin and cool. When the old hut finally came into view in the waning light, I barely noticed the creek running behind it or the softly lit meadow. My heart pounded as much from desire as from the long hike, and all I wanted was his bed. He pushed back the deer hide covering the entry and turned to me with a silent question in his eyes. I nodded—meaning, *Yes, I am ready; yes, I am sure*—and he smiled and led me inside.

Following Wil into the hut and allowing him to peel off my clothes—each layer slipping to the dirt floor until I stood naked before him and then he then did the same—I was, for the first time in my life, free. We stood a moment, each astonished at the other's nakedness. Then he gently cupped my chin in his palm and pulled my lips to his. We slid onto the bed, so absorbed in each other that all existence felt condensed into that moment and place, into our skin and our touch and our motion.

Making love to Wil felt like arriving somewhere I had been crawling to get to for a very long time. In his arms, I became all the things it had never occurred to me to be before we met. I was beautiful and desirable and even a little dangerous. I was away from the farm overnight, a woman making choices and taking risks rather than an obedient and timid girl.

Afterward, I lay with my cheek against his warm shoulder as he slept, his arms engulfing me as naturally as if we rested in our marriage bed. I had never been held in a man's naked arms, had never even considered sleeping on a man's bare chest. Even as he lay beneath me, and I felt his breath and steady heartbeat and smelled the slightly sweet odor of his sweat, I could not fathom him. A silvery wing of moonlight reached through the hut's small window and illuminated his smooth face, his sinewy neck, one muscular arm resting outside the layers of pink quilts Ruby-Alice had given him. I tried to read in his broad hand some clues to his story—the red-and-black woven bracelet he never removed from his wrist, white scars striping his knuckles, the thick calluses suggesting the hands of a much older man. I wondered at the extraordinary power of his touch, how his caress had restored not only my ankle but something deep inside me I had not fully known was ailing.

I carefully pulled my own hand from the warm quilts and laid it across his, thinking back to the most remarkable thing I had witnessed those sure hands do, a week prior, which was to draw a puppy from death's sure grip. We had been at Ruby-Alice's place, and I was marveling at her shelves of knickknacks and her surprising love of pink. Even when praying for her soul as a young girl, I had never considered that she might sleep and eat and live in a small, warm home with little statues of angels and dogs and snowmen arranged just so. It was just then that Ruby-Alice had burst through the front door.

She was wordless, as ever, but clearly panicked, her wild eye beckoning Wil. Cupped in her pallid hands was a limp puppy. Its brown-and-white coat glistened with slick mucous. Clearly stillborn, the puppy's head lolled to one side. Its tiny, white-tipped feet lay flaccid. Without a word, Wil reached out. Ruby-Alice tenderly laid the puppy in his palms. Wil pulled it to his belly and began rubbing it up and down with his top hand, somehow both gently and furiously. He lifted the lifeless little body to his lips, blew softly on its face, then lowered it again, rubbed, breathed, rubbed. Ruby-Alice seemed wholly unaware of me, though we stood just inches apart, both transfixed. Wil rolled the limp puppy onto its back, exposing a belly bare and speckled as a toad, and rubbed, with just two fingers now, up and down the tiny chest. He lifted the body again to his lips and spoke quietly, words so faint and unfamiliar I could not understand them. Then he rubbed the little chest again, clasped the puppy to his heart, closed his eyes, and exhaled.

The puppy's first subtle squirm toward life was too surprising to believe. I thought I had imagined it, but the pup moved again, unquestionably this time, and again and again until it was wriggling in Wil's hands, as if born of his palms. The little creature stretched its neck, blind, nuzzling, searching for a nipple. Wil grinned, gave the puppy a quick kiss on the nose, and held it out to Ruby-Alice. She clapped twice and beamed, her crooked teeth ochre yellow against her pale face. She snatched the puppy to her sagging bosom, then vanished from the room as quickly as she had appeared, slamming the door behind her.

My mouth hung wide open. "How did . . . ?" I began, but before the question formed, Wil's mouth was on mine, and we sank to the floor. It took every bit of my strength to pull myself away from those hands to rush back home in time to fix supper.

A week later, lying naked on Wil's bare chest in the moonlit hut, I buzzed with desire now that those hands had touched my whole body. I tilted my head and gazed up at the outline of his lips. Unsure if I should wake him, I lightly kissed the soft flesh just below his collarbone. I could not help but kiss again. On the third kiss, he stirred. On the fourth, he bent to me and our mouths connected. Our bodies glided together in exquisite unison, knowing exactly how to move and where to touch, even though physical love was new to us both. We made love again, this time slowly and rhythmically, as if the first time had been mere rehearsal.

As we held each other in the autumn moonlight, breathless, aching, I could not have fathomed it, but our child began to grow.

Nine

I arrived back home the next afternoon—exhausted from little sleep and the long trek to and from the mountain hut—just minutes before Daddy and Seth returned from driving the Oakleys' cattle. Wil had escorted me through our back gate to the orchard's edge, kissed me goodbye, then disappeared into the trees. I strolled dreamily through the yard, hardly aware of my feet on the ground, until the sudden sound of Daddy's truck coming up the drive snapped me back to reality like the crack of a bullwhip. I ducked through the kitchen door, flung off my jacket and muddy boots, yanked my mussed hair into a ponytail, and hurriedly put a pot of water to boil on the stove top, not even knowing what I would put into it. Blessedly, Daddy and Seth took their sweet time unloading gear and tending to what had gone untended in the barn. I knew I'd get hell for not collecting the eggs and feeding the animals that morning. I recalled the particulars of the lie I'd told Uncle Og about nursing Cora's illness and steeled myself in anticipation of telling the story again.

By the time Daddy and Seth entered, just as tired as I was from the looks of them, I had cheese sandwiches and cold sweet tea on the table, green beans and onions crackling in the fry pan, and potatoes boiling in the pot. I stirred the pan to look busy as the men removed their jackets and Seth darted through the kitchen. I asked Daddy how the drive went, making my voice sound casual and honeyed, as if the girl who spoke wasn't a woman now, wholly transformed. He grunted grumpily that they "lost one," then exited the kitchen, leaving me to wonder whether the cow was missing or dead and why. I couldn't remember a time when Daddy didn't bring all the cattle down to winter pasture safely, whether driving for Oakley or Mitchell or as a hired hand. Intuition told me, correctly, the loss was somehow Seth's doing.

First Daddy then Seth reentered the kitchen and sat at the table. At late afternoon and the end of a hard drive, they were ravenous, devouring each item I placed before them.

Og wheeled into the kitchen and whistled, "Well, look who's home."

Mortified, I looked up from the sink where I was draining the potatoes to find that Og was in fact speaking to me. My stomach lurched but revived when I saw Daddy's and Seth's attention still focused on their food, both apparently assuming Og's comment was directed to them. My hands shook as I began mashing the undercooked potatoes with butter and milk.

"A rough one," Daddy replied, briefly eying Seth.

"Go ahead and say it," Seth challenged, but Daddy scooped more green beans onto his plate and ate them in silence.

Og dished up his food and looked from Daddy to Seth to Daddy again, a delighted twinkle in his eye at the obvious quarrel between them. I delivered the potatoes to the table, desperately wanting to find some excuse not to sit. But I was so hungry, my body seemed to sit me down and plate up my food without my mind's consent. Wil had had a stash of pork and beans at the hut, a cold can of which I had shared with him for breakfast but burned off hours earlier.

I tried to eat daintily and come up with something to say that might distract from my awkwardness, from Daddy and Seth's antagonism, but nothing seemed correct.

"More interested in roping yourself an Injun than them wanderin' heifers, that it, Sara?" Og provoked.

Seth slammed both palms on the table with such force that the utensils jumped and tea slopped from the glasses. His chair clattered backward to the floor as he stood and huffed out of the kitchen, kicking the wheelchair as he went, giving Og a jolt and an excuse to roar hoarse, mocking laughter.

Daddy watched Seth leave, shook his head, then crossly confirmed to Og, "That's 'xactly it. Lost us a calf."

Wanted placards describing Wil and promising a twenty-dollar reward still adorned Iola. For all I knew, they hung in neighboring Sapinero and Cebolla, maybe as far as Gunnison or beyond. I wondered how many other men who knew nothing about Wil were out there searching for him. I tried to change the subject, but truth and timing were not on my side.

"Sorry the potatoes are so lumpy, Daddy," I ventured.

He just shrugged and lifted another spoonful to his mouth, saying, in his own wordless way, that the food was fine.

"That's what you get for rushing 'em," said Og.

My heart plunged at the reference to my belated homecoming. I felt the first thin layer of my secret peeling away.

"How is poor Cora feeling, by the way?" asked Og with a sugared voice, glancing at Daddy and then at me. The false politeness in his inquiry, the way he tilted his head in faux sympathy, only made his question more sinister. He knew.

Daddy looked at me quizzically, and I stared back, wide-eyed. I was caught in my lie as sure as a coon in the headlights of a speeding truck. To make matters worse, devastatingly worse it would turn out, Seth reentered the kitchen just then, charging toward his jacket and the back door until he noticed Daddy's and Og's eyes on me and stopped.

"Still ailing," I managed in a small voice.

"Nice of you to spend the whole night caring for her," Og said as the final blow to my cover.

I lifted my tea glass, steadied it on my lips, and swallowed, watching Daddy's brows knit.

"Cora ain't ailing," he said, and my gut churned. "She met us at the pasture to help collect the horses and dogs. Looked fine."

Seth was watching the scene unfold from the back door, slipping one arm slowly into his jacket, then the other, his eyes glued on me.

I did what I could to salvage my scheme. I talked too much, nervously, stupidly, about Cora taking a turn with breakfast, about how she tossed all night with fever, moaning for Jesus in her sleep, but came around this morning with some biscuits and bacon.

Og sniggered and then, miraculously, as if throwing me a lifeline after causing the boat of my deception to tip in the first place, said nastily, "The gal does love her some bacon."

Daddy puzzled over the information for another moment, then told me to get the chickens tended and went back to his meal. Seth still stared at me from across the room, a grin now creeping across his face. He zipped his jacket with a quick jerk and disappeared out the back door, the screen slamming like a gunshot in his wake.

I could feel Og's eyes on me. Had I met his gaze, I might have found a slight gleam of apology, but I refused to raise my head. My appetite was gone. I stood, piled my half-full plate with the empty dishes from the table, and went to the sink to begin the washing up.

From the direction of the barn, I heard the fierce rumble of Seth's roadster roaring to life. He revved it over and over again, as if purposely taunting my nerves. When the car's yellow hood first came into view out the window over the sink, my mind failed to make sense of what I saw. Seth had become obsessed with the car lately, often with Holden Oakley and Forrest Davis by his side, all three leaning under the raised hood, rowdy and greasy, Lucky Strikes dangling from their mouths. After years of watching Seth tinker with the faulty engine, I never expected the car to actually drive. When he rolled slowly past the kitchen window, hunched over the steering wheel and peering at me in triumph, he raised his hand to his forehead and saluted me with mock regard. He paused and revved the engine to a shocking crescendo—causing Daddy to rush to the side door and Og to holler in exasperation from the table—then he sped away down the drive, leaving tracks like two deep claw marks and a fog of dusty exhaust in the air.

That evening, Seth did not return for supper. No one mentioned it, as if his empty chair had never held an occupant. Daddy asked me if I'd got caught up on my chores in the coop and the barn. I said I had. Og said nothing. After Daddy and Og left the kitchen and the dishes were done, I tromped up the stairs and closed my door more loudly than necessary to announce an early bedtime. I tucked a pillow under my bedspread in a human-shaped lump and put on an extra sweater before tiptoeing back downstairs, noiselessly pulling on my boots and wool coat, and slipping out the back door.

Shivers shot through me as I crossed the yard, less because of the late-October air, so cold it stung my nostrils, and more in anticipation of Wil's embrace. I shook from nerves, too, constantly checking over my shoulder, peering into the moonlit night to my left and to my right, afraid of being followed, of leading Seth or one of his cronies right to the man they sought. By the time the arched cottonwood came into view, along with the reassuring outline of Wil leaning casually against its trunk, I had worked myself into such a twist of excitement and fret, I burst into tears. I ran toward him, and he received me in his outstretched arms.

We ducked through the willows and sat together in a small clearing, face-to-face, my hands cradled in his. We spoke of love and danger and Seth and his kind. He smoothed my hair and wiped the cold tears from my cheeks. I looked into Wil's gentle, dark-brown eyes and mustered the courage to betray my own heart.

"You should leave this place," I told him, both believing and despising my words.

Wil let the idea hang a while in the crisp air between us. Then he grinned at me—as he had on our first exchange at the corner of North Laura and Main, and as he had when I stood naked before him at the hut—with appreciation for something within me that no one else, least of all myself, had ever perceived. I felt crazy inside, my suggestion so at odds with my desire that it was as if some other girl had spoken.

He shook his head. "There are more folks like Seth than stars in the night sky," he finally answered, meaning to be dismissive and comforting but having the opposite effect. For what he said was surely true: Where was Wil to go where there wasn't a hate-filled boy like Seth ready to blame his troubles on a brown-skinned boy like Wil? I knew he wouldn't run.

"I'll go as a river," said Wil. "My grandfather always told me that it's the only way."

I nodded as if I understood what he meant, and we made plans to meet the following day.

WITH MY JUDGMENT CLOUDED by craving and Wil's confidence that our love would outlast Seth's fury, I continued to meet him whenever I could. All logic called us foolish, but we refused to listen. Still, I was careful. I snuck off only when unnoticed, or so I believed. Seth was scarce. He did his chores, even more quick-temperedly and sulkily than usual, and showed up for occasional meals, but mostly he was out joyriding in his roadster. There was no more talk of any "Injun," and each day it became easier to believe what I desperately wanted to be true: that Seth had forgotten about Wil.

I cannot say on which of our meetings I unknowingly led Seth to him. But a week after Wil held my hands among the willows and told me he would not leave Iola, a week, to the exact hour, after he brushed tears off my damp cheek and tried to kiss my fears away, Wil failed to show up at our meeting place.

As I paced in the frigid November night waiting for him, back and forth in front of the arched cottonwood, shining my flashlight into the silent fields and ditches along the road, it became clear he would not arrive. I rushed to check the clearing in the willows; then I ran to the orchard's edge, the bend in the creek, the Gunnison River bank, the spruce on the hill, every secluded spot where we had ever met, praying in between that I had merely misunderstood the rendezvous point.

Breathless, I unhooked Ruby-Alice's gate, creating a frenzy of barking and scurrying among the creatures in the yard. The door to her old barn stood open, but, inside, only a few chickens and a frightened bat stirred when I called Wil's name. One dim light glowed in the house. I longed for Wil to receive me there, just as he had that warm autumn day, mere weeks earlier and yet a lifetime ago too, when I was so sure I would find him behind that pink front door. Moving slowly through the yard as if through mud, I knew that he was not there. I peered through the window to find Ruby-Alice stretched out on her sofa, her white face and hair glowing like the moon the night sky lacked. She clutched a quilt to her chest, looking both dead and desperate to hold on to something of this earth.

I crumbled to the ground, having exhausted all possibilities other than the hut, which sat so high and inaccessible in the Big Blue it might as well have been on the top of the world. A small dog crept to my side in curiosity at my whimpering and licked my pant leg. I kicked it away and it snarled.

I don't recall the walk home or hauling myself up the stairs and into my bed. I only remember that that is where I was, still fully clothed, wide awake well past midnight, weeping, when the roadster growled through the yard. The sound rattled my window and my bones. When I heard the side door open and close, I leapt from my covers to rush out of my room and down the stairs to confront Seth in the kitchen.

He had not turned on the light. His dark figure sat, hunched over, on the bench by the back door. By the size of his shape, I could tell he still wore his jacket, his boots. Surely he knew I stood in the kitchen doorway, but he sat silently, immobile. Whiskey and cigarettes and car exhaust wafted off him. I reached for the light switch but thought better of it. I did not want to see his face. I knew everything I needed to know.

"I hate you, Seth." I spit it into the darkness like sour bile that had been building in my gut my entire life.

"Got me better'n that reward, Torie," he slurred, surprisingly tenderly, like he was sharing good news with a friend. "Got me better and then some," he added, followed by a tired sigh and an inebriated chuckle. "Better and then some," he repeated to himself, with just enough incredulity bubbling through the drunken pride that I realized, with a sickening shudder, that Seth had not merely run my Wil out of town or captured and surrendered him to the authorities. If I turned on the light, I was sure I would see blood on his hands.

I spun away and dizzily crawled up the stairs on all fours, hardly noticing I had limbs beneath me, trembling down the hall and to my bed like a sickened animal.

. . .

IN THE WEEKS OF waiting for my fears to be confirmed, I went about my chores feeling barely in my body, zombielike and ill, finding the daily rising, arcing, and setting of the sun insufferable.

"You sick?" Daddy opened my bedroom door one morning when I failed to rise for breakfast.

I gave a muffled grunt from under the covers.

"Dr. Bernette need fetchin'?" he asked.

"No," I croaked.

Daddy closed the door and headed down the stairs. Raw guilt clawed at me as I imagined him making his own breakfast, so I rose to cook, and the next morning I did the same, and I continued, day after day, doing what needed to be done, despite feeling both numb and pained all at once.

By nightfall I'd be exhausted by charade and grief, but each night, after the last chores were done and the house was dark and quiet and Og and Daddy had settled behind their closed bedroom doors, with Seth out who knew where, I donned layers and snuck into the frigid darkness to search for Wil. Frost salted the tree limbs overhead, and dead leaves crunched beneath my boots. Just as I had done on the night of Wil's disappearance, I walked and walked, visiting each place where we had met, wishing at every turn to see his silhouette leaning patiently against a tree, his bright grin lighting up the darkness. All the while I knew I was flirting with madness, all hope just a trick of my yearning. He was nowhere to be found.

At Ruby-Alice Akers's window, night after night, I peered in to find her alone, sleeping corpse-like on her sofa. Her dogs, inside now because of the cold, slept in little balls all about the room. As I retreated through her oddly still yard, I wondered if perhaps

Ruby-Alice's constant bicycling was her roaming the day as I roamed the night, searching against all reason for the loved ones she had lost, and I wondered if whatever madness of grief that had infected Ruby-Alice had come to claim me too.

ONE MORNING IN LATE November, as I was standing in the rear aisle at Chapman's, choosing a box of baking soda, as if a box of baking soda mattered, two ranchers leaning against Chapman's deli counter were talking loudly enough that I overheard snippets of what I could not bear to hear: *A body. Bottom of Black Canyon. That Injun boy. Nearly skinless. Drug behind a car. Tossed.*

A human being can only hold so much. Within me I already carried enormous bundles of grief and guilt and love and fear and confusion and, though I wasn't yet fully aware, a child just forming in my womb. The men's words rammed to get in, but I could not hold them. Even the few I absorbed were too much. I fell to my knees and vomited.

Mr. Chapman ran from behind the counter to my aid. He pulled me up from the mess on his otherwise spotless floorboards, guided me to a stool, and brought me a cup of water. Others fussed over me— though I can't recall now who they were, a blur of extended hands and gentle voices and worried eyes—while Chapman mopped the floor. I gathered myself enough to apologize and shakily exit.

A light dusting of snow had fallen the night before, and the sun's reflection off Main was unbearably bright. I shielded my eyes as *drug behind a car* echoed in my head. *That Injun boy. Nearly skinless.*

I stumbled away from Chapman's to try to make my way back home, avoiding the corner of North Laura and Main. Above Iola glowed the Big Blue wilderness, its fresh white snow warped and unlovely through my tears. Wil could have chosen sanctuary in those mountains. Instead, he chose me. I tried to bear the unbearable by imagining him there now, tucked beneath quilts in the hut, sunlight streaming through the one small window to land softly upon his perfect skin. And yet. I knew the truth: that the world was too cruel to protect an innocent boy or measure what we can and cannot bear, that the Black Canyon had become Wil's deep and terrible grave because he had stayed to love me.

PART II

1949-1955

Ten

1949

That winter was the driest on record in Gunnison County. The temperature in Iola routinely dipped well below zero, but the snow mostly refused to fall.

While Daddy worried about the following summer's low rivers and potential drought, I appreciated going about my chores without having to shovel or trudge through the usual drifts. Exhaustion sistered my grief throughout that long, eerily brown winter. At times, I could not find the strength to carry a basket of eggs from the henhouse, couldn't raise and stretch and pull a rake through Abel's stall. I remember being barely able to lift my arms to properly wash my hair while sitting in my Sunday bath. Instead, I gazed across my body and contemplated my growing breasts, my swelling belly. The once thread-thin veins in my hands and feet bulged like young snakes beneath my skin. I had stopped bleeding each month. Naive as I was, I'd assumed grief was making me heavy, pooling my blood and longing and sorrow until, blessedly, I would eventually explode. It was not until the first flutters of life—so subtle at first, like a butterfly winking an eyelash, then stronger, like a tiny bird in my belly—that I fully understood the true source of my bloat and fatigue.

I spent that winter hiding my growing form from the men in my house. It was simple at first, a matter of wrapping an elastic bandage around my plump breasts, just as I had when they were mere buds as a shy adolescent, and wearing layers of sweaters and skirts against the moistureless cold. Daddy was distracted by hauling hay and cutting fence stays on the Mitchells' ranch and rebuilding a collapsing wall in our barn. Uncle Og stayed in his room most days, swigging whiskey and listening to radio programs and whatever else he did in there to pass the days until spring allowed him to roost on the porch again. Sometimes I'd catch him looking at me when I was dishing up a meal or hanging laundered clothes in his armoire, just looking, not with detectable suspicion or malice or pity but with eyes that seemed to say he had just noticed I was there, an actual human being, living with him under the same roof. He knew something about my secrets, but he never said a word.

Seth was mostly absent. From the day Wil's body was discovered, Seth had one reason or another to be away from Iola. First it was a hunting trip with Forrest Davis, where they were gone two weeks and brought home only three grouse and one paltry elk, a yearling at best. Then it was some work on the rail line that Holden Oakley had heard of, down south near Durango, employing the two boys and Davis for near a month. Seth returned with a wad of cash for the household jar; stayed a few days helping Daddy finish the high places on the barn wall and getting drunk in town every night, never speaking to me or looking my way; then taking off again for a construction job in Montrose. Daddy didn't mind as long as Seth kept contributing to the family till. In fact, Seth's sporadic absences seemed to relieve Daddy. No one in town had tied Seth to Wil's death, though it might have been easy to do for anyone who truly cared to find the culprit. I could tell Daddy had his suspicions.

I couldn't bring myself to confront Seth. Once Wil was gone, I was so overwhelmed by all that had happened, I retreated back into the role of obedient girl. I sought comfort and safety in the daily habits on the farm and distanced myself as much as possible from the horrible act: I never gazed at the rear bumper of Seth's roadster in search of rope marks or blood, never allowed my mind to visualize Wil's flesh against gravel, never demanded that Sheriff Lyle investigate the murder or pointed my finger at my brother. In short, I was a coward, just as Seth knew I would be.

And yet, my growing belly ensured I could not hide in routine forever. By February, I had to resew buttons to widen my skirts. Every morning, I was ravenous and nauseous all at once. Ordinary morning aromas—the eggs, the pepper, the ham, the biscuits, the butter, even the scent of the animal pens and stacked firewood that blew in with the breeze when Daddy entered—each penetrated me so thoroughly I frequently fled to the toilet to vomit. By late March, I had grown out of all my clothes except for one A-shaped frock. My cheeks rounded, my fingers plumped, my belly protruded like a cantaloupe beneath layers of increasingly suffocating sweaters. By April, I knew I had to leave home.

I began plotting my exit as if for another girl. I had not had many friends growing up, imaginary or otherwise, so it wasn't for anyone in particular I began stashing supplies in an old canvas backpack—rope and jerky and matches and candles, a pot, a hatchet, mason jars and tins of pantry staples, a knife, vegetable seeds, knitting needles, yarn, a cake of soap wrapped in waxed paper, one of Og's giant sweaters—just for some girl who was in trouble, some girl who had to flee. I pondered the route for her, felt relieved for her that the high-country snowpack was light, tried to think through for her all the necessities and potential pitfalls. Until that cloudy mid-April morning when Uncle Og wheeled back to his room after breakfast and Daddy loaded Trout in his truck and drove away to assist Mr. Mitchell with the calving, I had, on some non-sensical level, refused to believe the girl who was pregnant, who was heading to the mountains to save herself and her family the shame, who would keep her baby safe from her murderous brother, was actually me.

I fed Abel a bucket of oats, then saddled him and led him from the barn. I donned the heavy backpack full of supplies, awkwardly mounted the horse, and trotted away from the farmhouse and through the still-dormant orchard. I did not look back.

I RODE ABEL ALONG Willow Creek and up a rocky incline until I was so high above Iola I could look down on the little square footprint the town made in the meandering valley. The Gunnison River appeared as a gray ribbon through the center, the water low and sluggish from drought and cold, the rails and Highway 50 running alongside it. I could make out Ruby-Alice's dark pine patch southeast of downtown and, next to it, our long drive. My eyes followed the pale gravel to the two whitish blocks that were my home and barn, bordered by the bare bristle of the early-season fruit trees. The Mitchells' lightly greening pasture was freckled with large brown dots beside small brown dots—the heifers and their newborns—and, somewhere among them, the pinpoint that was my daddy. On the far edge of the valley, smoke rose above scorched earth where someone, Mr. Clifton I guessed by location, or maybe the Oakleys, was burning fields in preparation for planting. I felt a pang of guilt at not getting the garden in before leaving. The onions had been planted last fall, and Daddy could find hands to lay the potatoes, but putting in the kitchen garden once the weather warmed would be women's work. I wondered if Daddy would find the seeds I'd left labeled for him and plant them himself or simply go without. I could barely grasp that whatever he chose, however he ate and washed and managed, was no longer my concern. I turned and continued higher, putting all I knew behind me, climbing over and down a ridge to the top of another rise—far out of sight from town but not so far that Abel couldn't find his way home again—and dismounted.

My pack nearly pulled me over as my feet landed. I held Abel's reins for balance and felt the pressing weight of doubt double the burden of my pack. For a long while I stood at the horse's side and contemplated what to do next, feeling equally afraid of my options, unable to move either forward toward my plan or backward toward home. I doubted my strength, both physical and mental, and felt tempted to remount the loyal animal waiting patiently for some decision. I lay my face on Abel's neck, aware that releasing him meant relinquishing all ties to the familiar. Once he turned and trod down the hill in that slow, sure way horses do, instinctively navigating back to where he knew sweet alfalfa and a soft bed of straw waited, I would be wholly alone, a tiny speck of a girl in a vast and unpredictable wilderness.

Abel breathed deeply and rhythmically beneath my cheek. His chestnut hide was warm and damp, soft as spun cotton. I was eight years old when I witnessed his birth. Summoned from my bed by my mother just before sunrise, I sat on a straw bale with her and the boys, mesmerized as Daddy expertly pulled one branchy leg, then another, from the mare's bloody hole. Abel slid out into this world with such force that Daddy fell over backward with the slimy foal in his arms, half cussing, half laughing, then gazing at the dazed newborn as if cradling his own baby. My mother named the colt Abel right then and there, telling Daddy that Adam himself couldn't have looked upon his child with more awe.

"Not Cain?" Daddy teased—a different man back then, with flickers of humor and lightness—before releasing the colt to lean into its mother's muzzle.

"Not Cain," my mother replied tersely, never one to joke about anything biblical.

My young mind couldn't quite comprehend that a horse who had not existed moments earlier suddenly had a body, a name, a life, had become a part of our farm, just like the peach trees and the creek. Mother heaved an exasperated sigh at Daddy's wit and walked back to the house to start breakfast, Daddy washed up in the deep barn sink, and Cal and Seth gathered feed pails and rakes to begin their morning chores. But I couldn't pull myself away. Something had been made of nothing right before our eyes. I cautiously approached the newborn Abel where he lay and reached out my hand to touch his slick, new neck. He looked up at me with soft, curious eyes that told me he didn't understand his arrival any more than I did.

I now rubbed that very same place on Abel's neck, then kissed him goodbye. I backed up and said, "Git on now." I dropped the pack to more easily wave my arms and shoo him down the hillside.

"Go on home, Abel. Git!" I hollered, unsure of my choice even as I was making it.

The horse turned downhill but would not proceed.

"Git! Git! Go on now!" I shouted at him, making windmills of my arms. Abel didn't budge. I continued shouting at him while weighing the idea of just keeping him with me, remounting and going forth into the mountains with the comfort of both friend and transport. But I had caused enough trouble. As badly as I wanted Abel to stay, I couldn't take Daddy's horse, nor could I put Abel at risk in the unknown. With tears welling up, I grasped a baseball-sized rock and threw it at Abel's rear haunches. He startled and took a few steps forward when the rock struck the ground near his hind feet. I found another rock and threw it, hitting him just above the tail. I threw another, then another, sobbing now at the absurdity of my actions against an animal I loved, and he started lumbering down the hillside, reluctant, frightened, occasionally looking back at me as if to pose a question he didn't know how to ask.

I had been a good girl. I had been obedient and obliging and respectful to my elders. I had read my Bible. I'd laid peaches into the bushel baskets as if each peach was made of thin glass. I kept the house clean, the bellies full, the laundry folded, the farm tended. I didn't ask too many questions, never let anyone hear me cry. All on my own, I figured out how to carry on without a mother. And then I'd happened on a filthy stranger at the corner of North Laura and Main, and I fell in love. Just as a single rainstorm can erode the banks and change the course of a river, so can a single circumstance of a girl's life erase who she was before.

Yelling and throwing rock after rock, tears streaming down my face, I hurled all my fear and grief at the poor horse. As it was for me before I met Wil, all Abel knew was loyalty and obedience. Every rock I threw at him taught him what I had learned: for every ounce of good in this world, two ounces of bad outweigh it. You can be a good girl, a good horse, you can obey, you can love, but don't expect that if you do right then right will come to you.

The final rock clipped Abel's jaw and, to my horror, made him bleed. He took off down the hill away from the girl who was once good to him. I fell onto my pack and cried just as the clouds parted, the noon sun making salty crust of my tears.

I pictured the farmhouse kitchen, still as midnight, the stove cold and vacant. Daddy would be lunching at the Mitchells', so Og would be the first to know I had fled. Even before he'd reach the kitchen, he'd notice the absence of aroma, and when he entered to find no one to serve him, his suspicions about me would be confirmed. He wouldn't telephone to alert Daddy or tell him what he thought he knew. Both responses teetered too close to caring. When Daddy came home in the evening, tired and bloodstained from calving, he'd first discover Abel saddled and loose in the yard; then he'd step inside to find no meal waiting. It was hard to imagine my father pondering my absence, considering me, the actuality of his daughter, as more than mere fixture, simple house servant, the correct and predictable girl. I pictured him tentatively entering my bedroom, finding the note I had left for him on my bed, and slowly opening it with his chafed hands. I lamented that I had not written more, that I hadn't had the courage to tell him the whole story. The note read:

> Daddy,
>
> Gone away for a spell. Had to take care of something important.
> Please don't go looking for me. I'll be home when I can.
> I love you.
> I'm sorry. Don't worry.
>
> Victoria

Lying on my pack, I wondered, when morning came—with the calves still arriving and both Mr. Mitchell and the heifers dependent on Daddy's skillful hands—would he return to the work that needed to be done, or would he search for me? I didn't know. I hoped my signature—*Victoria* rather than *Torie*—would imply that I had matured outside his notice, that I was old enough now to make this choice. He had not once in my entire life called me Victoria, neither in anger nor affection, and so he might see this girl who had fled, this young woman named Victoria, as someone altogether new.

It occurred to me then that it was Torie who lacked the wherewithal to rise and move forward, but Victoria—Wil's Victoria—had a woman's strength to go on.

I, Victoria, rose to my feet. I hefted the pack onto my back, ran my thumbs between the straps and my shoulder bones to adjust the fit, and began walking. Not entirely sure I knew the way to the hut where Wil and I had lain together, I summoned instinct and even the baby in my womb to guide me. Absurd as it was, I had little else but magnetism to get me there, an unlikely trust that my baby and I would feel a pull to the place of our becoming.

I hiked through the trailless landscape, trying not to picture Abel trudging in the opposite direction in the seemingly endless hills of sage and rock. I searched for something familiar from my trek with Wil those many months ago when autumn was turning to winter. I imagined us then, giddy with love as we walked side by side, how beautiful his smile was and the ease with which his hand glided in and out of mine, how he bent to pull a branch of sage, twisted it until the leaves burst, inhaled it with pleasure, then held it to my nose. As if to conjure a piece of him, I bent to tug a stalk of sage, tore it as he had, and tucked it in the pack's strap. Its pungence revived a hazy memory that seemed to guide me in the right direction. Soon I crested a hill to find a row of tall sandstone pinnacles that confirmed my recollection. Wil had called them sentinels and pointed out how each seemed to link hips with the other. I hiked down the hill and around the four jagged towers. Beyond them, I now knew I could find my way. I hiked through the leafless aspens, each dappled with ripening auburn buds, and up another hill. I sat there a spell, winded but encouraged, drank from my canteen, then trudged down into a dry wash and up a final slope of aspens mixed with pine and the occasional mounds of receding snow. Through a clearing, I could see it—the small log hut where Wil had taken refuge. It was even humbler than I remembered, barely bigger than a horse stall, set directly on the crooked earth and roofed in haphazard layers of rusty tin.

"Just an old abandoned hunting hut," Wil had said when I wondered aloud if we were trespassing. "Nobody's missing it but the spiders and critters I shooed out."

A pang in my heart reminded me again that if Wil had hunkered down here for the winter, coping with snow and frigid cold and hunger, he would have had a better chance at staying alive than he did moving closer to town. I didn't always know where he slept once he moved down from the hills—Ruby-Alice's house or barn, I supposed—but I did know with stinging certainty that he'd left this safe haven because of me.

I entered the muddy meadow. Dropping the heavy pack, I settled on its spine and surveyed my surroundings. I had reached the hut, but now what would I do? To enter the room where our love had flowered yet where Wil would never return felt excruciating. To remain outside fully exposed to the wild felt equally impossible. To begin setting up camp and establishing a life in this place was absurd. I sat for a long while, paralyzed with fatigue and indecision.

As cool evening descended and the forest grew dim and sinister, I had no choice but to stand and enter the hut. I imagined Wil grasping my hand, helping me to my feet, and guiding me, pushing back the deer hide hanging at the entrance, inviting me in, just as he had the first time I had crossed the threshold. Once I stepped inside, I saw that the little room was just as he had left it—tins of pork and beans were stacked neatly in one corner, an aluminum canteen hung from a rusty nail, a jar with a half-melted candle sat atop a box of matches. It was easy to believe he might return any minute. The bed was piled with Ruby-Alice's quilts. I placed my pack on the dirt floor, too exhausted to rummage through it for food. I removed my boots, timidly lifted the edge of the bedding, and crawled inside, feeling my baby fluttering inside me. I inhaled long and deeply, hoping to catch Wil's scent. Whether the blankets still smelled of him or whether I conjured the fantasy to keep myself from going mad with grief and fear, I curled into the perfume of him and blacked out everything else to fall asleep.

The entire next day, I surrendered to exhaustion. I left the quilts only to relieve myself outside the hut and eat cold soup from a can. I had never in my life stayed in bed all day. Even when ill, I'd helped Mother with the chores, and after she died, I completed my tasks every day, no matter the circumstances, just as she had done. The freedom to lie in bed with no duties and no one to answer to could have felt like a luxury but instead felt all wrong. I drifted in and out of sleep, my strange torpor beleaguered by anxiety about laziness and choices and the unfamiliar noises surrounding the hut. I dreamed of Wil, sometimes caressing, sometimes laughing, and, for the first time, of him dying behind that speeding roadster, his skin tearing away like fine paper wrapping. I woke sweaty and panicked in a ray of warm sun streaming through the tiny window, unable to locate myself for a bewildered instant. Unmoored from the attention and judgment of others, I curled into a ball and mourned with an agony I'd never thought possible. Once unleashed, grief's dark grip held Mother and Cal and Aunt Viv nearly as much as Wil, four thick fingers squeezing my heart like a fist around a sponge, wringing out my tears, my guttural howls. That night I slept deeply, dreamlessly, greedy for refuge.

The next day, I forced myself to rise. I ventured into the frosty morning to do I knew not what but understanding that something needed to be done to begin my life in this place. The morning after that, and the next and the next, sheer will drove me to do the same.

Once up, I was jumpy. I was not so much lonely as intensely aware of my aloneness in the seemingly endless radius of wilderness. Ordinary noises frightened me. I would startle at the sharp snaps of deer crossing downed timber or the clatter of falling branches kicked loose by a squirrel or the wind. Even silence un-nerved me, giving me sudden feelings of being watched from a distance or stalked from the pines. I'd spin around to catch sight of it—the imagined bear or cougar or who knows what—and find just the quick flick of a curious chipmunk or nothing there at all. I'd attempt refuge in the hut, only to sit stiff and alert, listening intently to the hum of the creek behind me, anticipating the thud-ding footsteps of man or beast disturbing the river rock on the path to my vulnerability.

I tried ways to secure the old deer hide that hung from the crooked doorway, but I had neither nails nor hammer and realized that even if I did, I would be sealing myself in as much as keeping intruders out. Most nights ended with me tucked in the blankets, the long knife I had taken from the farmhouse kitchen clutched in my fist, my wide eyes staring unwaveringly at the door. Eventually drowsiness would overtake my fear and I'd close my eyes, reluc-tantly releasing myself to whatever would be. In the morning, I'd be amazed at the good fortune of waking, still whole, the knife protrud-ing like a slim fish frozen mid-leap from the hut's dirt floor.

I wasn't homesick; that was certain. Though I felt a vague pining for Daddy and the orchard from time to time, each had already become hazy to me, as if from a half-forgotten dream. Mostly, I felt great relief to be freed from Seth and Uncle Ogden and everything to do with them. No matter how unsettling my solitude, I would not return home. Weary and edgy, I spent that first week determined to set up my camp, to pretend, at least, that a new home could be of my own making. I had Wil's child to care for now, and though my longing for Wil often felt unbearable, I had to keep my sanity, to center my attention on what made me want to stay alive rather than dwell too long on why I might rather not.

DIGGING A LATRINE SEEMED a logical place to start. But the ground proved so firm and my trowel so small that I progressed by mere tablespoons. In frustration, I threw the trowel into the creek, where it lay rusting for days. I needed success at something, so I chose my next jobs carefully: refilling my and Wil's canteens from the pebbled edge of the stream; cutting a pine bough to sweep spiders and webs and mouse droppings from the hut; building a fire ring, gathering wood, and constructing a stick A-frame I hoped would be sturdy enough to suspend a pot. I tied a rope from one thick aspen limb to another, lugged out the pink quilts, and hung and beat them with a branch. Dust escaped and swirled away on the breeze like little dancing ghosts. I retrieved the trowel from the creek and dug more earth from the latrine. I notched tally marks into the hut wall to track the passing days.

I knew I would eventually need to learn to gather food, but I still had a good stock from home—jerky, canned soups, dried beans and oats, preserved peaches and pickled eggs, a tin of crackers—and the stack of pork and beans that Wil had left behind, so I put off the task until I understood more about my surroundings. I watched for fish in the creek eddies and in a beaver pond I found downstream from my camp. Nothing but stones glistened through the clear waters, but I told myself I'd find trout when I needed them. Whether I would actually be able to catch fish with neither pole nor line nor hook was something I was not yet prepared to discover. For better or worse, my survival would come one day at a time.

My first venture into the dark forest on the other side of the creek was to search for raspberry plants. I knew it was far too early for the fruit, but I wanted reassurance I'd have berries come July. I found a stretch of shallows upstream from the hut with four tortoise-shaped stones that made for easy crossing. I picked up a stick the shape of a baseball bat for protection, but my first steps into the forest assaulted me not with foe but with fragrance. My sense of smell was so acute in pregnancy I often felt wolflike, able to catch scent on everything around me. The woods were pungent with sharp pine and musky earth and moist layers of decay. Even the boulders smelled of metal and moss. The mixture was strange but not unpleasant. I inhaled deeply and carried on.

As I wandered farther into the woods, my heart sank. Most of the ground was still covered in a crusty layer of snow, ankle-deep in some places, knee-deep in others. The tall pines, broad and black and crowded, barred sun from thawing the forest floor. I realized that, at this altitude, nothing wild would be edible for months. Even the emerging sprouts from seeds I'd brought from home would surely freeze and blacken if planted any sooner than mid-May. It dawned on me why digging the latrine had been so difficult. The ground was not hard packed. It was still frozen. I nudged a patch of snow away with the toe of my boot. I kicked at the earth and jabbed it with my stick. Solid stone could not have been more unyielding.

Defeated, I plopped down on a stump with a sigh. I peered about the forest, at the layers of life and death suspended in the cold stillness and half-light, all silent but for bird chatter. Downed timber was strewn amid rocks and fallen branches and pine cones. Massive russet trunks shot upward into the canopy of boughs. Dozens of saplings pushed toward life, some barely tall enough to poke their bristled heads above grass stubble and snow, others emerging from the centers of decaying logs like infants from opened bellies. There was beauty to this chaos. Every piece of life here had its role in the eternal business of living. I felt small and unnecessary but not entirely unwelcome.

I stood and continued through the snow, deeper into the woods, each step cracking the quiet. As I hunted for anything that might eventually feed me—feed *us*—my baby churned within me, swimming in my womb with more vigor and presence than ever before. He—as I would later learn, my baby was a boy—gave what could be considered a kick for the first time, and I laughed and rubbed my round belly through my wool sweater, sure I was caressing his minute foot on its smooth, immaculate sole. He pulled his foot away then kicked a second time, and I laughed again at our game. I was not truly alone in these strange woods after all.

Weather arrives quickly in the mountains. I had known this my entire life and learned to read the sky as accurately as a school text. I could watch a storm rise and blacken, then perfectly time my exit from the orchard or the animal stalls or even Main Street to be flying through the kitchen door just as the first crack of thunder shook the valley. But everything I thought I knew about land and sky was put to the test once I was deep in those hills, like learning to read all over again.

The storm started as a rush of wind through the highest pines. The treetops began to sway like drunken giants before I even felt a breeze. The songbirds hushed, issuing a warning I didn't understand. Then everything around me, even the baby inside me, went perfectly still.

As if in sudden exhale, a cascade of wind surged like a transparent tidal wave across the forest floor, flexing the young pines and scattering debris. The wind hit my face like a smack from an open hand. It was cold and moist, and suddenly I could sense what I was in for even before the dark clouds fully overtook the sky, making quick evening of midday. I spun and, guided by my own footprints, I ran, scrambling over rocks and downed trees, dropping my stick, slipping in the snow, rising, running, then slipping again. Ice crystals topping the old snow sliced my palms and sprayed my face each time I fell. I cursed myself for straying so far from camp, for being lured too deeply into the forest calm that I knew could change so quickly. When I finally reached the wood's edge, furious rain-dappled wind lashed at me. I pushed against it and rushed across the creek toward my camp, slipping off the last stepping-stone in my panic and plunging one foot deep into the frigid waters.

Thunder grumbled overhead. I tried grabbing the pot of beans I had left soaking next to the fire ring, but as I did so, the full ferocity of the storm unleashed in torrential, sideswiping rain. The pot slipped from my trembling hand and dumped my precious food like worthless pebbles in the mud. A lightning bolt cracked the heavens overhead, instantly followed by another white flash and another. Thunder roared. I struggled against the cold rain, stumbling and slipping on the slimy earth until I finally clambered through a wide puddle at the hut's entrance and dove inside. My frozen, quivering hands could barely grasp the deer skin and yank it across the doorframe.

Rain pummeled the hut. Leaks sprang through the rusted tin roofing in every corner. I rushed to catch what water I could in the few empty tin cans I had saved, but I was helpless against the other drips. The dirt floor darkened in spreading circles of brown mud under my cold, wet feet.

The downpour turned deafening, like a million coins hurled onto the tin roof and against the single window. Lightning flashed bright white through the glass, followed immediately by an explosion of thunder so mighty it rattled my heart. Right then, as if someone had pulled a trigger, I collapsed to my knees. My body folded; my fore-arms and face crashed to the muddy floor. The hard ball that was now my belly, my baby, slammed against my thighs. Other than my violent trembling, I could not move. I was struck by an overwhelm-ing, immobilizing sorrow, as if the dark storm had permeated my interior as thoroughly as it had overtaken the afternoon sky. Why did I believe I could survive here? Because my eyes had traced these distant ridgelines all my life? Soaked and quaking with cold and fear, I understood that horizon is not home. I did not belong to this place.

Just before I lost consciousness, a cry seared through me, louder than the relentless cacophony of the storm, announcing with om-inous clarity what I could no longer deny: my plan would never work.

Eleven

What I remember most vividly about waking the next morning is the cheerful bird chorus that had replaced the fearsome storm. I was groggy at first, unsure where I was, but I could recognize the long trill of red-winged blackbirds, the hollow triple coo of a mountain dove, the chatter of chickadees and finches and sparrows outside the hut.

I vaguely recalled that I had woken on the muddy floor in the night and recovered just enough of my senses to remove my wet boots and socks and crawl from the ground into the bed and the blessed mound of quilts. As birdsong awakened me, I tucked myself deeper into the bedding's warmth. I rubbed my belly to encourage some sign of life and felt great relief when my baby gave three soft kicks.

The skin on my arms and forehead felt tight and crusty with dried mud. My ears and damp head felt frozen. I added a woolen hat to my long mental list of supplies I had either forgotten or hadn't wanted to steal from Daddy or foolishly never thought of or simply couldn't carry: a proper shovel, a tarp, a bucket, pencil and paper, a gun.

I was considering all the things I would have to learn to do without when I heard that voice again, just as I had heard it the night before, the grim and clear proclamation that my plan would never work.

My plan would never work.

I felt foolish and frightened, ensnared by my own idiocy as much as by cruel circumstance. My bladder ached to empty, but I simply couldn't pull myself up and face what lay outside the cocoon of the blankets. I didn't belong here, or anywhere, and I had no idea what to do.

I thought back to the long-ago morning when I woke to the first day of a motherless life. I had dreamed all night of Sheriff Lyle's black-and-white patrol car and my father's private collapse in the yard. I opened my eyes knowing that my mother, my Cal, my aunt were not at home, not anywhere, and nothing could be done about it. The golden morning light streaming into my bedroom felt intolerable. I did the only thing I knew to do at barely twelve years old. I leaped from bed into my dark closet and closed myself in.

Hours later, Seth discovered me there but let me be. Then Cora Mitchell tried to coax me out, but I wouldn't budge. Daddy never came. I imagined that he was down the hall in his own closet, hiding in the mothball dark like me. That afternoon, someone placed a plate of food outside my door, and the smell was too tempting for a hungry child to resist. I crawled out hesitantly to warm scoops of unfamiliar casseroles, presumably cooked and delivered to our family by sympathetic townsfolk, and I ate, first delicately but then in heaping, gulping bites. I despised myself for doing it, for nourishing myself, for continuing on, but I couldn't help it. A force larger than myself moved me forward, from primal hunger to that initial curious creep out of my bedroom and down the stairs, to eventual regularity and the assumption of my mother's role as caretaker of the family. I did not choose so much as succumb to necessity.

Similarly, whether my plan to live out my pregnancy in the wilderness and bring Wil's and my child into this world would work or not, I knew I had to continue on. I had to empty my bladder. I had to eat. Just as I had stepped into a motherless life, I would step into the life of a mother. I would heed the call of necessity. I would rise.

When I lifted the hide and stepped out into the birdsong and cool morning air to squat near the hut, it was as if the storm had never happened. The meadow spread out before me, damp and perfectly still. Spring was beginning to unfold in each new leaf and blade and bud. The rising sun lit only the tips of the surrounding peaks with a glow as soft as hand-churned butter. The foothills and valley stood in shadow, waiting patiently for light to feed their patches of greening, to dry their mud and melt the waning snow. I took a deep breath of this calm, held it in the taut balloons of my lungs, and slowly let it go.

Surprisingly swiftly, the sun's radiant ball emerged piece by piece from behind an eastern peak's jagged ridge to spread pale light across the valley. It reached where I stood first, bathing me in subtle warmth, reflecting off the droplets clinging to every leaf and stalk around me, illuminating tiny fluttering insects and sparkling stretches of spider's webs invisible just an instant before. The sunlight touched the white aspen bark and the budding red branches of the thick willow maze lining the creek. Inch by inch the light crept. Within minutes, the entire valley floor woke along with every possible shade of spring, yielding to the dawn and the songbirds' celebration.

When the sun topped the ridge and unleashed its full warmth and brightness, I tilted my chin upward to face it. In the steady rise of morning, I recognized that I had been given another day. Tomorrow, perhaps, I would be given yet another.

In contrast to the hopelessness of the previous night's storm, the morning felt like possibility. My plan might not work, but, in the kind gesture of the sun's rising, it felt equally likely that it could. The birds prattled on, now diving and swooping and twirling all around me. Somewhere in their revelry I found a nudge of encouragement.

So I kept on, day by day, and gradually I began to relax, yielding my dread to some level of trust. Comfort certainly did not arrive all at once, and, often, just as I glimpsed it, a noise or another storm would frighten me and set me back. But I soon realized that even more important than planting seeds or digging the latrine or establishing my routine of daily living, I needed to quiet my mind. Worry and fear would not change the outcome of my situation or my fate. Horizon might not be home, but I found a way to stay.

In time, I began to notice the soft twilight across the meadow as more beautiful than ominous. Most sounds and silences became merely themselves and, eventually, just familiar background to daily living, more music than menace. Throughout that first month, a fragile camaraderie with the forest grew. I increasingly moved through my days in accordance with the rhythm that all nature's creatures obey by instinct and millennia of habit—lives patterned by the rise and fall of the sun, the dictates of coolness and heat, the body's hunger and need for sleep, the spectacular sweep of storms, and the black or luminous nights, depending on the cycle of the moon.

As the ground thawed, I finished digging the latrine. I stuffed my pack with food that might attract bears and roped it to a high aspen limb on the far edge of camp, just as Wil had done. Along the hut's warm south side, I planted the seeds I'd collected from the kitchen garden the previous autumn. I drank creek water that tasted of river stones and poured it, so cold and clean, over my naked body. I took the time to wonder at the world—the total silence of a trotting fox, the perfect symmetry of a beaver lodge, how butterflies arrived like a toss of colorful confetti just as the first tiny blossoms of nectar unfurled, the daily parade of sandhill cranes migrating overhead who knew exactly where to go. I collected and chopped mounds of firewood; knitted loose yarn netting and dipped it into the beaver pond to snare an occasional young brookie; hacked out a high-backed chair from a stump and sat there most evenings, wrapped in a quilt, observing the sinking sun and dwindling forest sounds, hooting back to the owl I nightly heard but never saw, admiring the stars as they poked through the sky's black canvas one by one. On moonless nights, I stared up at the staggering haze of the Milky Way and, never having learned the names and shapes of proper astronomy, invented my own constellations among the glimmering stars: hands in prayer, peach blossom, piglet's tail, trumpet.

In the midst of this eternal cadence, as balance to the withering of my fear, my child and I grew. By the end of May, my belly was round and taut as a melon, my whole body fleshy and fertile and surprising, my child stretching and punching and turning within me.

One night, as low clouds hugged the valley, I curled us—my unborn child and me—into our nest of blankets and imagined all the animals in the forest doing the same, bedding down, curving into warmth. I considered how some forest mothers felt their babies kick within them just as I did, how others nursed and nurtured and protected their offspring just as I would. I thought about all the life beginning, enduring, and ending around me, from the biggest bear to the tiniest insect, to the seed and the bud and the blossom. Here in the forest, I was not alone. I was sure it was something Wil had been trying to explain to me all along. I wrapped my arms gently around the globe of my belly, embracing my baby but also something more, an indescribable immensity of which I felt a part.

I thought back to the many nights I had tried to fall asleep in my bed at home while Seth and Og argued downstairs or Seth's friends drunkenly hollered at one another while revving the roadster's engine in the yard. I remembered what I had tried to forget: the few times I was awakened by my bedroom door handle being jiggled in the dark—by one of Seth's friends, or maybe even Seth himself, testing the lock, succumbing to a dare or mad desire or a dark, desperate weakness—and then footsteps shuffling away, defeated, saved.

As I drifted off to sleep in my new forest home, woven in some great and mysterious tapestry, the only sound I listened for was the steady pulse of the vast collection of beating hearts, the inhale and exhale of a million lives being lived alongside mine. I realized I had never been less afraid in my life.

Twelve

J une made promises.

The weather was warm and mostly clear. The days were long and—devoid of housework and farm chores and putting meals on the table—astonishingly spacious. The hours I spent sitting in the meadow or strolling the woods, immersed in my own observations and thoughts, felt less awkward and idle and more vital by the day.

Beyond a few small trout, I had no luck harvesting food, but ripening raspberry bushes abounded on a southern hillside and tiny leaves were emerging in my garden, assuring nourishment come July and August. Though I hadn't yet snared a rabbit or a grouse in my makeshift trap, I felt hopeful my skills would improve with practice and necessity.

One violet twilight, I sat motionless on the grassy edge of a small neighboring meadow. My snare—a little prison box I had fashioned together with twigs and yarn—was propped at a slant on a Y-shaped stick and baited with clover flower. I waited stubbornly, or perhaps just naively, faithful to my method. Bats dove and spun above me, plucking miller moths from midair. Night noises roused cricket by cricket. A doe appeared on the meadow's edge, tiptoeing from the aspens. She straightened her neck in surprise, blinked, and lightly stamped her feet, unsure what to make of me. Her black eyes glistened and blinked again, and her white tail feathered back and forth in indecision. Still as stone, I gazed at her. I had seen many animals since my arrival—ground squirrels and tree squirrels and bullet-nosed chipmunks; marmots and rabbits and porcupines and foxes and a lone coyote hunting in a field; herds of deer and elk moving across the hillsides—but this doe was the first to seem as interested in me as I was in her. We locked eyes for a long while.

The doe turned gracefully back the way she had come and pranced out of sight. Seconds later, she reappeared, followed by a delicate spotted fawn. I gasped at the simple beauty, and they looked toward me in perfect unison. The fawn crept closer to her mother with noiseless, careful steps. They crossed the meadow fluidly, side by side, then disappeared into the foliage. Suddenly, the shrubbery rustled where the doe had first emerged. I braced for a predator in pursuit. Instead, a second fawn burst forth, smaller and even more delicate than the first. He rushed across the clearing to keep up with his mother and sibling, so scrawny and oblivious it made my heart ache.

I saw the doe again a few evenings later—her favored fawn at her side, the runt several lengths behind—as the trio cautiously approached the creek near the hut. After they tested me again the following dusk, they frequented my camp for their evening drink. I felt camaraderie in their trust and relief each time the weakling fawn emerged from the bushes in determined pursuit of his family.

The month passed one step at a time: one waking, one fire, one pot of oats, one walk in the woods, one attempt to catch food, one sunset, one can of beans, one night. I hauled fallen branches from the forest to build a lopsided fence around my garden. I dribbled creek water from the canteen onto the emerging greens and lay a quilt over them each night to protect against the frost.

When I remember June of 1949, I see my seventeen-year-old self sitting naked at the creek's edge after bathing, sun pouring across my young body like warm honey, my belly a pale and mysterious globe, my breasts so full and strange. My baby tumbled in my womb and kicked at my heart. Sunflowers and purple lupines and pale-pink wild roses ornamented the hillsides. Magenta spikes sprang up from the stream bogs, each stalk a tiny circus of pink elephant heads, their trunks lifting to the sun. I caught grasshoppers just to study their tiny grinding jaws. I counted a dozen different colors of butterflies. Delicate happiness pushed through the mud of grief just as surely as the summer forest blossomed from winter.

But as June ended, my strength began to wane. Worse, the cravings began. My meals the past two months had certainly not been hearty, but they had sufficed. True, I took inventory of my food daily—read like a verdict the dwindling cans in the hut's corner and the decreasing weight of my stash every time I hauled it down from the tree—and tried to eat as little as possible to conserve my stores. As July arrived, hot and dry, my jerky and jarred peaches and pickled eggs were long gone and the canned goods nearly depleted, but greens and sweet peas were maturing in my small garden, with beets and cabbage to follow, and, eventually, potatoes and carrots. Little brookies and fat rainbow trout swam the beaver pond. Raspberries were slowly ripening. I wasn't worried.

The desire for impossible food began subtly. One evening, as I sat in my hollowed stump, awaiting the deer family and knitting cotton diaper squares as the sun slipped behind pink-and-gray-striped clouds, I thought of my mother's holiday ham. Daddy slaughtered a hog once every few months, so we ate plenty of pork throughout the year, but Mother's holiday ham was special, glazed in brown sugar and roasted whole, the drippings thick and sweet as molasses. Strangely, it was those drippings I most longed for, or even a hunk of fat. I imagined slicing the dense, greasy belly meat and sliding piece after piece past my lips. When I came back to my senses, I was appalled at my ridiculousness. It had been years since such a ham had been served at our table, and I had never liked the fatty part.

The next day I craved fried chicken, and, later that week, I couldn't stop thinking about gravy, dark and rich, slathering a plate of biscuits or just eaten with a spoon. I ate the first tiny pea pods from the garden, but even after so much care and anticipation, they did not satisfy. I plucked bitter, unripe raspberries and longed to douse them with cream. Elk stew, ham hocks, thick slabs of bacon, pastry dripping with butter, sliced potatoes smothered in cheese—increasingly, I could think of nothing but food. Day and night, I dreamed of it with a yearning so powerful I'd find myself salivating and, more than once, breaking into tears when fantasy crystallized back into famished reality. My hunger was not unlike my yearning for Wil when I had first arrived to this place. I knew I had to get control of my thoughts. But, this time, I simply couldn't do it.

I hadn't had any recent luck catching trout, but suddenly I felt desperate to snag one. For four solid days, I dropped my handmade net into the beaver pond, struggling against my girth to kneel, drawing nothing but dead reeds from the water. Panic gripped me every time I came up empty. Finally, a flash of iridescent scales glinted in the sunlit pool and I plunged my net. What I pulled up wasn't much—not eight inches long—but I rushed the fish back to camp, eagerly gutted and speared it, then roasted it briefly over the remains of my morning fire. I devoured it in seconds, bones and all. Splinters caught in my throat and I hacked and gargled to free them. Still, I craved more, even the bones, especially the bones. In retrospect, I know I was starving.

Along with the cravings, weariness and aches and sudden belly cramps troubled me, making daily tasks like fetching water and gathering wood increasingly difficult. I could barely bend to arrange kindling and light a fire without needing to sit and rest. When the first raspberries I had long been anticipating ripened to sweet jewels, I dragged myself upslope to pluck and gulp down every last one. But my legs barely held me as I hiked back down the hill and to my bed, and I never gathered the strength to climb to the berries again.

My belly grew so large that every ounce of the rest of me seemed relegated to its support. My limbs had withered. My feet ached. Lying in bed hurt my back. Sitting agonized my bladder and bowels. Standing strained my hips, and walking made them feel as if they might come apart altogether.

One moonless night—in late July or early August, I believe, but I had stopped keeping track of days with marks on the hut wall, along with every other nonnecessity—I tossed and turned in the bed in search of a suitable position, trying to purge the cravings and discomforts from my mind. After hours of this, I finally rose in frustration, not knowing where to go or what to do for relief. I lit a candle, pulled on the big sweater I had taken from Og, and stepped out of the hut into the cool, black night. Millions of stars winked above me, but I barely gave them a glance, so frantic was I to find something to soothe me. The garden beckoned me. I kneeled and pulled the first beet. It was no bigger than a grape, but I ate it, including the dirt residue and much of the stalk. I pulled another, and another, knowing I was ruining the crop, eating it before it had any real value, but I could not stop. The dirt crunched between my teeth, a grit both insufferable and somehow pleasurable, and soon, inexplicably, I was scooping handfuls of the soil into my mouth. The act was both so wrong and so right—I began to cry, overwhelmed by confusion. The tears salted the dirt as I licked my filthy palms. The baby kicked ferociously as if asking for more.

When I stood to return to the warmth of the hut, feeling ashamed and bewildered at my actions, my womb stiffened. The cramp started small and familiar, then intensified, extending and tightening its grip until my whole belly stood tall and rigid and I thought I might faint. I struggled back through the doorway to my bed. Eventually, the pain and tautness subsided. Even in my ignorance about giving birth, I recognized this as the first contraction. I was terrified. When sleep did come, I dreamed of searching for something I could not find. I woke in wet underclothes and bedding, moisture gluing my thighs.

They say there is a merciful amnesia that accompanies giving birth, and perhaps this is true, for I cannot recall many details of my son's arrival. But I do remember this: I knew I was too weak to do what needed to be done, and yet I understood I must do it anyway.

The contractions intensified for days, and I became more raw and more feral and afraid with each. It was the inescapability of the birth that most panicked me, as if I had mounted a wild stallion and had no choice but to ride until I was thrown. All thought of food vanished. My surroundings disappeared. I was nothing but body and opening and burn. When the pain became unbearable, I howled and snorted and fell to my knees in the middle of my camp, rocking on all fours like a miserable animal. By the time I was sure my hips would dislodge and hurl through space in opposing directions, I had somehow crawled into the hut. I don't remember stripping, but soon I squatted naked on the dirt floor, gripping the bed's edge.

I remember reaching my quivering hand to my crotch and touching instead the hard crown of a tiny skull. I don't remember pulling the pink quilts off the bed to the ground beneath me; I don't remember the series of pushes that thrust the baby slithering out of my body; I vaguely remember falling to my knees and lifting him, slippery as an eel, to my chest, our bodies still connected by the purple, pulsating cord. All I clearly recall of my son's entrance into this world is that he was not moving.

He was tiny and lifeless as a doll, his only motion from my quivering hands. My mind swam to reconcile the impossible with the actual. The potent life force kicking so insistently to be free had vanished. I knew something must be done to save him, but I was just a foolish girl alone in the wilderness with no idea what I was doing. *Of course the baby would die,* I thought in delirium and anguish, and I, withered and exhausted, blood streaming down my legs, was sure to follow. I could think of nothing to do but shout.

"Live!" I cried out, perhaps as much at myself as at the baby as he lay in my lap, so blue and so limp. "Live!" I sobbed, over and over again, as if mere words could raise the dead.

But then, I swear, Wil appeared at my side. He lifted our baby in the crook of my arm. He pulled my free hand into his, and together we began rubbing our baby's chest, just as he had done with Ruby-Alice's flaccid puppy. Gently at first, then vigorously, purposefully, Wil stroked my flat hand over our baby's heart, turned him and stroked his feathery back, turned him again, rubbing, calling him to life. Wil blew into the tiny blue lips. Still, our baby did not rouse.

Wil would not give up. Through my palms he rubbed quick circles across the baby's chest, over the thin strips of ribs, the fleece-soft purple flesh. Suddenly, like a switch abruptly and mysteriously engaged, the baby gasped. It was a raspy sound, deep and clogged and surprising. I turned him facedown and rapped his back, trying to clear his lungs, and when that didn't work, I flipped him back to face me and scooped my fingers through the mucus obstructing his minute, gummy mouth. He gurgled another breath, weak and uncertain. I lifted his mouth to mine and sharply inhaled, spat out the mucus, locked mouths again and inhaled, drawing up life as sure as sun coaxes sprouts from the soil.

My baby boy's first cry was the most beautiful thing I'd ever heard. I turned my astonished smile toward Wil, stunned to find him not at my side. He had been there, just seconds before, helping me save our child. And yet the only actuality of Wil was in the baby himself, pinking now and wailing. I cradled him against my chest with one hand and dragged another blanket off the bed with the other. I wiped and wrapped him, cooing unsteadily to soothe his cries. I knew I needed to find a way to cut the cord, but all I could do was cling to him and rock back and forth, weeping with joy and disbelief and gratitude. My baby lived. Perhaps I wasn't as foolish a girl as I believed, for I had made this new life and I had given it passage.

When he eased open his little swollen eyes and peered at me curiously for the first time, I felt wonder beyond compare. All these months I had believed this being inside my body to be a stranger, mere creature of mystery, or, perhaps, deserved atonement. Never had I imagined he would be someone I would recognize from some- where deep and unnamable within my being, *this* baby with *these* dark eyes, uncannily familiar.

He knit his tiny brows and we stared at each other a long while like two souls reconnected after being a universe apart.

Thirteen

The first time my baby nursed, after the drama and euphoria of his birth, my milk was as rich and yellow as butter. Pain pierced my nipple and signaled my womb to squeeze forth the placenta. I found my knife and cut the baby's cord; it squirted blood until I tied it off with a length of yellow yarn from my knitting bag and hoped for the best. Leaving the entire mess on the floor of the hut, I climbed into bed and tucked us under the two remaining unsullied quilts. I worried that the fragrant juices of birth might attract animals, but I could not muster the energy to rise and remove them. I marveled at my baby's perfection as he suckled: faultless lips, nose, forehead; the exquisite curl of each ear; the dark contemplative eyes, so like his father's. His family name would be Moon, I supposed, and I cooed nicknames at him like Moon Face and Moon Pie and the one that stuck, from the song "Blue Moon" and the Big Blue wilderness—my Baby Blue. I felt deeply weary in the wake of his delivery but overwhelmingly grateful—for his breath, for my milk, to be on the other side of his frightening arrival, to have a piece of Wilson Moon in my arms. In the sacred cocoon of new birth, we slept for days. Somewhere in the midst of that torpor, my breasts swelled and burned and I feared something was terribly wrong, but the milk still flowed, now white and creamy.

But what was left of my strength soon dwindled, and with it, the sole nourishment for the baby. I could not find the energy to fish. Even if I could have hiked the hillside where the raspberries grew, too many bears now frequented the patch. All reserves long gone, I had only the small daily harvest from my still-maturing garden, greens and peas, mostly—so foolish was I to plant slow-growing roots and cabbage—and thin carrots, pebbles of potatoes, and a few remaining beets, no bigger than Baby Blue's fist. I was so desperate that, as I finally wrapped the afterbirth in the top quilt and dragged it as far from camp as my slight strength would allow, I briefly considered eating from the placenta, just as I knew some other animal would. Sipping my own breast milk from my cupped palm also occurred to me. But I declined both possibilities as my final fall into indecency. The garden would have to do. But it was not enough, and I knew it.

When Baby Blue was little more than two weeks old—increasingly alert to life despite the fact that my milk and my mind were beginning to fail—I woke to a morning so dim and cold that it could have been the last limits of December twilight. It felt wrong from the instant I opened my eyes.

I set the sleeping baby to my side, tucking our shared quilts around the knit blanket in which he was swaddled. Shivering, I pulled on my big sweater and peered out the small window. Snow. At least two feet had fallen in the night. No matter that it was, I guessed, late August. Any weather is fair play in high-mountain whimsy. Perhaps folks down in Iola rejoiced in what must have been the first rainfall since spring across the yearning land. I, in contrast, did not even have to step forth from the hut to understand that the unexpected snowfall and frigid air had sealed my fate. My garden would be ruined.

The single difficulty in the decision to seek help was waiting for the storm to pass. Once I decided to give up, I wanted to get on with it. The skies did not clear or the temperature rise for two agonizing days. I kept the baby tucked under my sweater, bare skin to skin. We mostly slept and nursed. When warmth or milk was not enough, we both cried. I emerged on the third morning to summer sunshine and the earth greedily drinking the melting snow. By afternoon, little evidence remained except muddy patches in the shadows and the flaccid green slime that had been my garden. Nothing had survived. The tiny beets and carrots and potatoes were still edible, but their greens, and thus their promise, were laid to waste. I dug through the ruin to reap and eat what I could. And then I placed a fresh diaper square on my gaunt baby, wrapped him tightly in the knit blanket, clasped him to my chest, and started walking in a direction I thought most likely to yield another human being.

Months prior, when I had first arrived, I imagined how, when the day came to leave, I would carefully dismantle my camp. I'd till under the garden, remove the fire ring and the stick frame holding my pot, pull down ropes, clear out the hut, topple the hollow log I had used as a chair. I'd erase my summer of shame, and no one would be the wiser. But now as I walked away, too weak to even tidy the bed or put fork and spoon in the pack and hoist it on my back, I wondered two things: Who did I think was going to care enough about me to come sleuthing this place? And what had I planned to do with the most incriminating and enduring evidence of all, the baby himself? What good would a hidden camp be when I wandered into Iola with a newborn in my arms? I shook my head and began to walk, a lifetime older than that silly girl who'd arrived in April.

It was the longest walk of my life. I cannot gauge whether it was one mile or ten. I only knew I had to keep the nearly weightless baby clutched to my chest and to put one foot in front of the other. Delirium toyed with me, making the journey feel otherworldly. I walked with urgency and purpose, yet I did not know to where, and the surrounding forest felt adversarial in a way it hadn't in months— the late-summer sun a devilish lashing, the songbirds an incessant marching band, the terrain as lumpy and daunting as a field of skulls. Even the tall stalks of magenta fireweed mocked me with their elegant ability to withstand the snowstorm that had destroyed my hopes. When the baby cried weakly, I stopped walking and put him to my breast, knowing I could offer only a few disappointing sips of paltry milk, satisfying him for mere minutes before he whimpered for more. Like the parched landscape before the snow, my body was in drought. I had nothing left to give.

As I stepped into a clearing on my solemn trek, the mother doe and I startled each other. I hadn't seen her in weeks. Not five yards away, we locked eyes. We were both mothers now, but where were her fawns? The bushes rustled and her favored offspring emerged, tall and elegant. The fawn eyed me with wise caution as she stepped to her mother's side. The pair gracefully moved on. The second fawn did not follow. I sat on a boulder and waited. When the weakling never appeared, I sorrowfully hugged Baby Blue more tightly and stumbled on.

Fourteen

I was unsure at first if the long black automobile was a mirage. I had wandered for I don't know how long, searching for the rock pinnacles to guide my way but finding only miles of unfamiliar land. Aspens and willows had hours ago yielded to sage and juniper and rock, and then this: a black city car parked along a road near a clump of ponderosa pines. It was more than my muddled mind could comprehend.

I hid behind a tree and tried to make sense of the scene. Picnickers. A man and a woman, a red blanket spread on the ground displaying their meal: a golden bread loaf and a round of cheese, layers of pink ham like Mr. Chapman sliced so thinly behind his counter, and—could it be?—two gorgeous rosy peaches, big as softballs, atop a brown paper sack. My stomach ached at the sight.

But even more wondrous than precious food was a baby, swaddled in pale blue flannel and cradled in the woman's arms. He was larger but perhaps newer than Baby Blue. He writhed and kicked and howled like a baby should. The man stood to the side, smoking a cigarette and cursing two screeching blue-and-black Steller's jays perched on a ponderosa bough overhead. The woman opened her shirt and clumsily exposed one round white breast, as full and succulent as mine were drained and withered. Her baby pushed away, but the mother persisted. As the infant calmed and began to nurse, I knew what I must do.

There is a kind of sadness that transcends sadness, that runs like hot syrup into every crevice of your being, beginning in the heart then oozing into your very cells and bloodstream, so that nothing— not earth or sky or even your own palm—ever looks the same. This is the sadness that changes everything.

I assumed I had already known this deepest sorrow. To be sure, losing my mother, my dear aunt Viv, my Cal, had ripped a hole in what had been the tightly woven tapestry of my proper childhood, but my mother's Bible and the necessities of daily living instructed me it was a tear that must be mended. My dazed young mind accepted the answer of practicality and went forth accordingly. I swallowed my grief like a hard lump of cinders, and there in my gut it remained. And when I stood in Chapman's store and overheard the news of Wil's tragic fate, I did not return home to pick up a kitchen knife and hurl it at Seth in wild revenge but, instead, went on obediently cooking and washing dishes and tending to Abel and cleaning the henhouse in silent, secret tears. I kept moving. I ran away to the woods, made preparations, gave birth, stayed alive. Sorrow tried but did not claim me.

But sneaking over to that long black car, laying my baby down on the warm leather back seat, and leaving him behind unleashed a billowing grief that overtook my every cell. I didn't realize this at first, so dazed was I from hunger, so accustomed to enduring, to doing what needed to be done. When I clicked the car door closed and walked away from him, I did so almost as if I had set down a mere stone. Or if not a stone, a puppy then, or a hatchling, something I had needed to care for then pass along, a practical change of hands like the sale of a piglet from the sty or a sapling from the orchard. I did not nuzzle him one last time into the hollow of my neck or brush my cheek against his downy head in farewell. I did not inhale his smell and commit it to memory as I placed him on the seat or take one final gaze at his perfect lips through the open car window. Farm kids learn early on not to get attached to the babies whose fates are beyond us. I kept meaning to look back, to watch from a hidden place until one of the picnickers noticed my son—to know for certain he had been discovered, to see him lifted and embraced—but, instead, I ran. Weak as I was, I turned from the car and bolted from the clearing without so much as turning my head.

I clambered over rocks and branches and stumps, darted around sagebrush and boulders, inexplicably exploding from my fatigue by galloping through furrows and straight up hills, stumbling and falling, struggling to my feet and continuing on. What had I done? I was frantic, bewildered, with no idea of my direction. Had there been forest eyes to witness my retreat, they would surely have believed something dark and hungry chased me. No one could have guessed that my only predator was my own unimaginable act.

Finally, I collapsed on the forest floor. I lay on my back and heaved for air. All I remember is this: above me the sky was a fierce,

cloudless blue, and in it, circling, was a red-tailed hawk. I fixated
on her graceful flight as if it were the only thing left in the world to
believe in. She did not seem to be hunting but was enjoying a ride
on a private breeze. Round and round she floated, effortlessly, not
even flapping her wings. Round and round my eyes followed. I lay,
quaking and childless, far below her delight, overcome with loneliness. The kinship I had felt with all the world while pregnant was
gone. I wondered at the possibility that on the day Wil and I had
lain together—maybe even at the exact instant my back had arched
in love's ecstasy—this hawk might have returned to her nest to
discover it had been robbed, her babies gone. Was it possible that I
had been lost in my own elation as the hawk's disaster struck, just
as she was oblivious to my tragedy now?

For the first time, I wondered exactly what I had been doing the
instant my family's automobile had missed the curve. Was I playing
in the orchard? At the car's first tumble, as one by one those I loved
were flung through open windows, heads splitting on rocks, was I
biting into a sweet peach? And where had I been when Seth's car
lurched forward, that first catastrophic jolt to Wil's tied hands?
Could I have been such a fool to be pulling perfectly browned bread
from the oven as my Wil suffered the first sear of flesh against gravel
or as he took his final breath?

How absurd it was to desire the hawk to share in my suffering far
below. Like everything about my Baby Blue, I would endure the
agony of his loss alone. The fact that he existed at all—the impossibly soft folds of his neck, his sweet breath, his tiny, clutching
hands—was known and mattered solely to me.

And yet, I thought then of her—the woman in the white blouse,
the other mother.

I had only glimpses of her as I snuck closer to the car from behind bushes and trees, but I recalled her wavy, chestnut hair, short and swept stylishly to the side, and how she tucked it behind one ear when she looked down at her flailing infant. She was pretty, with round cheekbones and a delicate nose, but she was also pale and expressionless, tired perhaps from the drive, solemnly bouncing the baby and patting his bottom, encouraging him to quiet and latch on to nurse. She occasionally glanced up at her husband, who kept his wide back to her, cursing the blue jays then staring out at the woods, a cat's tail of cigarette smoke curling above his dark head.

My mind's eye envisioned what came next as clearly as if I had witnessed the scene: the screeching jays finally quieting, then the woman cocking her head toward the first soft cries rising from the car. At first, I imagined, she mistook the call for birdsong, but then her mother's instinct told her otherwise. I pictured her buttoning her blouse and handing her own infant to her husband, moving toward the car, cautiously at first, then with urgency, surefooted and quick. I saw her peer through the window and gasp before yanking open the car door and gazing down in disbelief. And then, I was certain, the woman hurriedly, instinctually, scooped my starving baby to her bosom and gave him her sweet, rich milk, the lifesaving nourishment I could not provide.

And while she held him to her breast, I imagined, I hoped, she would perhaps think of me. She would cast searching, sympathetic eyes into the forest, knowing that somewhere out there, a young mother, so like her, had laid her baby down and stumbled away in bewilderment. She would wonder at such an act, at what extreme circumstances might cause a woman to make such an impossible, stupid choice.

I lay on the forest floor, still hypnotized by the hawk's constant circling, and pressed my right hand—the very last part of me that had touched my child—firmly to my cheek. I imagined the imprint of his tiny head to be carved in the lines and folds of my palm and stroked my face over and over again, hoping he could somehow feel my touch.

I MUST HAVE SLEPT, for what I remember next is waking on the hard ground where I had collapsed, stones digging into my back, my head pounding. I lay there, unmoving, staring at nothing but dim dusk and one rose-shaped gray cloud. I replayed the day in my mind. When I had set out for help, I had had no intention of giving my son away. But when I saw the picnickers—the sleek black car, the full breast, the family—my baby's possible lives flashed before me. In one version, he would remain mine but he would continue to weaken and almost surely die, and if he managed to live, if we both did, where would we find refuge? In the other version, he would be gone from me forever to become another woman's son, but he would be nourished, grow fat, have a future, a father, a home. Like the doe whose instinct to favor her stronger fawn was surely at odds with her desire to nurture the weaker, a voice from a deeper inner recess than logic or love or even hope told me I must make a similar choice. I had walked unconsciously, dreamlike, as if some force other than the usual brain mechanism had moved my feet through the tall dry grasses and sage, over the rocky ground toward the car, moving forward without being fully aware of what I was doing until I did it. One moment, I was clutching his tiny body to my chest. The next, I was opening the rear car door, laying him down on the leather seat, closing the door with a quiet click, and walking away.

Darkness fell quickly, black and moonless. I stood and stumbled to a cluster of pines to lie beneath them, in the illusion of their protection, through the cold night. I faded in and out of sleep, agonized by dreams that my baby was crying for me and I searched and searched but could not find him. As soon as the faintest ribbon of yellow dawn appeared on the eastern skyline, I rose, shivering and stiff, and began walking, trying to retrace my steps from the previous day. By the time dawn fully broke, I had managed to find the clearing and was standing in the exact place where I had laid my baby down. The car and the couple were gone. Not a footprint or a tire track remained, as if ghosts had stolen my child after cruelly enchanting my mind. Half-dazed, I spun round and round, eying the scene in circular lap after lap as if one more look would reveal some evidence of his fate. A terrible panic gripped me that the whole episode had been delusion, that I had left him who knew where.

Suddenly, my eyes lit on a peach, propped on a tall boulder like an orange jewel in the brightening dawn. There had been two peaches on their picnic blanket. Now she had my child and I, her peach. She had left it for me, perhaps guessing from Baby Blue's feather weight that his mother was hungry, but, more importantly, she might also have known that I would return here, seeking some confirmation that he was in caring hands.

I approached the peach cautiously, not trusting my mind. When I reached out and found the fruit to be real and so perfectly ripened that I could feel Daddy's palm twisting it from its branch and Cora's tender grip as she placed it in a sack, I realized that our lives—mine and the family in the shiny black car—had intersected even before I had happened upon them. They had been to our roadside stand. Possibly, they had inquired about a pleasant picnic spot, a place to get off the highway for a spell, and had followed Cora's directions. As Cora pointed with her big arms, explaining the lefts and rights to this place, perhaps I had just begun my dazed wandering toward the very clearing she described. I had never possessed my mother's bedrock sense of faith in divine fate, but at that moment I decided that she might have been correct about God's will. My baby needed breasts full of milk, a mother who could care for him properly, a father of this earth, and these had arrived. I needed food and confirmation that my son had been found, and here I held a miraculous fruit in my hand.

The first bite was so exquisite it stung. I let its sweetness explode in my dry, lonesome mouth, then slowly savored the next several bites like salvation. In spite of myself, I began devouring the peach with immense, eager gulps, juice running down my wrists into my tattered sweater sleeves. In an instant, the precious gift was gone. I had sucked every shred of flesh from the pit, then licked my filthy hands and wrists for the last taste of juice.

Desperate for more, I exited the clearing where the black car had been parked. This led to a narrow dirt road that wound through the forest not a half mile before intersecting with a wider road made of dull yellow gravel. Had I been fully in my mind, I would have recognized where I was by then, but every effort was in simply moving my weak body forward, step by weary step. I chose the road's downhill slope less from directional logic than for avoidance of a climb. But it was the correct way home, as I discovered when that endless gravel road eventually began to run along Big Blue Creek and finally merged with Highway 50. Without so much as glancing for an oncoming car, I rushed stupidly across the hot black asphalt to clutch the guardrail on the other side. Below me ran the Gunnison River, slow and low; the rails stretched along its side. To the east lay Iola, the town and the life I had not allowed myself to miss until that instant.

I must have been a wild sight for the driver I flagged down. I was unconcerned, but with my matted hair and emaciated figure in filthy clothing, it's a wonder that he stopped for me at all. He was not a local man but had a kind face and agreed to drive me into town. Sweet aftershave and mint, cigarette, shoe polish, gasoline, leather—my sense of smell was so acute and unaccustomed to the ordinary odors of civilization that the car's interior nearly overwhelmed me. The man's pleasantries were the first words spoken to me since I had left home in April. They felt baritone and bouncy and sincere. Blessedly, he was not chatty. I rested my head against the warm glass, closed my eyes, and let the engine's vibration lull me toward sleep until I felt the automobile slow and turn off the highway, cross the bridge, and turn again onto the gravel road toward Iola.

There was our stand, so utterly familiar, the neat rows of perfect peaches, and dear Cora, unchanged, leaning against a post, charming an out-of-towner. It was the lure of those peaches that had pulled me from the hills, but now that they were near, I could no longer imagine myself among them, nor conversing with Cora, nor walking through my own front door. I had become a wild thing, an alien in my own land. I instructed the man to skirt the edge of town and turn on our road, but even as I did so, I had no intention of going home. The driver slowed to a stop in front of what he could not know was a house hidden deep in the dark pines.

"You sure?" he asked skeptically, eying the trees.

"Yes, sir."

Ruby-Alice Akers would receive me, just as she had received Wil. Of this I was sure. I thanked the man, crawled from his fragrant car, and stumbled through the pines to Ruby-Alice's gate. The little dogs and guinea hens and skittish chickens yelped and clucked and scattered.

Before I managed to reach the pink door, Ruby-Alice opened it in welcome. She guided me inside by one elbow, as if I were the fragile old woman and not she, and I crumpled onto her sofa. She looked at me with something like pity in her sunken eye, misgiving but understanding in her wild one.

Her blue, trembling hands tipped a glass of water to my parched lips. She fed me broth and bread. She brought me a fresh peach, sliced in bite-size pieces as if for a toddler, arranged carefully on a fine china saucer. Warm though it was in the small house, she covered me with a pink quilt, and I clutched it to my chest in memory of my baby and of Wil.

I slept for three days and nights, waking occasionally to receive the small portions of food and drink my body could hold. Ruby-Alice increased each feeding's size and substance, until, waking past noon on the fourth day, I was able to consume my first full meal in months. She had slaughtered and roasted a hen, and I devoured it as if I were a bear fresh from hibernation. I ate whatever she put before me: strawberries, fried potatoes, green beans boiled with chunks of ham, airy raspberry muffins split and mounded with butter. I ate until I felt sick, let an hour pass, then ate again. Ruby-Alice helped me bathe and gave me fresh clothes. She teased the tangles from my long hair, twisted it into a rope, and rolled it into a loose bun. Both of us accustomed to silence, the old woman and I did not speak, except for my many expressions of appreciation and her satisfied grunts in response. If she heard my whimpers and sniffles as I cried for my lost baby, she knew well enough to just let me be.

I would never have known Ruby-Alice as anything but a crazy old lady in need of God's help had it not been for Wilson Moon. I would not have known my own appeal, my beauty, my strength, or the precious feel of Baby Blue in my arms had it not been for Wilson Moon. I pledged to try to put these memories above the pain and loss as I eventually rose from the sofa and walked with Ruby-Alice to her gate. She allowed me a quick hug of gratitude around her bony shoulders before I stepped into the pines and made my way to the path leading to my family's farm. As I did, the long low whistle of the 5:47 sang me home.

Fifteen

No one was at the farm, not Seth or Ogden or Daddy or Trout. Even the chickens and hogs were missing from their pens. The house was cluttered with evidence of Daddy—old newspapers, stained coffee mugs, muddy boot prints, soiled clothes and work gloves carelessly tossed about—but Ogden's and Seth's rooms were both clean and vacant except for bare beds and dressers lined with dust. Several days' worth of dirty dishes layered the countertop and sink. The kitchen garden sat parched and unplanted. Only my bedroom felt normal, untouched since the day I left, the note for Daddy lying open on my bed. I sat and reread my words: *I love you. I'm sorry. Don't worry.* The note seemed naive and childish now. I wadded the paper into a ball and tossed it in the bin on my way out of my bedroom door. I did love my father, but I had shed the fear and obedience that had accompanied that love, and I had no idea who he'd be to me now.

The only one I truly owed an apology to was Abel. I found him in the barn, unkempt but well. He reared his head in greeting, his gentle chocolate eyes flashing recognition and relief. I caressed his sleek auburn neck in long, slow strokes, and he nuzzled my shoulder as if to say, *We're okay, you and me. Glad to see you made it back home.* At least that is what I hoped. I held a bucket of oats for him, and he ate.

I kissed the white star on the broad flat bone between Abel's eyes and believed at least for the moment that it was for hurting him alone that I might seek pardon from God or man or beast. Falling in love with Wilson Moon had been the most honest act of my life. The unforeseen ripple effects of an honest act do not make the choice less truthful. All one can do, I had learned from Wil, is to meet those ripples—as unimaginable or horrific or beautiful or desperate as they may be—with the best you had. I imagined Baby Blue, a full week older now, grown round and rosy with nutrition. Though my heart ached and sorrow ran like thick tar in my marrow, I knew it had been another honest act to lay my baby down.

In the distance, I heard Daddy's truck laboring up the long drive. I steeled myself and left the barn to meet him. He did not notice me walking toward the truck as he parked and exited, but Trout leaped out after him and sped to me wriggling with joy. Crouching to pet the old dog, I looked up to meet my father's pale gray eyes. They were blank as river stones, looking back at me as if I were some fool or stranger or both.

"Daddy," I ventured, but he merely turned and walked toward the kitchen door like he had not seen me at all. He was thin, hunched, and clothed in filthy coveralls. His cap was missing, and his balding head was pink and raw from sun. Three deep wet coughs as he disappeared through the doorway told me he was not well. I nuzzled Trout a while as he squirmed and whined in celebration of our reunion, and then I stood and followed Daddy into the house.

He was already fixing his supper, as, I supposed, he had done every evening for the past five months. Surprised at his fluid movements with knife and spatula and skillet, I stood by the side door and watched him work. He knew I was there but did not look up from the steaming beef and onions he stirred on the stove top. I did not suspect he was preparing enough for me to eat as well, but I nevertheless went to work setting the table for two and filling glasses with sweet tea from the pitcher in the fridge. I took my place at the table and waited to see if he would serve me. Finally, the skillet appeared near my right shoulder and a heaping spoonful landed on my plate. He scooped a smaller portion for himself, returned the empty skillet to the stove, and sat across the table from me. I didn't force conversation he was not ready to have, didn't feel the need to nervously fill the void with chatter or explanations or questions, so we ate in silence that evening except for several bouts of his gurgling cough and, at the end of the meal, his gruff insistence that he do the washing. I didn't know whether his silence was an expression of unforgiving anger or a wall against topics he wanted to avoid, like the reason for my leaving or where I had been, but the quiet suited me fine.

After dinner, I walked among the fragrant fruit in the orchard beneath the last pale-pink licks of sunset. Full bushel baskets at the end of each tree row awaited transport to the stand in the morning. I anticipated the comfortable familiarity of loading the old truck, riding by Daddy's side to the stand, falling into Cora's welcoming embrace, unloading the baskets and arranging the peaches just so.

I twisted a perfect peach from the bough and sank my teeth into its yielding flesh, the unmistakable taste of home. I sat down on a broad stump to breathe in the still twilight and quietly weep with longing for my baby boy.

At breakfast the next morning—also prepared and cleaned up by Daddy despite my offer to help—a few more words were exchanged, and during the drive to the stand a few more. At lunch a few more words, at dinner a few more, and so on. He was a slowly melting icicle and I a patient stream.

Within the week, we were sharing chores side by side and conversation had developed an uneasy flow. All the while, Daddy's cough grew deeper and more persistent. Over peach-raspberry pie I'd made as an apparently irresistible final peace offering, I learned that Sheriff Lyle had questioned Seth about "the trouble with that Injun boy," as Daddy put it, and Seth had left town on what I gathered was Lyle's demand.

I set my pie plate to the side and pulled a deep breath.

"Seth killed that boy, Daddy," I said after a long silence, my heart twisting at both the truth and inadequacy of the words.

Daddy's already solemn face collapsed into a sullen mixture of disgrace, disappointment, and regret. He stared at his coffee mug and wrapped both rough hands around it as if he needed something solid to hold on to.

"I 'spect," was all he said, and all he'd ever say, about the death of Wilson Moon.

I never knew whether Daddy also supposed that Wil had been my lover and the cause of my leaving home. I wanted to tell my father he had a grandchild, a perfect baby boy, but the words refused to leave my mouth.

"And Ogden?" I asked instead.

Daddy merely grunted and waved the question away with his fork. I knew well enough to let it be.

That night, Daddy began coughing up blood. His hacking and sputtering grew as we washed the supper dishes. He spun away from me with each attack, then turned back to the sink as if hoping I hadn't noticed. When he came in from evening chores, he could barely sneak a breath in between bouts. He refused my offer to fetch Dr. Bernette and went to bed early.

All night long his coughing slapped the black silence between our bedrooms. When the coughs turned so violent and constant that I couldn't stand it any longer, I tapped on his door and entered. I found him sitting up in a pool of dim bedside light spitting bloody mucus into a bowl.

"Daddy," I said softly, unable to hide my shock and pity.

He glanced up at me with the look of an animal who knows the end is near, that sad mixture of fear and resignation, then looked down again at the bowl and awaited the next rise. He was so thin and small in his nightshirt he could have been a child. As I approached his bedside, he raised his hand to signal me to stop.

"Daddy, let me help you," I begged.

"Nothin' to be done," he answered hoarsely. "Git on back to bed."

I lay awake the rest of that long night listening to him struggle. Now that my son was gone from me, my father was my last link on earth. Each cough was like a fraying of my final family thread. When I had pictured the faraway farm from my retreat in the Big Blue wilderness, I had assumed it carried on essentially unchanged below. But I had been so wrong. Everything except the peaches had waned, and I returned to an even more broken relic of who we used to be. I'd always believed it was the men in this house who held the place together. It never occurred to me that I was more than housekeeper and hand, that the heart of our family and home had somehow become me. As Daddy weakened, the orchard and I were all we had left.

One of the last things my father said to me, in the midst of delirium from fever and failed lungs a few weeks later, was that I looked just like my mother now that I wore my hair long and spun into a bun on the back of my head.

"She was a beauty," he said with rare wistfulness, sweetly recalling his lost love but also implying he thought I was beautiful too.

I held his hand as he drifted in and out of sleep, relishing the way his fingers intertwined with mine, committing his every freckle and fold and gnarled knuckle to memory.

Sixteen

1949-1954

Daddy died the Saturday after the final crop was picked and delivered. As if he had it all carefully scheduled, the first morning the temperature dropped below freezing, the hired hands pulled the last peaches and Daddy failed to rise.

I sat at his bedside, with Trout curled solemnly at my feet, and gazed sadly down at my father. When I reached out for one final touch, I never imagined a hand so cold.

Nearly everyone in Iola showed up for Daddy's graveside funeral beneath the bluest autumn sky. After, when folks gathered for food and respects back at our farmhouse, I learned from Sheriff Lyle that it was Daddy himself who had turned in Seth. Lacking solid evidence, Lyle couldn't make an arrest, but he assured both Seth and Forrest Davis they'd be in for trouble if they stayed. The pair headed out to California in Seth's roadster, Lyle explained, "taking their mischief with them."

"It was a hell of a lot more than mischief," I said, clenching my jaw.

Lyle nodded solemnly, his eyes searching and apologetic. I could tell he wanted to ask me questions but was politely holding them back.

"You should know your Daddy was out looking for you every day after that, driving to Gunnison, Sapinero, Cebolla, riding Abel into the hills," he said, moving the food around his plate but not eating. "I think he figured you'd come home if you knew Seth was gone. Asked me to keep a lookout."

I considered that information, wondering what all Daddy knew, wondering if roaming the hills had given him the cough that grew to claim his lungs, if I was the cause of my father's undoing, like I was the cause of Wil's.

"I might have," I answered grimly, the unimagined alternative to treating my baby as if he were an unwanted thing stinging the back of my throat like swallowed wasps. I was sorry I ever doubted my father's devotion. It was too late to thank him and far too late to bring his grandson home.

"He even had me relocate your uncle," Lyle continued.

"Relocate?" I asked, having difficulty reconciling the term with what Daddy had eventually told me about Og—that the "free-loader" had had kin all along but only contacted them once there was no longer a woman in our house to do his bidding.

"Turns out Ogden had a mother," Lyle said.

"Everyone has a mother," I said rudely, fatigued by the demands of the day.

"Not everyone has a mother who'd been searching for them for pert near eight years," Lyle said. "Your father discovered a letter.

Had me come pick up Og, drive him to Salida, and put him on the first train to Denver. The deuce swore at me the whole way."

"What did the letter say?" I asked.

"Said she didn't believe the notices she received saying both her boys died in the first months of the war. Said God wouldn't do that to a mother."

"God would," I said, thinking, *God will or He won't.*

"God didn't," he replied. "Somehow this old woman knew that. Tracked down her son and begged him to come home."

"Mother's intuition," I said, envying her, for I had no idea what God had or had not fated for my own son, had not a clue where he could be found.

"My office tried to find that dead boy's kin," Lyle added, searching my eyes to gauge if I knew anything and if this was all too much. "I figured he had a mother somewhere too."

My heart sank. "He had a name, Mr. Lyle," I said.

"That Moon fella," he corrected. "But a drifter's hard to track. Last records we found had him at an Indian school in Albuquerque, but no tellin' which reservation he'd come from. He'd run away from the school a few years back. That's all we could dig up."

With that, it was indeed too much. I took my leave of Sheriff Lyle and the whole crowded scene of black dresses and casseroles and hand-tugging sympathy.

I soon found myself walking alone in the orchard, my orchard now, among the falling yellow leaves and the few pieces of rotting fruit refusing to release from the trees. Wil had a home he never found his way back to, where he knew the land and the land knew him, where, perhaps, his family waited for him still. I had heard of Indian children being removed from their reservations and placed in special schools. Even though I had grown up believing that nothing mattered so much as where you came from, I had never considered what each of those children was forced to leave behind. Wil hadn't told me about his past, maybe because he missed it too much, or maybe because it didn't matter anymore. I hadn't asked questions, but he seemed to me both a child of somewhere and nowhere all at once, his peculiar loveliness perhaps born of his homeland but ripened in the leaving, the resilience required to carry on. I only hoped our baby had the same strength to adapt.

Less than a month after my father took his last pneumonic breaths, the final train heaved through Iola, the conductor pulling the whistle extra loud and long. The Denver & Rio Grande Western had done away with passenger cars a decade earlier and, after nearly seventy years, had decided to also halt the cattle and coal cars in order to shut down the whole Western Slope operation that fall of 1949. Many said the line had been fool's folly from the start, the arduous process of laying track through the Black Canyon to Cimarron costing more lives and money than authorities of the time dared to admit. But, for me, those train whistles had set the rhythm of life. They had even brought Wil to me. An eerie hush fell on Iola on that first whistleless day. "Like a death," some folks lamented. "Like constant night," said others. Little did we know that this was just the first silence, that one day the whole of Iola would be swallowed up, every sound, every structure drowned and gone.

AFTER DADDY PASSED, I kept the farm running as best I could for several years. The Mitchells were of great help for a while, and I hired hands when needed. I replanted the kitchen garden and repaired broken fences. I kept the irrigation ditches flowing and the moth grubs and scale and raccoons away from the trees. I pruned, fertilized, mulched, watered, thinned, and harvested. When a block of trees got too old to produce, I hired hands to help me remove them, painstakingly grafted new shoots, exactly as Daddy had taught me, and planted a new block on a resting patch of soil, just as my family had done for generations. I suppose to the outside eye all appeared in order, but every morning I rose with a stabbing truth in my heart: my love for the place was yet another withered leaf on my barren family tree.

Loyal old Trout had died on the center of Daddy's bed the very day I hauled away the final box of my father's belongings. I dug a deep hole by the pond and stroked his exquisitely wooly chest one last time before wrapping his limp body in a blanket and placing him in the earth. The next winter, I discovered Abel lying on his side gasping for breath on a patch of ice outside the barn, his tibia jutting from a bloody rip in his lovely auburn hide. I couldn't bring myself to shoot him. Instead, I caressed his perfect neck, just as I had at his birth, while the county veterinarian gave him the injection that stopped his heart. I retreated to the barn and wept while the vet and her assistants hauled him away. With that, my only family became a few mean chickens.

Try as I might to deny it, the hollowness with which I conducted my days and tended the farm grew daily. I spent many afternoons at Ruby-Alice's place just to be elsewhere, to help in her garden or coops or kitchen, comforted to be where Wil had once dwelled and by the old woman's strange, quiet presence and the sleeping little dogs.

When at home, memories haunted me. The certain weight of a pillow or a bag of rice might suddenly feel like my Baby Blue, and, though I knew it was madness, I couldn't stop myself from cradling it. Several times I woke in the night so certain he was crying for me at the faraway hut that I rushed down the stairs and didn't come to my senses until reaching for my boots. Some evenings I'd sit alone with my supper at the long kitchen table and, plain as the plate, I'd see Seth's roadster slinking past the window, hear the low snarl of its demon engine devouring the long drive.

One spring night, as white moonlight crested the far hills and cast black shadows across the front porch, I was certain I saw Seth peering at me through the parlor window. I leapt from Mother's chair, and, I am ashamed to say, I hid. Crouching in the broom closet as if a broom closet could save me, trembling like a pathetic rabbit, I suddenly recalled washing my bedding earlier that day and hanging the quilts to dry on the porch instead of on the laundry line in the muddy backyard. What I saw as my brother's menacing face was merely a patchwork square. I pulled myself up and tried to reclaim some dignity by marching straight to the porch to pull and fold the bedding.

No matter how many years passed, I saw them: Wil on the fringes of the orchard, waiting for me, reaching his hand out to mine; Daddy among the shaggy trees, expertly twisting a peach from its hold; Mother tending the kitchen garden, gathering fresh greens for supper; Cal calling to me from our tree house as if it hadn't long ago fallen to ruin; Aunt Viv and Uncle Ogden, both still so full of life, sneaking kisses on the front porch. There had been promise and love in this place once. One by one those hopes had perished. I imagined how my son might have revived it all had I had the courage to bring him home. I pictured it until it burned—him toddling across the kitchen floor, calling me his mama, then, in time, growing long and lean, running through the orchard with his father's grace-ful gait. Instead, only one good thing remained on our land, and that was the peaches.

When the government man knocked on my front door one hot July afternoon in 1954 and asked if he could bend my ear a spell, I poured us two tall iced teas, then joined him on the porch to listen. I had heard rumors about a proposed dam to be built downriver and the possible buyout offers for the valley's land. All Iola was in a fury over the idea of losing everything to a new reservoir. The uproar was both expected and proper, not only against drowning our town but also against choking the wild and wonderful Gunnison River. The plans were misguided at best, tragic at worst, as countless other projects in the name of progress across the west had proven to be. I knew it was all wrong, but sitting there listening to the govern-ment man make his offer, I realized that I secretly, shamefully, wel-comed the plan. I longed for erasure. I told the man I'd think about it and sent him on his way.

I was the first in Iola to sell out. That September, the govern-ment paid me handsomely for my acreage, though the price proved small compensation for the indignation I then suffered from my townsfolk once news of my betrayal spread. To say I felt hated would not be an overstatement. Local folks I had known my entire life stopped buying our peaches and looked away when passing me on Main. Even the Mitchells cut off our ties, either out of genuine anger or perhaps fear of being ostracized by association. Against her father's wishes, and clearly more from obligation than desire, Cora stayed with the stand until the end of that peach season, her once jolly demeanor chilled to cold politeness to every out-of-towner and, especially, to me.

As Cora heaved herself into her truck after we sold our last bag of peaches and I began boarding up the stand for good, she stared at me through the open window as if I had changed beyond recognition.

"You know your Daddy's rollin' in his grave, Torie," she said. "One full turn for every dollar you 'cepted from those gov'ment men."

I thanked her for her many years of loyal service, then reminded her I didn't go by the name Torie anymore.

The afternoon sun filtered through the dust trailed by her truck tires, making the ordinary road a strange sort of beautiful as she drove away.

I had loved Cora Mitchell, just as I had loved a hundred other particulars of my life in Iola. But tragedy and grief had gnawed at every last thing I knew to be true about that place. I nailed the final board across the vacant stand and whispered an apology to my grandfather. I did not offer the same nod of regret to my father, however, for, contrary to Cora's judgment, I felt confident that he lay still and calm in his grave. Regardless of what Cora or anyone else had to say, I knew with certainty that Daddy would have supported my chance to flee this town and all its memories. That is, as long as I did right by the orchard, as I intended to do.

MY GRANDFATHER, HOLLIS HENRY NASH, had been crazy to try to adapt Georgia peaches to the high arid west, but that hadn't stopped him from trying and, after much trial and error, eventually succeeding in the most unlikely place, in the cold thin air of Iola, Colorado. Or so the story went as told throughout my childhood, and, thus, it was the only explanation I knew. I had many times witnessed Daddy defend our orchard against naysayers,

some disbelieving its existence even while holding the round weight
of one of our perfect peaches in their palm. Both the proliferation
and quality of the orchard had apparently been somewhat of a bio-
logical miracle from the start. Famous peaches or not, Mother had
taught us the sinful nature of pride and that our farm was a good
place to call home and not a source of bragging rights. That is, until
I had to decide what would live and what would drown. So much
had passed from my life that was unsavable. I had never known my
grandfather Hollis, but for him, and for Daddy, I was determined to
save the orchard.

Unfortunately, I had no idea how to do so, and I was entirely
alone now that the town had turned its back on me. Ruby-Alice
seemed of no help beyond a dependable ear for my troubles, but, in
a way, it was through her I found a guide.

Each year since I had befriended Ruby-Alice—or, more accurately, since she had so kindly befriended me—she had withered.
The ancient woman from my childhood memories was young compared to who she had become. Her discarded bicycle had tarnished
in the yard for several years by this point, a favorite perch for her
hens and dogs. Her groceries and animal feed were delivered from
Chapman's, and, otherwise, she had no contact with anyone but
me. Her spine was as curved as the old cottonwood where Wil and
I used to meet, her icy blue eyes tilting toward the ground most of
the time, one eye still wild and piercing, the other grown viscous
and recessed. Her thin limbs shook. I felt sure she appreciated my
visits, though I had little evidence other than an occasional pat on
my hand and perhaps a meal painstakingly prepared for two.

It was during one such supper a few weeks after I closed up the
peach stand that Ruby-Alice let out a faint high cry like a rusty

wheel, then collapsed into her plate. I leaped up and lifted her, light and limp as a bag of feathers, and carried her to the sofa. I rushed for a telephone, which, of course, she did not have. Despite the urgent need to dart along the path to my farm to call for help, I simply couldn't leave the food splattered across her wrinkled face. If she were to die while I was gone, she would not die soiled. I wet a kitchen rag and delicately wiped her thin skin, returning some small dignity, just as she had once done for me. Then I ran home, breathlessly repeating over and over my childhood adage, *GodHelp-RubyAliceAkersAmen.*

In the ten minutes it took me to rush to my phone, call Dr. Bernette, then drive Daddy's truck back to the old woman, she did not stir. I squeezed her tiny wrist to feel her pulse, soft and unsteady as first raindrops. Breath only minutely rose and lowered her bony chest. I remember those long, silent minutes—before Dr. Bernette's arrival, then the chaos of the ambulance and red stabbing lights and rushing men and yipping, panicking, scurrying hens and dogs—as wrapped in a sort of timeless bubble. Unlike all the other deaths I had experienced, this passing held the eternal logic of a long life simply falling back into everything else. "Ashes to ashes, dust to dust," Mother would have said with every confidence in the divine wisdom of mortality. I held Ruby-Alice's impossibly slight and silky hand and said my farewells.

But, like a final rebellion against expectation, Ruby-Alice did not die. I didn't know this as I spent the night at her house to calm and tend to the animals after the ambulance took her away, as I sentimentally lay one final time on her sofa, wrapping myself in her pink quilts and contemplating her strange life. When I arrived at my farmhouse with the sunrise, the phone was ringing. Dr. Bernette said he had been calling for hours. He said that Ruby-Alice had sat bolt upright in the middle of the night and hadn't lain down since, that the hospital had asked him if she had kin who could speak for her since she was silent as a post.

I drove Daddy's truck to Gunnison and told the hospital clerk that Ruby-Alice was my granny. I filled out forms. I combed her hair. I spooned green Jell-O to her trembling lips. I slept at her bedside in a stiff chair. She'd roll toward me slightly when a nurse came at her with a needle or would sometimes lift her face toward mine for no reason at all, a sort of acquiescence in her wild eye and, I think, gratitude in the thin slice of the other. It was plenty thanks for me.

When Ruby-Alice slept, I escaped the hospital's sterile whiteness to stroll Gunnison's broad streets. The cafés and bars and colorful cars on Main Street felt lively and interesting at first, but it didn't take long for the bustle to overwhelm me. On the second day, I bypassed downtown to stroll the college campus instead. I had never seen such manicured lawns, green even in October, a host of yardmen raking the yellow leaves nearly as quickly as they fell from the cottonwoods. The curved concrete paths linking the tall red brick buildings thronged with students—clean-shaven boys in smart sweaters and belted trousers, girls in tight wool skirts and pressed white blouses. I had never before considered that women went to college. In Iola, girls rarely made the trip to Gunnison for high school. I certainly hadn't seen the point. The girls I passed on the campus were as curious to me as zoo animals. Little groups traipsed by in their high heels or black-and-white saddle shoes, drumming a hollow tune on the walkway. I was only thirty miles from home but felt I was in a foreign land. I had not yet decided where I would move when the government purchase was settled and I finally left Iola, but I decided right then and there it would not be Gunnison.

Outside a white stucco building, an elaborate garden with dozens of unusual plants caught my eye. I wandered through its center, especially admiring the strange and wonderful trees, each with an unpronounceable name printed on a rectangular metal card staked in the ground. The garden path ended at a glass front door, the entrance, I realized, to the college's science hall. I peered through the glass and saw a long corridor lined with numbered doors, all closed except for one labeled *Office*.

I took a deep breath and entered.

The blond woman sitting behind the desk gripped a coffee mug in one hand and filled out a form with the other. Before she even looked up to acknowledge me with polite, inquisitive eyes, she reminded me of whom my Aunt Viv might have become had she lived to middle age. The woman had style and assurance and an air of competently handling multiple demands at once. A black-and-white nameplate in a rectangular silver frame read: *Louise Landon, Secretary.*

"Tell me what you need, dear," she said, at once hurried and helpful.

"I'm Victoria Nash." I held out my hand and she dropped her pen to shake it. "I don't go to school here. But I need advice." I spoke of my family's famous peaches and the government plans to flood Iola. She said she had heard of both. She listened to me intently, knitting her brows and ignoring her cooling coffee.

When I finished explaining my dilemma, she snatched up her black phone receiver. As she dialed in quick, efficient turns, she glanced my way and declared, "What you need, Miss Nash, is a wingnut botanist."

Miss Landon walked me upstairs to Dr. Seymour Greeley's office after she briefly explained my situation to him over the phone. On the way, she pointed out his laboratory through a hall window—a jungle of vines and leaves and roots in a mess of pots, tubes, buckets, and aquariums. Miss Landon chuckled and told me not to worry.

"Trust me," she said. "He's your man."

Seymour Greeley was waiting for us at his office door. I had never met a professor, but his round black spectacles and slim frame beneath an oversized tweed jacket seemed to fit the bill. He was younger than I'd expected and his manner both more nervous and gracious. His reddish hair was mussed like he played with it too much. His smile was awkward but genuine. I liked him right away.

"Nash peaches," he said as he eagerly extended his hand.

"Victoria," I replied, extending mine. He clasped it and shook with great enthusiasm, as if meeting someone of importance.

"Seymour Greeley," he said. "Students call me Greeney, because I'm a plant man, you see. Come into my office." He placed his hand on my back to guide me. Miss Landon flashed a satisfied grin and took her leave.

His office was a muddle of books and papers and plants. He sat behind his desk and motioned for me to take the other chair. I moved a stack of papers and sat. He leaned forward on both elbows and listened to me describe my orchard's fate. When I finished my speech by imploring him for help, he ran his hands through his hair and frowned.

"I'm guessing you don't mean grafting scions and starting over?" he asked.

"No," I replied, not even knowing my plan until I had to say it aloud, "I want to save them. To move every last one."

"I see," he said thoughtfully. "Even the old ones? I fear it's hardly worth saving the old trees."

I knew he was right. My family's trees produced quality fruit for longer than most, twenty to twenty-five years, before starting to wither. Grandpa Hollis and Daddy had both kept a careful rotation scheme, always one patch of cover crop lying in wait for a newly grafted batch of saplings when an elder block had to be torn out and mulched. I knew the rotation well but hadn't wanted to admit I couldn't save them all. Our farm had just one block that would soon age out, four long rows of gnarled old trees that I loved, planted the year I was born. It would pain my heart to leave them behind.

"Okay," I replied sadly. "I agree. But that's just one block. We have a dozen more blocks that need to live."

Greeney's frown deepened. He stared off toward his bookshelf in thought.

"I can't make promises," he finally said, and he went on to explain the complexities of transplanting. Some of his terms I knew from being among trees all my life, but some, like soil pH and sunscald and root tangle, sounded like fancy science for an orchard that had long known just how to grow.

"Our roots are strong," I said.

"Oh, this I believe," he replied. "Your trees are legendary. But they are strong in their own soil. Displace them, and . . . well, I just want you to understand. We might lose the lot."

"I have to try," I said, and I meant it. I spoke calmly, but his hesitation and warnings stirred panic inside me. Sitting there in this stranger's messy office, I was suddenly certain I simply would not be

able to go on without the orchard. I could not save Wil or my family members or our farm. I could never again hold my baby. But I
could save our trees.

"Please, sir," I implored him.

He nodded, then softened his brows.

"Then I, too, shall try," he said kindly, and he smoothed his wild
hair. "It will be a challenge and an honor, Miss Nash."

"Victoria," I said again with a smile.

THE HOSPITAL RELEASED RUBY-ALICE the next morning.
Her doctor, who looked more of a cowboy right down to his buckle
and boots, told me her heart was a fickle old clock. I took this to
mean it would tick until it no longer could, and that would be that.

As I helped Ruby-Alice into the truck's passenger seat, a young
couple exited the glass hospital doors. The man had his arm around
the woman's shoulder, and she carried a newborn too loosely in her
arms. The tiny head poking from the blue flannel blanket had a
swirl of jet-black hair just like Baby Blue's. I swallowed hard and
stared, holding back the urge to snatch the baby from her and run.
When the woman glanced at me with the wide, worried eyes of a
new mother, I wanted to tell her to hold that baby tight.

The entire drive down Highway 50 along the curves of the Gunnison River back to Iola, I wasn't thinking about peach trees and
the risks of transplanting. I couldn't get that woman's eyes out of
my mind. I thought about her baby, what kind of life he would have,
whether his mother would rise to the task, and what kind of mother
I would have been, had I given us—my son and me—a chance.

Hungry animals greeted me at Ruby-Alice's gate. I left her sleep-ing in the truck while I fed them, first the five little dogs, then the guineas and chickens. I lifted one of the dogs as it finished eating to cradle its smooth body against my chest and cup its black head in my palm. I soon found myself lifting each little dog into the pickup cab. Ruby-Alice woke as the dogs swarmed her feet and jumped onto her lap, and she reached out a trembling hand to touch each one. I shooed hens into cages and lifted them and their feed sack into the truck bed. I had decided: the old woman and her brood would be coming home with me.

Inside, I found a burlap market bag in the kitchen and stepped into Ruby-Alice's bedroom to gather some clothes. The room was sparse and orderly and just as pink as the rest of the house. I pulled two green sweaters and a stocking cap from a wall hook and packed them in the bag. I felt like a prowler sliding open her dresser drawer, looking for whatever might be useful, nightgowns maybe, or under-clothes. What I found instead was a strange collection of items ar-ranged neatly in a single layer as if in a museum display: an ivory hand mirror, an embroidery hoop, a silver pocket watch, a mahog-any pipe, a fishing reel, a folded men's handkerchief embroidered with a little brown bird, a small doll in a muslin dress with a painted porcelain face, two gold wedding bands tied together with twine. Each was old and worn but polished and free of dust, all of an era that made me believe these were special relics, belongings, I as-sumed, of the family members Ruby-Alice had lost all at once to the flu. I couldn't read the story the items told—if the wedding bands were her parents' or her own, if the doll belonged to a sister or a cousin or a daughter—other than to understand that the story was about love and sadness that had proven too mighty for Ruby-Alice to bear.

I slid the drawer closed, feeling guilty for the trespass. I pulled two pink quilts from the bed and added a few figurines from the living room shelves to the bag, and then I returned to the truck. The old woman had fallen back asleep with one of the dogs on her lap. Neither of them stirred as I started up the truck and drove us home.

Once settled in Og's old room, with her things around her and her dogs curled on her bed, the old woman seemed agreeable enough to the move. She slept peacefully most hours and received food when I presented it to her lips. It felt good to have hens in the yard and someone to care for again.

Greeney and several graduate students arrived two weeks later, unloading all manner of scientific gadgets and getting straight to work. They gathered data for weeks. I mostly stayed out of their way except to answer questions and offer freshly canned peaches and, as the days grew cooler, deliver jugs of hot coffee with a shoebox full of mugs. By the time December snow began to fall, Greeney had a plan. We would find a plot of land over the West Elk Mountains in the lush and low North Fork Valley, spend the winter preparing the new soil to match our farm's rich loam, and, come spring, scoop deeply into my family's orchard and move the trees one by one. It was no more impossible than my grandfather's original dream, as Greeney liked to remind me, and he had found a university grant to pay the bill.

"Miracle peaches from the start," he'd say reassuringly. Then he'd frown, like a scientist who didn't actually believe in miracles at all.

• • •

I SETTLED IN FOR my final winter in Iola. Calm cascades of snow fell like sifting flour across the farm, silencing all creation and encouraging rest. I welcomed the quiet and eased into the gentle days. Change was coming. As I phoned a realtor to make a sight-unseen offer on acreage Greeney had found for me near the little town of Paonia, I knew I needed to gather my strength for spring.

My next task was to decide, piece by piece, which parts of my old life would travel with me. I hauled in bushel baskets from the barn and placed them in the parlor corner alongside a stack of clean white dishcloths. Each evening, after Ruby-Alice was fed and the dogs brought in for the night, I'd sit on the gold sofa surrounded by my family's things and try to pack for the move.

I often recalled the government man who had sat on the same sofa during his second visit, his thin legs crossed and his smooth hands folded delicately on one knee, and the casual way he'd informed me that everything I left behind would either be auctioned off, burned, or drowned. I had turned from his eager blue eyes to survey the parlor. My mother had lingered in each precise stitch of the muslin pillows and framed embroidery; her porcelain cross collection was displayed on the high white shelf; her favorite pale-blue vase sat atop the white doily on the oak end table. Daddy was in the shiny chestnut radio he'd brought home against Mother's wishes, Cal in the handmade checkerboard, Vivian in her favorite chair. I shook my head and assured the man that nothing would be left behind.

"Please sign here," he had said, handing me yet another document and pointing to a vacant black line across the bottom, smiling skeptically, saying, "Just in case."

I rolled my eyes at the absurdity and signed.

Yet once the bushel baskets waited, I couldn't wrap a thing. I tried. But the sofa without Mother's pillows and the end table without the blue vase felt all wrong, so I put them back. The radio hadn't worked for years. The checkerboard contained both Cal and Seth; to bring one boy with me meant to also bring the other. Vivian's chair was terribly uncomfortable. *Mother's desk, then*, I thought, but as I delicately opened the drop leaf, I found it to still be entirely her own, the contents perfectly organized. Night after night, I'd stoke the wood stove, then sit by the parlor window to watch the falling snow. I told myself it was simply too early to pack up. Surely, I'd find the wherewithal come spring.

Seventeen

1955

The February morning dawned crisp and clear. After breakfast, I helped Ruby-Alice out of bed and to the toilet, then guided her by one skeletal arm to a chair by the window. Whatever countenance she once possessed had grown unreadable, but I think it pleased her to look out at the jeweled snow and deep-blue sky. I brushed her thin hair. She reached a wobbly hand toward me, grazing silky fingertips across my wrist, acknowledging our odd little friendship as all that stood between us and lonesomeness.

Later, I fed Ruby-Alice oatmeal with honey, then resettled her into the quilts for a nap. I pulled on my snow boots and blue wool coat for a quick walk to town. I had only two stops—a few groceries at Chapman's, a new axe handle at Jernigan's, then home. Friendly chitchat certainly wouldn't slow me. Not so much as a tolerant nod had come my way in months. Folks were angry enough at my selling out, but ever since rumor had spread that I'd forced Ruby-Alice to sell out too, and had taken all her profits for myself, I was a true pariah. In reality, I'd never spoken to Ruby-Alice about the dam or the government offers, figuring her peace of mind on the day she died was all the wealth she'd need.

As I trudged down the long drive, the winter air, usually sharp as a snap, felt sun-softened and smooth in my lungs. The snow glowed bright as wonder. Starlings chattered and darted among the bare cottonwoods, a sure sign of oncoming spring. As I passed Ruby-Alice's property, I recalled the solace of that little house among the pines, where I first felt Wil's embrace, where Ruby-Alice cared for me after I emerged from the Big Blue. A twinge of wistfulness tugged at me for all I'd leave behind, for the unsuspecting landscape carrying on as it always had but doomed to be drowned. But, as I approached town, I thought of how this place also held the cruelty of ignorance, where some folks believed a lonely old woman was a devil and a beautiful tan-skinned boy was an outlaw and a skunk. That same misconceived ire was aimed at me now, and no amount of nostalgia made me want to stay. I walked down Main and up Chapman's steps dreaming of the day I'd drive away.

As I stood in the entry unbuttoning my coat, Mr. Chapman glanced at me with cool indifference over the heads of customers seated at the deli counter. I didn't care. Even when two customers swiveled on their stools and I was face-to-face with Millie and Matthew Dunlap, I felt emboldened and immune to whatever they might say.

I suppressed an eye roll as Millie sweetly sang my name, "Well, Torrrrie Naaaash."

The Dunlaps had sent me a few hands from the flophouse that autumn, as they thankfully had each harvest since Daddy passed, but ever since news had spread of my sellout, they'd stopped re-questing deliveries or frequenting the stand.

"Ma'am," I replied, then nodded at Matthew before he abruptly turned away.

"Oh, don't *ma'am* me. It's Millie, hon, just Millie." She rose from her stool and came at me like a tree falling too swiftly to outrun. "How long has it *been?*" She grabbed my shoulders, stopping short of a hug. "Look at you! I'll be darned."

Her round face was wrinkled and pale as a cabbage now, but the half-moon curve of her brown eyes still falsely implied harmlessness. I'd learned long ago not to trust those eyes or her singsongy tone of friendship. Nearly seven years had passed since that awful morning in the flophouse kitchen and her sudden revulsion at my inquiry about the boy she called a "filthy Injun," but it might as well have been yesterday to me. Her eager grin in Chapman's doorway re-minded me why, other than business basics, I had long kept my distance.

She asked if I'd gotten the harvest in properly, clearly expecting thanks for sending hands, which I gave her. Then she prattled on about weather and other nonsense while my mind sought a way to flee.

Before I could escape her, she showed too many teeth and said, "And, heavens, how nice it must be for you to see your brother again."

I looked at her as blankly as if I had received a slap.

"What?" I said. I had heard her words plainly, but they flew straight from my ears to my gut, skipping my mind.

"Seeing Seth again," she repeated. "How nice for you two." She swiped at my arm like a playful cat.

I had not heard my brother's name spoken in years. I'd assumed Seth had been erased from the communal memory, just as we in Iola never spoke of a failed crop year or a careless combine accident as guard against shame or bad fortune.

"Matty and I were so surprised to hear that Seth didn't know *a thing* about you taking the money from those government men, seeing as half that settlement would be his and all." Her moon eyes arched higher.

"Seth . . . ," I croaked, the name burning my throat, "is in California."

"Oh, heavens no." She pawed at my arm again as if flabbergasted by my stupidity. "He was for a spell . . . out near Fresno, I believe he told Matty . . . but he's been Montrose way pert near a year now. West of the town. Working sweet corn. We've seen him over there at auction, time to time, then just a few days ago after the picture show. Of course, he's not much for talk. You know Seth."

She let that comment hang on me, studying its effect.

Yes, I know Seth, I wanted to spit back in her face.

"Not sure what the poor boy was more upset about when we chatted," Millie continued, her fake sweetness turning sour. "Hearing 'bout you selling out or you taking in that crazy old Akers woman and getting her to sell out too." She paused cruelly then shrugged. "But he said he'd pay a visit, so I suppose you all worked it out."

Seth. In Iola. I was out the door and running home before Millie Dunlap, her damage done, could saunter smugly back to her stool.

I flew through the kitchen door winded and flushed. Without pausing to catch my breath or remove my boots, I ran to Ruby-Alice's room and threw open her door. I'm not sure what I expected to

find—Seth hovering over her, weapon in hand, or, worse, the bloody
aftermath of his invasion—but I found her exactly as I'd left her,
napping soundly, her shallow breath slowly easing in and out. Two
of the little dogs curled by her side glanced at me lazily, then went
back to sleep.

My hands shook as I filled a glass at the kitchen sink. I gulped
the full glass, then refilled it and drank again. Seth's roadster still
haunted the window in front of me. I would never stop picturing
the car's slither and roar on the other side of those panes the night
Seth first set out for Wil. I expected to see Seth there now, recreat-
ing his sinister salute. But he was not there. Nor was he in the
parlor or upstairs or in the barn or hiding in the dilapidated pens
where he used to tend the hogs. The smooth snow revealed no
footprints to or from the orchard. I spent the entire day looking for
him in every possible and impossible place. When I wasn't looking,
I was listening, my whole being on guard like a threatened dog. I
drew every curtain, locked every window and door. I did not sleep
that night.

Lying in bed on that moonless night, I eyed the doorknob, just
as I had so many nights as a girl. Repugnance gripped me, for Seth,
yes, but also for myself. I had spent too much of my life afraid of my
brother, afraid of things I could not name.

Then I remembered those first endless nights in the mountain
hut, so sure that something wicked lurked outside, and the nerve
that daily grew within me to face whatever would come. I remembered the terror and joy of giving birth, of creating a life and bringing it into the world, and the courage of laying my baby down and
walking away to save him. I remembered coming home and facing
Daddy and loving Daddy and competently carrying on after he was

gone. I remembered angrily yanking down those quilts I had once mistaken for Seth's face on my porch and vowing that night to not let him haunt me anymore.

I threw off the covers and rose. If Seth was coming, I'd damn well be ready.

THE NEXT MORNING DAWNED gray and solemn. The colorless sunrise found me sipping coffee in the dim kitchen, Daddy's rifle by my side. I hadn't touched the gun after he died, or for years prior, not since he'd taken me shooting a dozen times when I was thirteen, lining up Coca-Cola bottles along the back fence. I was a reluctant and imprecise shot at first. But Daddy was as insistent as I was obedient, so we kept at it. Eventually, I hit all six bottles in succession, then asked if I could be done. I hated the weight of the gun in my arms, the deafening boom, the kickback against my small shoulder, the acrid smell. I even hated hitting my mark, all that flying glass mimicking how the bullet destroyed a life. The gun now sat propped against my kitchen chair, but I had no intention of firing it. If Seth did show up, I wanted the gun in my hands. I needed him to see straight away I was no longer the girl he remembered.

I went about feeding the chickens and dogs and hauling firewood and cooking Ruby-Alice's morning oats, determined to be unafraid, the gun never far from my side. The longing to leave the farm grew by the minute, and I finally began packing, pouring my nervous energy into filling four full bushel baskets before noon and returning to the task after lunch. Suddenly, the move could not come soon enough.

I hauled a picking ladder from the barn into the parlor to reach the porcelain cross collection Mother kept on the high white shelf. The old ladder creaked and wiggled beneath me, but I lingered on a high rung, admiring the display, recalling the Christmas mornings when Mother would unwrap the new cross Daddy had bought for her, how she always acted surprised and pleased. Each was about the size of my hand and glossy white, ornamented with lapis-blue painted flowers or ribbons or birds in flight. Daddy special ordered the crosses from a Sears Roebuck catalog at Jernigan's, every December without fail, and I felt the tenderness in that tradition as I polished and wrapped each one. Among them was a broken cross, I knew, so I searched it out to lift it with extra care. Rubbing my fingertip across the jagged seams where Daddy had glued it back together, I relived that awful Christmas morning when Seth, furious at some perceived tease or taunt, reached for the closest thing to hurl at Cal. Mother's gift hit the parlor wall, then fell in pieces. Silence crushed the room as we awaited Mother's reaction. She merely set her jaw and stared down at her clasped hands. Seth's tantrums usually incensed her, but this time I could tell she was just plain sad. Daddy ousted all three of us from the parlor, and I spent the rest of that Christmas morning crying in Abel's stall.

Holding the glued cross, still feeling the melancholy of that long-ago day, I noticed a handmade wooden cross lying prone on the shelf behind the others. It was fashioned from two willow sticks joined at the center with a red Christmas ribbon. Long forgotten, I recognized it instantly. Seth had made it for Mother. He had placed it in a little box, tied it with a messy bow, and sheepishly presented it to her once we were allowed back inside for the brown-sugar-ham

Christmas dinner. Mother had received it politely yet somberly, then set it aside and got on with the meal. Seth didn't look up at her or any of us until we started passing the plates. Despite the bounty of treats Mother and Viv prepared only for the holiday, Seth barely ate a thing.

I stepped down from the ladder, the cracked porcelain cross in one fist, the handmade cross in the other. The pair held truths about my brother, about his impetuousness and rage, but also about some part of him that understood right and how to do it, some part of him that wanted more love than he had any understanding of how to invite. His fierceness and the resulting sorrows so crowded my memories that I barely recalled the boy who might carefully construct a willow cross as an offering of apology. Mother had saved both crosses. I felt like that should mean something to me. I held them in my palms and stared at them for a long moment before carrying them to the kitchen and dropping both into the garbage pail.

A FEW DAYS LATER, I was drying and shelving lunch dishes when I heard heavy footsteps on the front porch followed by three solid knocks. It was him, and I knew it. My nerves rattled, sending me scurrying about the kitchen nonsensically. In my many imagined versions of Seth showing up at the farm, a civil knock on the front door certainly wasn't one of them.

I took a deep breath and grabbed Daddy's gun. Walking down the hallway and through the parlor, I thought of all the ways Seth might still force his way in. I had, of course, moved the key from the porch beam where it had hung on a nail for decades, but perhaps he had his own key, or he would break a window or power through the door shoulder first. But as I moved closer, he simply knocked again, louder, sending the dogs closed in Ruby-Alice's room into a barking fit.

I gathered the courage to peer through the parlor window, and there, peering back at me, nearly nose to nose, was my brother. I leaped backward, my heart tumbling inside my chest.

"Open the goddamn door, Torie," Seth demanded through the window.

My brief glimpse of him told me little other than he was thinner now and wore a dark, shaggy beard that made him look more like a grown man than I had anticipated.

"Come on," he urged, his voice deep and coaxing. "I ain't gonna hurt you."

I paused to untangle my emotions and realized I wasn't afraid for myself. Whatever mischief Seth brought with him, if it was against me, I could handle him. If it was against Ruby-Alice, I wasn't so sure. When her dogs quieted, I approached the window again and, through the glass, I ordered him to sit himself down in the porch chair. He chuckled at my demand but did as I said.

I wrapped myself in a sweater. Then I clasped the gun and hurriedly exited, pressing the knob lock and slamming the door tightly behind me, eying him while I rushed to the far side of the porch.

Seth laughed hoarsely, then said, "I thought you hated that old rifle."

"I do," I replied, satisfied that it was the first thing he'd noticed, hoping it said all I wanted it to say about me.

There was a long silence as we studied each other. In a strange way, he was Seth but also not Seth. He smelled the same, like cigarettes and whiskey, but the stocky, dark-blond sixteen-year-old who had fled Iola had morphed into a brown-haired, brown-bearded man of twenty-two, his face chiseled with new angles and curves. He had deep frown lines between his thick brows and a long white scar puckering the skin of one cheek. His gray eyes felt familiar, still nervous and quick, but somehow softer, less aggrieved than those of the boy I knew. He was wide shouldered but skinny beneath his tan canvas jacket. His grubby hands were thick and gnarled like Daddy's and trembled a bit as he repeatedly rubbed them across the dirty thighs of his jeans. Something about his posture said he'd seen a lot of trouble these past six years, all of which I was certain he had brought on himself.

I couldn't guess what he was thinking about the changes he saw in me, but, beyond my new comfort with giving orders and holding a gun, I didn't much care.

"I run into the Dunlaps in Montrose and—" he began.

"I know. Millie told me all about that," I interrupted.

"Did she? I gathered you two weren't friendly no more," he said.

I shrugged. "She said you'd be coming here, for the money," I said.

"So, you're not surprised to see me," he chuckled nervously.

"Only surprised it took you so long to show up." I meant to insult his greed, but he replied as if we were having a conversation.

"Yeah, I reckon I couldn't decide what to do," he said. "I always told myself I'd never come back here."

I considered how he'd break that promise for a payout but not to attend Daddy's funeral. He knew that's what I was thinking, and he shrugged against my unspoken judgment.

"Maybe I came back for more than just money," he finally said.

"Like what?" I prompted.

"Maybe I've been needing to tell you things." He squinted up at me, looking a lot like the boy who'd presented that handmade cross to Mother after ruining our Christmas.

I wondered at the differences in how my brother and I bore our burdens. We weren't old enough to know how to reckon with loss when loss found us anyway. We had gone forward—without Mother, without Cal and Aunt Viv, with only a declining father and a malicious, ruined uncle left in their place—by being more solemn versions of who we had always been: I, the obedient girl; Seth, the angry boy. Neither of us knew another way. But loving Wil had peeled back my armor of timidity, and Baby Blue had taught me my strength. I doubted Seth had been so lucky. I braced myself for what he would say.

"I've been needin' to tell you," he continued, swallowing hard, "that I wasn't the one that killed that Injun boy."

I steadied my breath. I wanted to tell him Wil was no boy and no "Injun" but a man with a name and a loveliness beyond his grasp. But there was no point. Instead, I bit back, "Well, you would say that, wouldn't you? Coming here, hoping to get money from me. You'd say anything."

"No, Torie, really." Seth shook his head wildly. "It was that Forrest Davis fella. He was the one . . . who tied . . . who did that to the kid. I was there, and I shouldn'ta been, but I didn't do it."

I couldn't reply other than to visibly tighten my grip on the gun. Violence was as alien to me as Mars, but in that moment, I comprehended revenge, the explosion of it, the desperate bid to obliterate pain by inflicting as much as possible on someone else. I remembered that awful night when Seth had come home, drunk and triumphant, surely with blood on his hands, when all I could do was crawl away.

"If you were there," I said when I again found my voice, "why in the hell didn't you stop it?" I was trembling now, realizing I had always suspected the murderer to be Forrest Davis, but I also knew all along that Seth had been too weak, too misguided and blindly bigoted, to do anything but watch Wil die. "Why?" I repeated, wanting to scream it but steadying myself, fighting back tears. "Why didn't you help him?"

Seth stared at the worn floorboards for a long minute, then said, "I was a damn fool back then. An angry, stupid-ass fool."

His rough palms scraping the thighs of his jeans became the only sound between us. Then he reached into his jacket pocket for a pack of Lucky Strikes, dumped one into his palm, raised it to his lips, and lit it. Tobacco crackled the silence with each long inhale.

Clouds crept like a dozen gray snakes overtaking the previously sunny sky and casting long shadows across the snow. The smoke-soured air chilled.

"One thing I wasn't too thickheaded to understand," he said, shaking his cigarette at me. "I wasn't too stupid to know why you run off."

I bit my lip and waited for him to say he knew about the baby, that Daddy and Og and Lyle and the whole town knew about the baby.

"You were afraid we'd come after you too," he said glumly, taking another deep drag, flicking the ashes to the porch. "But I never woulda hurt you, Torie. Me and you . . . we . . . ." He stopped, looking back to the floor. "I didn't like it one bit when I snuck after you and saw you kissing that Injun. I'll admit that. Not one bit. But I didn't blame you. You didn't know nothin' about his kind, their spells and trickery and whatnot."

That Injun, I thought with disgust. *His kind. Spells and trickery.*

I remembered Cal's explanation of Seth's fury when we barred him from our tree house. *He's just jealous is all*, Cal had said. *Of you and me.*

"When Lyle started breathing down our necks and Davis reckoned we'd better skip town, I looked for you," Seth said. "I drove all the hell over the damn place. I wanted you to know, with Davis gone, with that Injun gone, it'd be safe for you to come home. Say you believe me."

I didn't. Or maybe I did. None of it mattered anymore.

"What do you want, Seth?" I said, deadpan, needing the encounter to end. "Why are you here?"

"I don't know," he said, throwing the cigarette to the floorboards and crushing it with his boot. "To get me that money. But now that I'm here, I . . . ." He paused, thinking. "Is that crazy Akers woman in there?" he asked, pointing at the front door.

"Nope," I said. "She died. A long time ago."

He scoffed, "That ain't what I heard."

I shrugged and asked again, "What do you want, Seth?"

"Well, I'm just startin' to wonder. Who's gonna live here after you're gone? Who's gonna work the land?"

Fish, I wanted to say. *And lake weed and rot.*

"Folks say the reservoir ain't really gonna happen," he said. "They say building that dam ain't possible. That anyone who sells out is a fool."

He might have been right or wrong about that, but I didn't care. I had a plan and an exit.

He went on, "If you don't want this place, maybe I do. I'm dog-tired of driftin' without no home. And no one else can tend to this here orchard the way I can."

"Fine," I said, pouncing on what I hoped was an opportunity. "Turn Davis in to Lyle, testify to what you saw that night, and it's yours."

"Two problems to that," he replied. "One, ain't nobody gonna care enough about some dead Injun kid from years back to put together a jury."

He paused to read my eyes, which told him, sorrowfully, that I knew this was true.

"And two," he continued, "it wouldn't matter nohow. Davis got himself killed in a fight, when we was out there in Fresno." He pointed to the white slice across his cheek. "The cuss damn near took me out with him." He paused again, then added, "That's all the justice there's gonna be."

My eyes stung. I needed him gone.

"I'll be out by summer," I said. "Stay the hell away from me, and I don't give a damn what else you do. Come near me again, and I'll pour gasoline over every inch of this place and burn it to the ground."

He snorted mockingly, "Not the orchard."

"I'll start with the orchard," I lied, staring him down.

His aggrieved eyes told me that at least one thing in this brutal world—the peaches—actually mattered to his ragged heart.

"Don't doubt me, Seth," I said, moving closer. "Stay away from here until after I'm long gone. Then take this land if it will have you. And if Lyle discovers you or the government men come for this place, that's nothing to do with me. You'll be trespassing, and that's your own hell to pay."

He looked puzzled at my compliance. But I had not given him anything I hadn't already promised to the flood. What happened to the farm once the trees were saved and I started my new life meant nothing to me. Seth, I told myself, meant nothing to me. If he did come back, the orchard would be gone, the farmhouse would be empty, but the ghosts of his regrets would linger. My revenge, and the only justice Wil would ever receive, would lie in Seth's haunting and the day the Gunnison River would rise to erase it all.

I lifted the gun, aiming the barrel directly at his chest.

"Now get the hell off my porch," I said.

Seth rose, looking at me with a face so worn and troubled he appeared eighty years old instead of twenty-two. He looked so sad that, just for an instant, I was again the little girl who loved her brother and wanted to untangle that love from fear and confusion, wanted to save him from himself and balance out all the bad in him, all the bad in the whole world, by being good. I wanted to tell him there had been more inside me than I'd ever thought possible, and, maybe, there was more inside him too.

Still, I held the rifle steady as Seth slowly descended the porch steps, walked down the long drive, and disappeared beyond the cottonwood trees. I didn't lower the barrel, didn't even draw a decent breath, until I heard a distant engine roar to life and a car driving away.

ALMOST AS IF SETH took winter with him, the melting began in earnest the next day. Over the next two weeks, the earth emerged in gradual, scattered patches and then all at once, as snow turned to mud turned to greening. While Greeney and his students finalized the soil preparation on the new land over the Elk Mountains, I pruned the leafless orchard limb by limb, except for the old trees I would have to leave behind. I reassured myself aloud that the up-coming transplant would work, that my trees and I would blossom together in Paonia come May. Even as I spoke, my stomach knotted around the possibility of failure. Sitting on the muddy ground with my back against the wide, twisted trunk of the old tree that I would miss the most, I clasped my hands for prayer. As my words rose skyward, I realized I spoke not to God but to Daddy, the one who knew and loved the orchard most of all. I asked for blessings and help, for miracle peaches and good weather, and I asked, if it all went terribly wrong, for his forgiveness and understanding that at least I had tried.

On the first of March, I stood beside Greeney and four of his students, burlap sheets by our sides. I nervously watched as two of the young men carefully dug around the first tree, loosening the soil until the roots began to pop free. As they lifted the tree from the earth, I fell to my knees and Greeney did the same, admiring the thick, tangled roots and clasping as much soil as possible against them. The two other students scurried to wrap the great root ball in the burlap. Together we eased the bundle into a wheel-barrow, then rolled the tree to the waiting flatbed trailer. I didn't take a proper breath until Greeney gave a thumbs-up and flashed me a hopeful grin. I smiled back, but, inside, I felt as though I might be sick.

Day after day, we continued, one tree at a time, until a flatbed was filled and hauled away and a new one took its place. The giant holes left behind in the orchard were like open wounds. I worried that the land felt the pain of extraction, a bloodless, quiet suffering of ripped soil and displaced rock and root, just as it would feel the final gasp for breath when the floodwaters rose. But if these mountains had taught me anything, it's that the land endures, riding out human folly when it must, reclaiming itself when it is able, and moving on. Still, some evenings I sat in cool blue twilight in the ransacked orchard and apologized for what I had done.

Ruby-Alice slept most days and seemed unconcerned with the plans and changes, but with the loading of that first flatbed, she began turning her head against food and drink. Iola was her home, and I could only guess she was refusing to be hauled away like the trees. Days passed with no nourishment or movement. When I sensed her time was near, I carried her tiny frame to Daddy's truck, shooed in her little dogs, and returned her to her house among the pines. Within hours of my placing her on the sofa where she liked to sleep and covering her with a quilt, her breath grew short and shallow with long gaps in between. She passed on as peacefully as anyone could ever wish, her blue hands folded on her chest, four sleeping dogs by her side and one curled on her shoulder. I kissed her forehead and felt glad for her life—so odd and singular, so strangely overlapped with my own—and glad for her death, the only one I had ever known to be correct.

"Go as a river," I whispered to her, as Wil might have done, and, I swear, I felt her spirit rise.

I EXPECTED RUBY-ALICE'S BURIAL at the Iola cemetery would be as our lives had lately been, just the two of us and the Big Blue wilderness hovering above. It seemed fitting to place her deep in that ground, where white daisies blossomed all summer and her lost family and mine and generations of townsfolk rested beneath humble markers. If the reservoir came, their remains would drown with the land or, as the government man had promised, be resettled high on a hill above it all, a monument to what and who had been. I boxed up the carefully arranged old items I had discovered in Ruby-Alice's dresser drawer and gave them to Reverend Whitt to place in her casket before it was sealed. He asked if he could say a few words the morning of the burial, and I agreed.

Twittering sparrows and perfect golden sunshine accompanied me on the walk to the cemetery. I would bow my head at the grave-side while the old man said a prayer, then I'd say my farewells. A new life was unfolding before me. I never stopped questioning the choices of my past, but in the known world, each step surely unfurls the next, and we must walk into that open space, mapless and with-out invitation. Wil and the Gunnison River and the layers of life and death in the forests of the Big Blue continued to teach me this. Right or wrong, my next step lay before me, and I tried my best to trust it. This funeral would unknot my final tie to Iola, and soon I'd be on my way.

As I neared the tidy cemetery, my eyes at first disbelieved the sight of the gathering crowd. But it was true: two dozen townsfolk were entering through the white wrought iron gate, dressed in proper black, some holding bundled sage tied with ribbon in lieu of flowers not yet bloomed. Tradition reigned over all else as I took my place among them. The reverend recited psalms. The white peaks sparkled. We all joined hands and sang together, as we always had, our community funeral song, "In the Sweet By-and-By." I looked around at the solemn, weathered faces—at the Mitchell family and Reverend Whitt's three sons and Dr. and Mrs. Bernette and Mr. Jernigan, some old classmates I barely recognized by then, the ranchers Daddy had worked for, and the other regular folks from around town, minus, unsurprisingly, the Dunlaps and the Martindells. There was not a bad apple among them. These were the decent, hardworking people I had lived among all my life, who showed up for funerals and fiercely protected their own, however blindly. I couldn't imagine where they'd go and who they would be and what they would defend after the flood changed everything, how they'd piece their hearts and lives back together and go on.

I thanked each person for coming as they exited the gate. Many shook my hand, letting bygones be bygones, at least for the moment. I wondered who among them might have attended Wil's funeral had they been given the chance. Not all, I decided, but, yes, undoubtedly most, which sent fat tears for all I had lost and misunderstood streaming down my cheeks.

Reverend Whitt and his sons completed the burial, loaded their equipment into their black truck, and drove away. I stood for a while at the fresh mound among the eight small headstones on the Akers family plot, feeling for Ruby-Alice a certain relief that she finally lay among them.

My family was buried on the grassy rise above. I strolled through our plot and touched the arched wooden markers, saying the names aloud. When folks had gathered there to hold hands and sing for each of them, I had assumed that, when death someday came for me, my own funeral would look just the same. How strange, I thought as I said a final goodbye and walked back down the hill, that I couldn't picture what my life would look like now, let alone my death.

• • •

By mid-month, Greeney and I had overseen the removal and transport of every precious tree. It was with those final trees that I, too, left Iola.

The caged hens waited on the gold sofa alongside the packed bushel baskets of home goods and crates of canned peaches and Daddy's orchard tools and whatever else the student helpers could fit into the bed of the old truck. Greeney and the students then loaded into their own vehicles to drive ahead of me to the new orchard. I returned to the side door to walk through the house one final time but stopped myself. I had already perused its silent rooms and made peace with the memories and the items I would leave behind. Instead, I loaded the final basket into the passenger seat. It was flagged with a blue ribbon to mark its contents as special: Mother's porcelain crosses, framed embroidery, and her Bible; Daddy's flannel shirts; two of Ruby-Alice's quilts and my favorite of her figurines. I called the little dogs from the house and the yard and settled them in the back seat. Then I closed the kitchen door with a tug.

I started down the long driveway, trying not to look back. But I couldn't do it. I parked the truck and got out to take one long, final look at the place that made me. Then I returned to the truck and kept on driving. I would leave my past behind and try to build my life again, hoping not for miracles but simply for strength in new soil. I figured that if my trees could survive, uprooted and against the odds, then, damn all bad fortune, so too could I.

PART III

1955–1970

Eighteen

1955

Driving down Grand Avenue for the first time, I thought Paonia too fancy for me.

I peered over the steering wheel at the proper sidewalks and curbs, the colorful Paradise Theater with a framed picture show placard, and a tall building with *Hays Variety* painted in red cursive across yellow bricks. The café had a green awning and clean glass doors and a chalkboard notice for a trout-and-waffle special. A few folks glanced at me curiously as I drove by, and I could barely stand the embarrassment of my intrusion, the truck's grumbly engine disrupting their quiet spring afternoon.

But after I turned off Grand onto Second Street and crossed the railroad tracks toward Minnesota Creek, orchards and pastures and open land unfurled before me. A distant pine forest climbed to a swayback ridge linking two snowcapped peaks, one jagged and forbidding, the other smooth and gentle like a whale's back. I grabbed

Greeney's scribbled note from the dashboard and followed his remaining directions: a left at a red barn, a right across a drainage-ditch bridge onto a nameless dirt road, another left.

My new farm greeted me then, expectant and strange, like a distant relative I had never met. The cornflower-blue farmhouse needed painting and a new metal roof, but it was square and charming, with a broad front porch and a row of white mullioned windows across the second floor. The grassy yard was small, yellowed with dandelions and shaded by greening cottonwoods. Budding lilacs and other shrubs I couldn't yet name lined a rusty wrought iron fence. I followed the gravel drive around to the long side yard, past a brick patio bordered by a raised kitchen garden and weedy flower beds, to an old garage, its wide door opened to the blank interior. I paused there a moment, feeling like a trespasser, but the gravel drive continued on, so I did too—past two weeping willows and a sagging shed skirted with the dormant sticks of a raspberry patch, past a large barn gone gray with years but still straight and sturdy. My heart raced as the orchard came into view.

There were the trees. My trees. A few still lay unplanted, tipping at odd angles in their burlap root sacks beside their awaiting holes, but most stood tall in long, straight rows, every trunk staked and mulched, every bare branch reaching for a new piece of sky. It would be foolish to say the trees welcomed me, though I would have gladly accepted some reassurance that the move agreed with them and I hadn't made a terrible mistake. Instead, all I could glean from them and their replacement soil was that a new journey had begun. I had no idea what would happen now. I was wise enough to know only one thing: the land would decide my fate.

Greeney and several students heard the truck approaching and ran into the orchard road with raised arms, waving and cheering and laughing like victorious children. I honked wildly in response and felt more hopeful than I had in a very long time. Not far away, a long, deep whistle blew, and, for the first time in years, I smiled at the familiar rattle and hum of a passing train.

I WALKED THE ORCHARD that day and touched every single tree, counting, blessing, and encouraging them aloud, as I did twice per day for weeks thereafter. I pruned and watered and fertilized in accordance with Daddy's inherited expertise, my own instincts, and Greeney's recommendations, slowly coaxing up subtle signs of life.

In the evenings, I went about the strange business of setting up housekeeping in what felt like someone else's home. The old house smelled like only old houses do, like stories, like decades of buttery skillet breakfasts and black coffee and dripping faucets, like family and life and aging wood. The Paonia farmhouse in some ways resembled my own in Iola, but it was not my family's stories and habits and history scenting its walls. With no idea what ghosts I moved among, I struggled to settle. I positioned the gold sofa for the best mountain view from the sitting room window and slept there each night. I carefully arranged Mother's crosses on the mantel. I placed my white dishes in the kitchen cupboards and lined the pantry with a dozen mason jars of last season's peaches. The previous owners had left behind a long pine dining table, perhaps proving too cumbersome to move. Upstairs, two full beds with oak headboards and matching bureaus seemed to be waiting for me to properly settle in and accept the true owner's hospitality.

In those first weeks, when not in the orchard, I wasn't quite sure where I should be. Planting the kitchen garden with the seeds I brought from home helped, as did walking Ruby-Alice's dogs along the country roads and ditch trails. Greeney or one of his students stopped by to gather data every Thursday, and I'd invite them in for lunch and an update on our progress, still slow and uncertain. When neighbors stopped by with welcoming casseroles or freshly baked pies or jam from their grandmother's recipes, I received their offerings kindly and exchanged phone numbers. Their chitchat was friendly enough but didn't veil that, to most of them, a young woman living alone and running an orchard seemed both odd and doomed to fail. Most had heard of Nash peaches, but my trees and I were in real Colorado peach country now, they said, alongside the best cherries, pears, and apples in the state. Some folks implied and some outright stated that if my trees lived, which was yet to be seen, I shouldn't expect to be special. I nodded and shook hands and told them that suited me just fine, though I suspected the first time they opened a sweet Nash peach to pull its ruby center clean off the pit and take their first bite, they might reconsider. I prayed they'd have the chance.

One dim morning in late April, I sat on the sofa sipping coffee and looking out at the rain. The world was fleecy and silent. Lead-colored clouds layered the valley floor. I had by then memorized the new view from my window—the distant pine forest's rise to steep rock, the rock's sharp rise to serrated cliff band on Mount Lamborn, and the smooth, timbered slope up neighboring Mount Landsend—but that morning, little was visible behind the gray flannel. Only the tips of the two peaks stuck above the clouds, one jagged point and one smooth, both stabbing skyward, catching the first hint of violet sunrise. The world seemed upside down in that moment—the inversion of land above cloud, cloud below land— the whole of it beautiful and disconcerting all at once.

When the rain eventually stopped, I pulled on my muck boots and headed to the orchard. The sodden soil smelled rich and sweet but different from home. Birds were still and quiet. A distant train whistle blew. Thick clouds hovered all around, slowly rising to erase the mountaintops and any hope of sun. The mood was fitting for that morning's grim task. My trees had finally sprouted shiny green leaves and, among them, pea-sized buds, the miraculous promise of life and flower and fruit tightly bound in each. But that day, I went from branch to branch with clippers and killed every last one. Each snip upended all I had ever known about the sacredness of a peach bud, about caring for it like a jewel until it unfurled into a delicate pink blossom. Greeney's research had convinced him there could be no fruit the first year after transplanting, maybe even two. Clipping the buds turned the tree's energy back down into its roots, he said. Sacrificing these buds meant stronger growth later on. I had to believe him. But with every clip, with every precious bud dropping to the ground in waste, my gut ached and I wondered what Daddy would say. When the rain started up again, light and misty at first, then fierce and hard like falling pebbles, I just kept clipping, my tears mixing with the rain on my cheeks. I turned my face to the sky, eyes closed, arms out in a kind of surrender, and let the shower soak me clean through.

That night, I again slept on the sofa beneath Ruby-Alice's quilts. Two of her little dogs lay at my feet and two more curled on the floor next to me in a white slice of moonlight. The oldest dog had been missing for days, lost or snatched by a coyote or just gone off to die as old dogs will. I wondered how Ruby-Alice would feel about that and tried to feel the same, as silently stoic about missing creatures as she was about most everything else. I thought then of that speckled puppy Wil had saved with his charmed hands and wondered what had become of it and why I hadn't noticed, and suddenly, absurdly, sorrow for that puppy I hadn't thought of in years consumed me. I clutched the quilts to my chest and cried as the slow moonlight inched from the floor all the way across my body. When it reached my face, I closed my eyes to the light and quieted, knowing my tears were not really for the puppy.

I dreamed that night of walking a long, wide road holding a swaddled infant. My left arm cradled the baby under his padded bottom, my right arm wrapped his back, and my hand palmed his silky head to my shoulder. His breath tickled my neck like a tiny feather. I knew I must get the child somewhere, that his life depended on this arrival, but even as I hurried toward the destination, I did not know where to go. I kept on, frantically rushing the baby to somewhere that was nowhere. Suddenly, my feet began losing traction. I peered over the bundle to examine my next careful step and realized I was walking on nothing. The ground beneath my feet, the earth that should have been so solid and sure, had turned cavernous, utterly devoid of light and substance. My heart pounded. I had to keep walking. I stepped gingerly forward, as if on ice I feared could not bear my weight but must, tightening my hug around the baby, who trusted me not to fall. And then, I slipped, and we tumbled together into bottomless darkness. Spinning and sinking, I clung to him with all my might. But the force pulling him was too strong. Just as he ripped away from my arms, I jolted awake.

I leapt from the sofa, sweaty and trembling, and paced nervous circles. I had dreamed of Baby Blue before, of course, dozens of times in the years since his birth, but rarely with such terror. The nowhere of the dream disturbed me as much as the letting go.

I pulled my jacket over my nightgown. As I stepped into the yard, the night creatures quieted. The cool air was fragrant with wet earth. A bright half-moon inched toward the western hills. I stood awhile looking out at the shadowed landscape. When I first met Wil, I couldn't understand why he proclaimed that one place was the same as another. I didn't believe he thought that even as he said it, and I didn't believe it still. But I understood now what he might have meant, that when no place will receive you, everywhere becomes a kind of nowhere, all ground as uncertain as in my frightening dream.

As the moon's tip disappeared beyond the horizon and the sky grew black and sprayed with stars, I knelt in the damp grass and asked the land for its blessing. I wanted to make a home here, for me and for my trees. In exchange, I vowed I would love and care for this piece of earth until the end of my days. Waiting to hear some sort of answer, I quickly added to my request what I wanted most of all but had never allowed myself to admit: that if, by some miracle or fate, my child came back to me, this land and I could nurture him together, teach him that one place is not the same as any other, that this small patch of the vast and unknowable world was where we were held as kindred.

All the night sounds that had hushed when I first stepped into the darkness started up again just then—the cricket song and pulsing katydids, the spring peepers wailing from the wet reeds, the hollow call of an owl in the distance—and, as I stood, I took this chorus as an agreement to my offer, or at least, I believed, it was a maybe.

A LOUD KNOCK AND barking dogs jolted me from a deep sleep. It took me a groggy moment to rise from the sofa and locate the front door. I hadn't hung any mirrors yet, but I was sure I looked a mess after the fitful night. I wiped my puffy eyes and anchored my hair with a clip before approaching the door, then, realizing I still wore my nightgown with two dried grass stains at the knees, I turned back to hastily pull on the trousers and sweater I'd left on the floor the previous evening. When I opened the door, the bright morning sun hit me like a firecracker. I winced and squinted at the tall dark shadow on the porch.

"Miss Nash?" said a baritone I recognized as the realtor whom I'd often spoken with over the phone and signed papers with by mail but had never met.

"Yes," I rasped.

"Ed Cooper," he said, stepping closer and extending a hand. "Your realtor? I'm terribly sorry. Did I wake you?"

To the best of my knowledge, no one in farm country slept past 6:00 a.m., and there it was, by the looks of the sun, well past 9:00. I started to make excuses for myself and my disheveled appearance, but his pale blue eyes were gracious and unconcerned, so I decided to just invite him in for coffee.

"You don't care for the beds Mrs. Harding left behind?" he asked, passing the sofa strewn with quilts and pillows and my dirty nightgown.

"Not yet," I replied.

He chuckled as if he wasn't sure what that meant but liked it anyway.

I put the kettle on to boil and apologized for my lack of chairs. He shrugged and leaned one shoulder against the kitchen wall and asked how I was getting along. He wore a white collared shirt, black pants, and black pointed shoes that had lost their shine. His mostly gray hair mismatched his youthful face and manner. His wristwatch and wedding ring were the same shiny gold as the two ink pens tucked in his breast pocket.

"I'm getting along well enough," I replied unconvincingly.

"Well, you know, it takes a while to settle in somewhere new," he reassured. "What questions are on your mind?"

"Yes, I do have a few," I said, spooning instant coffee into two white mugs. "I've been wondering about the folks who sold this place. Why did they leave?"

"Aw, that's a sad story, really," he said, shaking his head. "Kind folks. They ran variety apples. Some sweet corn. But then, you know, hard knocks. Their boy was killed in the war, and then their daughter ran off with a Mexican hand, and you remember the drought of '49? Mr. Harding had turned to drink by then. They lost most everything that year; the trees just shriveled up to nothing." Ed said that Mr. Harding had tried working coal up valley in Somerset after that. It was a heart attack in one of the deep shafts that killed him. Mrs. Harding had waitressed in the diner and minded the counter at Hays for a time but couldn't pay the bills.

"Lila is her name," Ed said. "Nicest woman you ever did meet."

I poured the boiling water into the mugs, stirred, and handed one to him. He accepted it with a nod.

"And what about the land?" I asked.

"Oh, it turned to weeds and waste. Can you imagine? In these parts? Might have been saved, had they showed it some care or asked for help. That scientist friend of yours, the professor? Darnedest thing. He called me the same day Lila Harding walked into my office all welled up with tears saying she needed to sell off."

We both paused on that for a moment and sipped our coffees.

"It's real fine what you and the professor have done here," he said, gesturing toward the window.

I smiled politely and replied, "I'll give it my best. If the land will have me."

"Well, the Hardings weren't the first to be taken out by sorrow and the whims of weather. I wish you and your peaches better fortune."

"Cheers to that," I said.

We clinked mugs, and I wondered on what day, what hour, the Hardings' good fortune had taken a turn and if mine, after so much struggle and loss, had now turned the opposite way. I pictured myself falling to my knees in the wet grass in the middle of the night, asking for a chance.

Ed went on with details about the town and its surroundings, some of which were of no interest, like gossip about my neighbors or where to find the best burger or eligible bachelors downtown. But other information proved valuable—where the rail lines came from and where they went; where to find the best produce stands and the farmers market on Tuesdays; which plumber would update my irrigation lines and which mechanic could fix the old tractor rusting behind the barn and who I should call if my drainage ditch clogged with spring runoff or ran dry in the fall.

"The river here, that feeds my ditch," I said, realizing it was the first time I'd claimed anything here as mine. "It's called the North Fork?"

He nodded.

"The north fork of what, exactly?" I asked.

"Well, the north fork of the Gunnison, of course," he said.

"The Gunnison?" I couldn't believe my ears.

"Sure. Just after the Gunnison runs through Black Canyon, the North Fork feeds in at Roger's Mesa." He brought two flat hands into a V to illustrate the confluence, then pointed south. "About fifteen miles down valley." Then he chuckled, "Well, those same Gunnison waters first come right through Iola. So you know them well."

"Yes, I do," I said.

He meant this as comfort, and I accepted it as such, but my sentiments about the Gunnison had become as turbulent as the river itself. I pictured its route, from its up-valley headwaters in Almont where Daddy and Seth used to drive the cattle down; through the town of Gunnison, through Iola and my homeland; past the union with Big Blue Creek, where my tears for my baby still flowed; then carving through the Black Canyon, my Wil's tragic grave. That length of the great river told my story. I felt equal parts love and anguish for its winding path, and awe that it had followed me here.

Ed finished his coffee and set his mug on the kitchen counter. As I led him to the front door and he stepped into the sunshine, he told me not to be a stranger, that Zelda was his wife's name and he'd love for me to meet her.

"And there's a moving sale at the Walker place this Saturday, right down on Dry Gulch Road," he said, pointing from the porch.

"Get yourself some furniture and stay awhile, Miss Nash." He gave a friendly wink then added, "Don't worry. The Walkers are not another sad story. They came from the city and want to go back. Go figure."

"Go figure," I echoed with a smile.

Folding the pink quilts on the sofa, I thought about what Ed had said of the complicated lives that previously inhabited this old house. I thought about the Harding son who'd left the farm's peace for the hell of war, and the daughter, who fled with what I could only assume was a forbidden love. I'm sure the boy was remembered as a hero and the daughter as a rogue, but the same wild boldness to walk out this front door had driven them both to elsewhere. I thought of Mr. Harding drinking away the pain, and of Lila Harding, whose heart broke a little more each day. And I thought of my own restlessness since my arrival and how much I resembled Ruby-Alice sleeping night after night on the sofa.

A decision suddenly crystallized before me. I lifted the folded quilts, marched up the stairs, and placed them on a shelf in the hall closet. I then bathed, pulled on a decent dress, and got in the old truck to drive to Hays Variety and buy myself brand-new bedding for the first time in my life.

When I returned, I chose the upstairs bedroom with windows facing the orchard. I made the wide bed with the crisp new sheets, a sky-blue cotton blanket, and a matching chenille spread I had spent half an hour choosing. I pulled white cases onto the four fat pillows I'd purchased as a final extravagance and propped them against the oak headboard. I stood back and admired my new room. Wil had liked to tease me that my name was fit for a queen. I smiled and told him to look, that now I had a bedroom to match. Sitting on the mattress edge, I stared out the window. My greening trees stood in tight, perfect rows. Beyond them, I could see all the way to the barbed-wire fence and silver metal gate bordering the back of my land and, beyond that, a neighbor's emerging hayfield and the distant North Fork River, glimmering and swollen with melted mountain snow.

I bought furniture from the sale Ed Cooper recommended and arranged it to my liking. I selected fabric striped with little yellow sunflowers at Hays and sewed kitchen and bedroom curtains. I clipped every last bud from my trees and watered and nourished them and bolstered my faith in the process.

And in the midst of my slow settling, I began weekly driving down valley along the edge of the North Fork River to the confluence with the Gunnison at Roger's Mesa. I'd walk the trail through the sage and wildflowers and willows, then remove my shoes and roll my trousers and wade into cold, rushing waters to stand in the exact place where the two rivers swam together to form one. The roar of their merging drowned out every other sound except their ancient conversation. I'd grip my toes to the slick stones below and balance against the current, close my eyes, and listen. I can't say exactly what those translucent waters told me. I only know that everything they said was true.

ONE DAY IN LATE summer of that year, I sat on the shore of the confluence letting my legs warm in the sun. Wil had often encouraged me to lie back on the earth rather than sit, to feel my whole body against the ground and gaze up at the sky, and I did so that day just for the pleasure of absorbing the world. I felt I could sense the vibrations of the rivers and rocks and perfect blue sky and busy insects, and when I stood, I felt bolstered and sure. I walked back down the trail and climbed into the old truck. Before I fully knew what I was doing, I found myself driving toward Iola. I was not entirely sure what unfinished business was pulling me there until the miles of sagebrush hills opened up into the Gunnison Valley, and I realized I was not traveling home.

Instead, I took a right off Highway 50 onto the gravel road paralleling Big Blue Creek. The truck groaned up the hill I had once stumbled down as a starving, dazed young woman. I was, for the first time, returning to the exact place I had laid my baby down. I did not know what I thought I'd find there. The nothingness of it, most likely, the utter vacancy of where I longed for him to be waiting for me, knowing, of course, I would not find him.

I wanted to tell him I was ready for him now. I wanted to tell him I knew the pain of displacement and how sorry—how deeply, profoundly, unutterably sorry—I was that I had given him away, that I hadn't known any other way to save him.

The gravel stretch led to a narrow dirt road, both steeper and longer than I remembered, that rose out of sage and scrub oak to curve through dense forest. My breath caught when I recognized the clearing. I pulled the truck in where the long black car had once parked and then stepped out onto the same ground where I had last held my child. With my hands crossed over my heart as if to keep it in my chest, I walked through the clearing to the fallen log where I could still so clearly see the woman nursing her infant. Starlings chattered on the same ponderosa bough where the two blue-and-black Steller's jays had cackled above her husband and his curl of cigarette smoke. The tree cast a wide shadow where their picnic once spread on a red blanket. I sat upon the log in the other mother's place and cried.

I can only liken the emotions I experienced that day to those of giving birth itself, the unfettered animality, the raw propulsion into something so beyond choice and reason that my sobs swelled to ragged howls. I wrapped my arms across my belly and doubled over, cradling the unnamable weight inside me that no amount of weeping could expel, the simultaneous cavern inside me that nothing but him could fill. I gulped the cool mountain air as if trying to taste him there, and, when my tears eventually calmed, I closed my eyes and listened as if I could hear him in the silent forest.

The boulder where the other mother had left me the peach stood at the clearing's edge. It was unlike the surrounding rocks—not round and blond, but bronze and orange and jagged, with three black stripes down its sheer face like claw marks. It appeared split in two, its other half worn down and carried away by the centuries. Of all that boulder had witnessed through time, my visits to this place had been as infinitesimal as a single raindrop. And yet the boulder stood for me as both monument and anchor, some tangible evidence that what had happened here in the summer of 1949 was not a mere dream.

I approached the boulder tentatively, though I cannot say why. Its chest-level flat top held nothing but a few copper-colored pine needles and a smooth, round stone. I picked up the stone and clutched it in my palm, remembering the peach. I leaned my back against the boulder and looked around. Magenta fireweed glowed in the afternoon light. Songbirds that had frightened away with my crying returned to the branches above me. I looked down and noticed a similar smooth stone to the one I palmed and bent down to claim it. Another rested in the moist dirt nearby, and I picked it up too.

And that is when I decided: I would gather six smooth stones and place them atop the boulder, one for each year since my child's birth. Next summer, I would return and add another stone, and again the next, and, in this way, I would have a monument of sorts, a place to feel him, an altar on which to offer a simple birthday blessing for my son.

I prayed that each of the years had been kind to him as I arranged the six stones, one by one, into a perfect circle.

Nineteen

1955-1962

Light slants differently through an autumn window than at any other time of year. This was true in my farmhouse in Iola and equally true in my new home. Regardless of the outside temperature or the color of the leaves, fall always begins with the first touch of direct sunlight on a southern windowsill.

Beyond that slant of light, the autumn of 1955 was different from any I had ever known. No ripe peaches waited to be picked. No thermometer required careful monitoring. No worries of frost or tipped baskets of bruised fruit or lack of hired hands kept me awake at night. I tended the trees each morning and evening, but they needed very little from me but patience. My days had not felt so expansive since that early summer in the mountain hut when I first learned to trust the hours instead of fill them.

That first spacious autumn in Paonia, after I completed my short list of farm chores, I took to wandering the banks of the North Fork

River to learn its ways. Round black rocks protruded like sleeping turtles from the low water, and I'd often leap from rock to rock to sit in the middle of the slow river and watch everything around me ready for winter. Rainbow trout fed on mayfly hatches in sun-filled eddies; plump brown cattails stretched above their long, golden skirts, preparing to burst; brittle fields of wildflowers released seeds every clever way; and above it all, red-tailed hawks and blue-winged kestrels hunted, and Canada geese migrated in long, symmetrical V's. Some days, I'd leave the river to drive the truck up to Lamborn Mesa and into the forest to just sit in the dappled sunshine and take it all in—the fetid, mossy, piney smells and the buzzing and tweeting and chatter all around. Each day, I was building a life of my choosing, and it was a good life. I knew what was missing, but I was also appreciative of what was there.

Autumn drifted into a mild and sunny winter, with just enough snow to be comforting but not so much as to be cumbersome. I gathered several mismatched chairs for the long pine table the Hardings had left behind. Greeney and his students were regulars at my table, as were Ed Cooper and his wife, Zelda, a buoyant blonde in colorful jewelry who always arrived with bakery bread and good conversation and an extra guest or two in an unsubtle attempt to socialize me. Ed and Zelda invited me to Christmas dinner for the first time that year. Their rowdy relatives from up and down the valley joined us in their tall downtown Victorian, and I'm sure I've never laughed so much in one day. In January, a new family moved in down the road and often sent their boy to my porch to borrow something—a cup of sugar or a tool or a lightbulb, as neighbors do. The mother was too shy or occupied, I suppose, to come herself, but her son, Carlos, was gentle and curious and the exact age of my Baby Blue. I'd hand him whatever he came for, along with a cookie, and we'd talk about silly things for as long as I could get him to stay. Standing on the cold front porch, watching him go—as he stopped in the yard to play with the dogs or roll a snowball, smiling and snotty and red cheeked, straight black hair sticking out from his stocking cap just as I thought my son's might—I couldn't help but imagine that the bundled child was my own, and from that day forward, Carlos became my measuring stick for how much my boy had grown.

Come spring of 1956, folks were too busy on their farms to gather. I gladly pulled into the tempo of daily work as my acreage woke from winter. Twice as many peach buds as the previous spring emerged like plump, shiny promises. We shared a longing— those buds and I—that they simply be allowed their unfurling. But Greeney advised one more year of rest, and I again spent weeks clipping buds. I agonized about the task far less than the year before, for I saw evidence that Greeney's methods were working and we all just needed more time. I fertilized and pruned and pulled weeds and waited. I planted my kitchen garden and repaired water lines and cleared ditches and studied the nuances of my new land, getting to know it acre by acre.

That summer, I returned to the clearing and placed a seventh stone in the circle atop the boulder and said a blessing for my son. That, too, tormented me less than it had the year before. I sat upon the log beneath the birdsong and pine and spoke to him, telling him I was making a new place for us, if a new place was what he needed. And I spoke to her, the other mother. I thanked her and wondered aloud where she and my son might be.

My memory loses track of the details in the years that passed after that. Troubles came and went, like troubles do. Ruby-Alice's little dogs died or disappeared one by one. I threw away for hog slop most of the first two years of my peach crop. I battled frost and drought and pests and broken equipment and loneliness and count-less other trials. But I had no complaints about my life. The new land had chosen to keep me, and I responded with every bit of de-termination and care that this honor deserved. Paonia and the North Fork Valley held me in their comforting rhythm and tem-pered my grief. Autumns brought canning days and long hours of neighbors helping neighbors; then came quiet winters of good food and time to read and snowfall and my holidays with the Coopers; with springtime came work and wonder and an abundance of fruit blossoms on nearly every farm. I mostly recall the long, hot sum-mers, tending to the orchard and walking along the river and re-turning to the clearing each August to place a stone, and, finally, blessedly, after several years of waiting, that first crop of bountiful Nash peaches from every transplanted tree, followed by summer after summer of the same.

It's not that I didn't think about Iola in those years. Ed Cooper kept me updated on tidbits he'd hear about the reservoir plans, until he lost interest in the slow, complicated project and stopped men-tioning it at all. Every August, after leaving the clearing, I'd pause at the intersection of the gravel road with Highway 50, knowing I could turn right, to drive along the Gunnison River and the rusted old rail lines to at least pass by what I'd left behind in Iola. But each time, I chose to go left toward what was now my home, averting my eyes from the concrete and cranes and bulldozers eating the river valley at the burgeoning dam site but grateful to see the Gunnison River still flowing free.

. . .

ONE COOL, CLOUDY JUNE day in 1962, I finished my chores and drove into town for a few supplies and, after, though I thought it foolish to pay for coffee I could make better at home, agreed to meet Zelda Cooper at The Diner. Conversation with Zelda was always interesting and enjoyable. She was smart, well-read, and self-assured, and she often made me laugh. I suspected her to be the source of the bachelors knocking on my door over the years, and though I wasn't interested in the men, I felt grateful Zelda considered me. Other than my curious bond with Ruby-Alice Akers, Zelda was the first actual friend of my life.

She wore lime-green pedal pushers and an orange-and-pink striped shirt that day. Her bleached blond hair puffed from a green headband and ended with a flip curl around orange rhinestone earrings. She made the other diners—myself and my old cotton dress and dull brunette braid included—seem unaware the sixties had arrived. I tried to picture myself dressing like Zelda Cooper and, even in my imagination, could never do it. I once reminisced to Zelda that even this humble main street had felt too fancy for me when I'd first arrived in Paonia, and she threw her head back and whinnied like a pony.

The waitress delivered our coffees and two slices of streusel cake. Zelda gossiped and I listened. She fluttered her fingers and asked me if I liked her nail color.

"It's called Bashful Blue." She smiled with exaggerated coyness.

"Oh, that's you all right," I joked, as if friendly banter came easily to me, and she giggled like a schoolgirl. Zelda's ease often made me extra aware that I had spent more of my life among trees than humans. If I made any conversational missteps, she blessedly never complained.

Zelda went on about her nail polish as I glanced at a neighboring table. The rancher there had unfolded his *Delta County Independent* and pulled it close to his face, as a barrier against our chatter, no doubt. The newspaper's headline was bold and black: "FAREWELL IOLA, SAPINERO, CEBOLLA—WESTERN SLOPE TOWNS EVACUATED FOR NEW RESERVOIR."

My face fell. Zelda looked about worriedly. I pointed to the headline and tried to explain all it held for me.

"Well, sugar," she said, not unkindly, "you've known for years it was coming."

I nodded. She was right. But it wasn't until that moment I'd truly believed that towns could actually be erased from the map, from their own land, that people could be forced out, their homes and livelihoods burned and drowned. I had resettled, but what about the others? I even wondered about Seth. If he had managed to stay at our farm until then, where could he possibly go next with no money or resilience or sense? I pictured the folks I grew up with loading their trucks with their belongings, herding their cattle toward safe ground east of Gunnison, shooing their horses and chickens and pigs into trailers. The evacuation must have been going on for months, and I had never even driven by.

"It's heartbreaking, absolutely," Zelda said. She took a sip of coffee and a bite of cake, then added, "But it's sure as hell nothing new. Think of the Utes."

Her candor took me aback. Most folks I'd known tended to think of the Utes with disdain or disregard or, most commonly, not at all.

She went on, "I mean, the only reason we're sitting here right now is they got forced off all this land we like to call our own. Just because people ignore that fact doesn't make it any less true."

Wil had never specified his tribe, and I was too shy and ignorant to ask him, but I wanted to reply to Zelda that, yes, I thought about the tragic treatment of native people, more than she could know.

"I'm not saying it's the same. I'm just saying the government can do anything it damn well pleases, and people suffer," she said. "And we don't learn one scrap from history."

She talked on about political affairs I didn't fully understand but knew I should, though I couldn't have cared less about them at that moment.

"Look at what Kennedy is starting up in Vietnam," she was saying. "Mark my words, that's going to turn into yet another damn mess."

I wasn't listening. I was wondering again about Wil and where and who he came from and how he ended up at that school in Albuquerque. And why, after he'd managed to run away, he hadn't gone back home.

And I thought about my own child in a new and troubling way. I knew from seeing Carlos that my son was becoming a gangly teen, surely with skin the lovely shade of his father's and questions about why he didn't look like his family. Did he wonder if he belonged? And if so, was it because the other mother had revealed to him his abandonment, or was it because he carried an uncanny memory of dislocation deep within his cells? I wondered if either of these wrongs could ever be healed in him or if they simply cut too deep.

The waitress refilled our mugs. Zelda paused for a moment to thank her, then started up again about Vietnam. I had no idea at that point where Vietnam was or why she was so concerned about it.

"You'd think after all the good men we lost around here to the war, people would be more worried about what might be coming," she said.

Two old farmers sitting by the window glanced at her disapprovingly, as if war was not hers to discuss.

"Did you?" she leaned in and asked in a whisper. "Lose someone to the war?"

She said "the war" as if there had been only one. But I knew what she meant.

"My uncle," I said, which was true enough. "And his brother." The fact that I had lost Wil and, in turn, my baby to a kind of unnamed war remained unsaid.

"My uncle too," she said. She looked wistful for a moment, then waved it all away. "But enough. Eddie would have a fit if he heard me talking politics again. He says it loses him clients." She rolled her blue eyes and changed topics, launching into her review of the film version of *To Kill a Mockingbird*, telling me I must catch it while it still played at the Paradise Theater. She'd be my date so she could see it again.

I read the book, I replied, and didn't want to ruin it with the film. Truth was, with that headline still staring me in the face and all our talk of displacement and injustice and war, I just couldn't stand more sadness.

On our way out, I took a newspaper from the stack and dropped a nickel into the coffee can. Zelda was a hugger and I was not, but I didn't mind her parting embrace that held me longer than usual.

I sat in my parked truck on Grand Avenue and read the *Independent* article. It turned out that the towns had been evacuating for the reservoir for three years, not months. The article said most folks had moved out in that time, reluctantly but without much protest, but some had stayed until this week's deadline. There was a quote from one of the holdouts—of all people, Matthew Dunlap. I shook my head, not sure I wanted to read what he had to say. The irony of his words sickened me: "This is America," his quote read, "land of the free. Where men have rights and are due their respect." He was later quoted again, making my blood boil: "A law-abiding man can't be kicked out like a dog. It ain't right."

Walking the orchard that evening, I felt grim and weighty. I touched each of my trees and surveyed the progress of the young green fruit, picturing the dozens of times I'd watched Daddy do the same in Iola. I imagined Wil at the edge of my new orchard with our son by his side. I told them all I was sorry the world was the way it was.

I later cut out the newspaper article—minus Matthew Dunlap's infuriating quotes—and tucked it into Mother's Bible. If Iola would soon be erased, my family would want me to save some proof it had once existed.

THE NEXT DAY, I made the two-hour drive all the way to Iola for the first time since I'd left. Or, more accurately, I drove as far as I could until I was stopped by a sheriff's deputy on the bridge. He leaned into the truck window without removing his sunglasses and asked my destination.

"Lake City," I lied, knowing that through traffic to the towns down south would need to be allowed to pass.

"You can head on, just no detour into Iola," he said. His patrol car sat on the roadside with red lights blazing as if for an accident.

"I hear folks are getting kicked out," I said just to hear his reply.

"Removed," he corrected in monotone. "Making way for progress, ma'am."

As the deputy stepped back and waved me across the bridge, I wondered at the limits of progress and if we'd ever know when we hit them.

I turned off at our abandoned peach stand, which stood boarded up and weedy, like an announcement that what was once alive here was now dead. I pulled off the road. Ahead, another patrol car guarded a white wooden barrier. I peered at the officer, hoping to see Sheriff Lyle, knowing he would receive me and let me through, but this officer was young and plump and stood with his arms sternly crossed, eyeing me as a trespasser. Beyond him was only stillness.

I took one long, final look at the road behind him, at the tips of familiar buildings and the bare school flagpole in the distance, the empty corrals and barns and abandoned wheelless trucks dotting the valley floor, and, though I couldn't quite see it, the fateful corner of North Laura and Main. I gazed once more at our stand. From its construction and decades of loyal patrons to its closure, dilapidation, and pending demise, that one weathered and lonely structure told my family's history in this valley, a story that now was done. I turned the truck around and drove away.

The officer on the bridge leaned against his patrol car and barely gave me a glance as I passed him again. After crossing, I pulled off and got out to look down upon the Gunnison River.

Its white waters rushed and tumbled with early summer runoff, so beautiful and unsuspecting of its fate. Looking down upon my river that would soon be a lake, I felt sure that after the dam was built, release gates would open to the lower Gunnison, and some of the current would still push on. No matter how slow and arduous its course, no matter what trickle seeped through, I knew it would find a way to keep flowing. And when it did, I, in my new life along the North Fork, would be on the other side to meet it.

IOLA AND EVERYTHING TO do with it grew small and distant in the rearview mirror as I drove west. I turned off the highway at Big Blue Creek, and the old truck grumbled up the gravel road. It was early for my annual visit to the clearing, but I yearned for the bird-call and a familiar place to rest.

When I arrived, I found snow still lingering in patches—under trees and in shadows and along the clearing's edge—but the log lay clear and dry in the sunshine, and I sat upon it, as I always did, where she had once sat. I thought of her, the other mother, as I always did while perched on that log. I thanked her aloud, as had become my ritual. Futile, yes, but it kept us connected in a small way. Maybe, just as she had sensed I needed that peach, she could also sense that I thought of her there, that I wanted to take her hand in mine, look her in the eyes, and simply say thank you.

Speaking to my son from that place had become more difficult with time. I used to sit on the log and simply tell him that I loved him, that I might meet him someday and hold his small hand and explain only the best parts about his father and his birth. I had imagined inviting him to live with me on my new land and teaching

him about his family's trees. But by June of 1962, he was no longer
a child who might so easily be mine or naively believe a candied
slice of his parents' tragic tale. I could now only think of one thing
to say to him. Two useless words when even a thousand could not
convey what needed to be said.

"I'm sorry," I said to the clearing. Barred from Iola, I felt a strange
hollowness, as if I had been orphaned myself that day.

Tiny footprints from weasels and squirrels ornamented the crusty
snow beneath the trees. I looked deeper into the forest and considered testing how far I could go. Only once in all my visits there had
I ventured beyond the clearing to try to find the mountain hut. I had
failed to get my bearings when nothing looked familiar and quickly
turned around rather than get lost. This time, I knew my footprints
in the thin snow would guide me back if I lost my way. But I pictured
the hut now, perhaps collapsed from avalanche or rot or sheltering
someone new—a sheepherder or hunter or runaway, his beans cooking in the pot I'd left behind, his night lit by my candles—and I
wondered, why return? When we—the meadow and I—had finished
with each other, we had no more business between us. Just as I had
relearned on the edge of Iola that very day—what I suppose Wil
must have known too—sometimes we simply cannot go back.

I sat a while longer, breathing in the crisp air; then I stood and
searched the ground for a stone, the thirteenth for my circle. When
I found one—smooth and oval and pale, like all the others I had
carefully chosen and placed—I kissed it and approached the boulder with it still pressed to my lips.

I saw the footprints first, in the snow surrounding the boulder
and in the mud surrounding the snow. Two sets of shoes. As I
neared, I could see that one set of prints were my size, the other,

slightly smaller. I looked around at the quiet woods, suddenly suspicious of eyes on me. But the footprints, revealing the many directions the visitors had moved about, were crusted over, several days
old at least. In all the years I had been driving to the clearing, I had
seen no evidence of other visitors. Only occasionally did I return to
find one of my stones out of place or lying beside the boulder,
nudged by creature or weather. Studying the footprints, my heart
raced. I rushed to see the boulder's top. My circle of twelve stones
was undisturbed.

But in the circle's center sat a round rock. I reached for it and
held it in my palm, marveling as if at an apparition. It was weighty
and round, undeniably the size and shape of a peach.

I glanced about the clearing again and again, eager for explanation. Not a bird or squirrel or branch stirred. Even the long whisps
of afternoon clouds paused in their approach to the sun. I stood in
that stillness for I don't know how long, listening. I held the round
rock against my belly and searched the whole clearing for clues.

Finally, when nothing and no one revealed themselves, I did
what I had come there to do. I laid a thirteenth stone in the circle
and said a blessing for my son. The clouds overtook the sky and the
afternoon grew too cool for my bare arms, but, still, I lingered.

I knew a round rock left atop a boulder was, perhaps, just a rock,
and the footprints merely traces of curious strangers who had found
my stone circle an odd work of art to which they added their part.
But I couldn't help wondering at another possibility: if, after all
these years, this place beckoned them, the other mother and my
son, just as it had beckoned me; if the circle of stones made them
wonder about me as I was now wondering about them, and if they'd
left behind a peach-shaped message just in case I'd find it.

Twenty

1970

As time passed, I fell more and more in love with the summer sunrise on my orchard. Every morning that began by stepping out the farmhouse side door into the sweet, dewy air, fragranced with ripening peaches and rich soil and overnight rain, was, to me, a good day. Just such a morning dawned crisp and golden in mid-August of 1970. I cranked the cool metal spigots to spill irrigation water into the soaking furrows, then grabbed an orchard basket and began to pick. The crop was uniformly fat, unblemished, and superbly sweet.

The land and the years had been mostly kind. It had taken Greeney and me nearly a decade to coax the transplanted trees back to their full yield and quality, and just as long to nurture the grafts into productive new blocks, but we eventually made Grandpa Hollis and Daddy proud. By that summer, every area stand carried Nash peaches, and loyal customers once again came from miles around. Greeney published articles and won awards and tenure for his part, and I spent all my late-summer and early-autumn sunrises picking peaches, just as I had as a girl.

I had continued my yearly pilgrimages to the clearing, but I hadn't solved the riddle of the peach-shaped rock. After finding the rock and the footprints in the snow that spring day in 1962, I went back nearly every week for months, hoping for evidence of the visitors' return or clues to their identity, but I found nothing. For several years thereafter, I scoured the clearing's edges on every annual trip, eager for—what?—any meager sign of them. Once I had even left a note, hastily written on a scrap of paper I found in the truck, too brief and vague and probably improperly anchored against the wind. It simply said, "Tell me." Still, nothing.

Eventually, I stopped looking for clues and let go of the desperate notion that the round rock had been left for me. I forced myself to believe that sitting on the log in that quiet, sacred place and adding another stone for my son was enough. The round rock had long sat on my bookshelf at home, not as a symbol of hope for a reunion with my lost child but as a warning against foolish wishing and the tricks the imagination can play when you too badly want what you cannot have.

I hired hands every harvest—local men and their sons and transient workers who knocked on my door—and they labored alongside me to ensure that every peach was plucked and delivered at the height of ripeness. That particular August morning in 1970, when the hands arrived, I took my leave and headed to the henhouse. The guineas scurried and screeched at my feet while I spread their feed and gathered a basket of beige speckled eggs. Zelda was coming for breakfast. She had put in her order and I was happy to

oblige: guinea eggs scrambled with garlic and spinach from the garden, my peach-raspberry muffins, and sliced peaches on the side,
freshly picked and sprinkled with cinnamon.

Ed and Zelda were the only people I knew in the valley who
didn't grow a bite of their own food. Zelda liked to say she and her
husband were built to buy and sell the land, not work it. This was
not a joke. The Coopers never got their hands dirty, rendering
nearly inexplicable the affinity between us. But I had come to love
them both over the years, and Zelda became one of my life's great-
est blessings. We didn't see each other often. I kept busy with the
farm and enjoyed being alone to wander the forests and riverbanks
or whatever else I pleased. Zelda helped Ed with his real estate
business, spent time with her big family down in Hotchkiss, and
made weekly trips to Grand Junction to shop. She also read insa-
tiably, and when we did get together, she always had something
worthwhile to say. She usually brought a *Reader's Digest* or *Time*
along, pointing to headlines and summarizing articles, reminding
me that there was a restless world churning outside the North Fork
Valley.

That morning, Zelda talked a mile a minute as we sat down to
breakfast at my long pine table, showing me articles about civil
rights and hippies marching for something called Earth Day and the
latest calamity in what she always referred to as "that damn Vietnam." I liked learning from Zelda. What I didn't like was her other
favorite subject, which was men.

"Did that cute beekeeper call you?" she asked. The late-morning
sun through the window ignited her blond bob like a halo, but her
hopes for me and the beekeeper were not exactly angelic.

"Oh, Zel," I sighed. "Do we always have to talk about this?"

My disinterest in men had long been her mission to correct.

"Yes, we do." She nodded stubbornly, pulling a warm muffin from the basket. "Did he call?"

"I don't want to date him," I replied.

"Who said anything about dating?" She winked, then bit into the muffin and moaned with pleasure. "For heaven's sake, V. I hear you. You aren't interested in marriage. Got it. But everyone needs a little . . . honey . . . from time to time."

She laughed, and I rolled my eyes.

"Well, what are you waiting for?" she said. "Warren Beatty to knock on your door?"

"Definitely not." I smirked and shook my head.

"Then for *what*?" She sighed and slouched her shoulders in dramatic defeat. Then her big eyes turned serious, beyond our typical jest on the topic, imploring me to explain myself. But I could not.

I had many times been tempted to tell Zelda the story of Wilson Moon.

"Nothing," I said instead. "I've told you. I'm not waiting for anything. Or anyone. Least of all for some beekeeper's *honey*."

I grinned, but Zelda, usually so quick to laugh, doubly so at anything risqué, did not break her gaze. She laid her fork on her plate and leaned toward me.

"What is it, V? Come on," she coaxed. "What aren't you telling me about why you won't date?"

How could I explain to her why a tragic first love when I was only seventeen years old prevented me from ever loving again?

"Let's finally talk about this," she was saying.

But all I could think of was the many ways I had failed Wil, and our son, that a life alone ensured that I would never betray them or anyone else again. I cared only for what I knew how to love, which was the land and the trees and the peaches.

"Did some bastard hurt you? Is that it?" Zelda asked, knitting her groomed brows.

"No, no," I quickly replied. "It's not that. It's . . . ." I so badly wanted to tell her everything. But my secret resided in such a deep lockbox, I had no idea how to open the latch and set it free. I did not fear Zelda's scorn. Still, I could not say the words. I could barely even explain my past to myself, other than knowing that a beautiful young man had died for me, that our baby was out there somewhere not knowing who he was or where he came from.

"It's . . . what?" She waited with expectant eyes.

"It's . . . nothing," I answered, again letting the truth pass like a floating seed unable to anchor.

"You're a lesbian?" she asked without judgment.

"No."

"You're into that nerdy scientist friend of yours?"

"Greeney? Oh, heavens, no."

Greeney had remained valuable counsel over the years and a welcome visitor from time to time. But his private life had never been my concern or something he shared. We talked about roots and soil and fungus and tasted peaches together with methodical precision.

"You're married to your orchard like some kind of tree nun?" she asked without irony.

"No." I smiled at her deadpan, considering the element of truth to her words.

She sighed and finished her eggs while I went to the kitchen to slice more peaches.

"So, no men, no babies," she said as I returned.

My heart dropped. Men, I could at least talk about. Babies, I could not.

The circle on the clearing's boulder by then held twenty stones, so many it wrapped around itself to hold them all, a long coil like a snail shell encircling the entirety of the boulder's flat top.

The gray, peach-shaped rock I had discovered years ago at the circle's center sat on the bookshelf directly behind Zelda's head.

"What about you?" I deflected Zelda's talk of babies. "You've never said why you and Ed don't have children. I've wondered, of course. But I didn't want to meddle."

"Oh, sugar, nothing you could ask me would be meddling," she said, fanning away my absurdity with her manicured hand. "It's wretched, honestly," she continued. "This body might look fantastic"—she swept her hands down the sides of her orange sleeveless mini dress as if her figure was a game show prize—"but it can't make babies."

Six times, she said. Six pregnancies. Six babies lost. With the sixth, she explained with a pitiful cringe, she miscarried at such a late stage that she actually held the tiny blue baby in her hands.

"Oh, Zelda," I groaned, remembering the agony of holding my own lifeless newborn and the sheer miracle of his first raspy breath. Tears welled in my eyes, as much from a remembered relief as for sadness for my friend.

"A boy," she said solemnly. "We named him. Joseph." She paused. "I carry him—all of them—right here." She placed her hand on her heart. "Eddie and I, we've gone on to make a good life. But there's always been missing pieces, you know?"

I knew. I wiped my eyes and just listened.

"You'll think I'm crazy," she went on, "but I used to look at our living room or the yard or around the tree on those Christmas mornings before you'd arrive, and I'd picture them, all of my children, being silly together and wrestling like puppies." She smiled weakly, then waved her hands in front of her face, pushing away the images. "Maybe I am crazy," she laughed.

I had never stopped seeing Wil and my son in my orchard, smiling from the edges or even working by my side. If she was crazy, then so was I.

"Know what else I think about?" she said. "My Joseph would be the exact age for getting drafted to that damn Vietnam. Plucked right out of the valley. I'll tell you what: if he was still mine, I'd run him to Canada or risk jail or hell to make sure he wouldn't have to go." She looked wistfully out the window, perhaps seeing her son standing there among the cottonwoods, and said, "Oh, I would have been a fierce mama bear, had I been given the chance."

I envied Zelda Cooper many things—her flair for conversation, her cleverness with politics, her close family and fashion sense and big unapologetic laugh, and, if I'm honest, even her wide aqua eyes and long black lashes. For her part, she often mentioned what she envied in me, saying she could never live on her own or walk in the woods alone like I did, could never begin to match my expertise in the orchard or the garden or the kitchen. I didn't know much about friendship, but I suppose we were like most good friends in that way, appreciative of our different qualities without being covetous. But that day, when Zelda spoke with the frankness of a woman completely at ease with her own troubled past, I was heartbroken for my friend, but I was mostly jealous of her unfiltered honesty, her utter lack of self-blame.

Maybe I would have finally just said it then, told her everything, had we not been interrupted by a knock on the side door.

I found Carlos there, holding his red metal toolbox. He was tall and broad shouldered and handsome, a young man of twenty-one and a fine carpenter. He came by whenever he needed money, knowing I'd always have work for him.

I invited him inside and he entered in his quiet, gracious way to sit with us awhile. Zelda chatted to him while he devoured three peach muffins and answered her questions with grins and nods. I just watched him, the way he ate and smiled and smoothed his black bangs off his forehead with his broad, calloused hand.

"What will you do if you get called up?" Zelda asked him before it registered with me that she was again talking of Vietnam.

"Take off to the backcountry," Carlos replied unhesitatingly through a mouthful of muffin, pointing out the window toward the wide wilderness of the West Elk range. "Those mountains there. I know 'em."

Zelda nodded and clasped his shoulder, as if wanting to root him where he sat.

"Good boy," she said.

He was young and naive and audacious in this plan, just as I had once been.

When I walked Carlos to the barn to show him the sagging support beam in need of reinforcement, he bent over his toolbox to get straight to work, but I couldn't leave. I stood at the barn door and watched him for too long.

"Carlos?" I finally said. He looked up. "If you have to go, please come by to say goodbye. I'll send you with some jars of peaches."

If he thought this request strange, he was too polite to show it.

"I'll try." He nodded politely, a young man's way of saying he probably wouldn't.

My heart ached as I slid the barn door closed behind me.

I reopened it.

"Carlos?" I said again.

He looked up with gentle dark eyes.

"What I mean to say is, I'll drive you. You know, if you need it. I know those mountains too."

He smiled and thanked me, and I pulled myself away, a terrible hollowness in my belly.

I returned to the farmhouse to find Zelda washing breakfast dishes, saying she needed to run to help Ed with a closing. That felt untrue. Instead, she seemed to be running from me. I thought I should apologize for something, but my lies to her, and to myself, were all by omission. I had nothing to take back.

"I'm sorry," I said anyway.

"Sorry for what, V?" she asked, clearly giving me one more chance at honesty.

I wasn't sure how to reply. "I'm sorry I made you talk about . . . your babies," I said stupidly.

Her look was as incredulous as it was pitying.

"Why wouldn't I want to talk about them? They're my babies. Plus, you didn't make me *do* anything. I've always wanted to tell you. I just wasn't sure you cared. Now, if they had been saplings . . . ," she tried to tease, but her laugh was too weak and her words too true.

"Whatever you're still not telling me," she went on, "that's your choice. But let me say two things. One, I know you are so tough, saving your trees and running this farm and working so hard and wandering about and every other damn thing you do all by yourself. But carrying your sorrows all alone isn't strength, V. It's punishment, plain and simple. Whatever happened to you, you've got to stop blaming yourself."

I felt like a child being lectured and just wanted her to go.

"And, two, I just sat here at your table and watched you look at that boy Carlos with the saddest eyes I've ever seen. Whenever you're ready to tell me what that's all about, I'll be here to listen."

I turned my head so she couldn't see my eyes.

She kissed my cheek, thanked me for breakfast, and paused on her way out the door, saying, "And I'll stop throwing men at you. I promise."

When I heard Zelda's car pull down the drive, I retreated to the orchard to pick. Row after row of perfect peaches surrounded me. The hired hands whistled tunes from the tops of picking ladders and set full baskets by the orchard road awaiting the delivery truck. Irrigation water flowed, and the August sun shone warm and bright. My entire farm and business ran like clockwork. A line of buyers undoubtedly waited for my fruit at every area stand. As Zelda said, I had indeed proved tough enough to work this land, and the land had proved generous enough to have me. And yet. In my most honest moments, I knew that sadness lingered in every leaf and root and in the pit of every peach. Quite simply, Wil and our son were not in fact smiling at me on the orchard's edge or working by my side, and no amount of imagining them would change that.

I had not yet made my annual summer visit to the clearing, telling myself I was too busy with this or that. More honestly, when I had placed the twentieth stone the previous summer and gazed upon the circle, a kind of finality had pressed on my heart. I had looked about the clearing and wondered, with the circle complete, with my child now a man, was this place done with me too? Unsettled by my morning with Zelda and Carlos, the clearing tugged at me to return and ask that question one more time.

A new blue Ford pickup sat aside Daddy's old truck in the garage. The rusted relic had become fussy and unreliable, but I chose it anyway. If this would be my last reckoning with the clearing, it seemed fitting that the old truck should be the one to take me there.

Much of the long drive back to the Big Blue wilderness was by then barely recognizable. New gravel roads and clusters of hastily built worker camps scarred the hills that once held only sagebrush and cattle. Backhoes and bulldozers sat idle, like sleeping yellow dragons after their damage was done. The rerouted Highway 50 rose and fell and curved through it all until the towering mass of concrete and rock forming Blue Mesa Dam emerged like a wide scar. I had seen its construction advance, piece by appalling piece, for many of the past several summers when driving to the clearing. Still, the actuality of the dam never failed to shock me. Worse, I braced myself for what I knew I would see on the other side: the sprawling blue reservoir where Cebolla, Sapinero, and Iola had all once stood, the Gunnison River choked and bloated a mile beyond its banks.

Fishermen and a few picnicking families dotted a sandy stretch of the reservoir's south shore, mistaking the scenery for nature. Surely, they found the new lake scenic, and I might have thought so, too, had I no history here, no knowledge of its artifice and the ruin strewn along its depths. I did my best to look away as I skirted the reservoir's edge, relieved to turn off onto the familiar dirt road leading to the clearing.

The old truck groaned up the long hill and through the woods. When I finally pulled off and parked, I gave the dashboard a grateful pat. A warm, sweet breeze blew through the open window as I studied the clearing from the driver's seat. Something in the harsh afternoon sunlight and the jagged shadows cast by the old ponderosa pine felt oddly stark and uninviting. As sure as waking to the summer snow that had sealed my baby's fate or opening my door to the government man offering to buy my land, I knew at first glance that it was time to walk away.

And in that shifting of my heart, I saw it: there on the boulder, in the center of my son's stone circle, in the exact place where I had once found a peach and, later, a peach-shaped rock, a plastic bag lay beneath a flat stone, its edges flapping in the breeze like a pinned bird.

I exited the truck slowly, steadying myself. My heart tumbled like a spring creek as I approached the boulder and saw a thick stack of pale-blue paper inside the sealed bag. My hand trembled as I reached out. I remembered reaching in just such a way when I knocked for the first time on Ruby-Alice's pink door, believing Wil would open it, and he did. I lifted the bag, knowing this, too, would be an opening that changed everything.

Dust and pine pollen swirled off the bag into the breeze. There was no way to know if the fine coating had been collecting on the plastic for a day or a year. No matter, I decided. It was there now, and so was I.

Through the plastic film I could see loopy script, like a hastily written letter. With the first line, my throat clinched and tears blurred my vision. It was not a letter so much as diary-like pages. The first words were all I needed to know that the offering was in fact for me, and that it had been left there not by him, my son, but by her, the other mother.

I wiped my eyes with the hem of my T-shirt and read the first line again through the plastic bag:

Baby at my breast, I heard birdcall.

I both longed for and feared every word that would follow. I carried the bag to the log and waited a while in the spot where I always sat—in her place—before opening the seal and pulling the pages into my lap.

A folded half sheet fell from the bag to the ground. I opened it to find a note in the same hurried handwriting. It simply read:

Forest Mother,

This is my story. An attempt, anyway. I thought I wrote this for myself, to try to make sense of it all, and to remember. But the hole in this story has always been you. Here, I finally tell you all you need to know.

The note was signed with a name—Inga Tate—followed by a phone number and an address, down south in Durango.

Reading the first few pages was like reliving that August day in 1949 through a crystal ball—the picnic on a red blanket, the screeching jays, the husband and the cigarette, the newborn fussing in her arms.

She had found my baby, she wrote, much as I had imagined—his cries rising above birdcall, then her rush from the fallen log to the car to discover him. I wept when I learned that she immediately, instinctively, pulled him to her breast to nourish him. I wept again when I finally learned my child's name.

"Lukas," I whispered breathlessly into the forest and hugged the pages to my chest.

I turned back to the first page. I took a deep breath to try to steady my hands and slow my mind. Then I began to read again.

PART IV

1949-1970

Twenty-One

BIRD

Baby at my breast, I heard birdcall.

Two jays perched greedily above us, shrieking like madmen, wreathed in slithering smoke from my husband's cigarette. The birds' black eyes pinned to the hastily displayed picnic on the red blanket: peaches on a brown sack purchased from an obese woman at a roadside stand, a paper plate of bread and ham sliced by a skinny shopkeeper in that nowhere river town where we stopped on our long drive home from the hospital in Denver.

The downed log made awkward seating for a novice nurser and ravenous infant. I teetered, attempting modesty but fumbling as I opened my blouse. Paul turned away. The baby pushed and punched until he finally grasped my ballooned breast and sucked. I longed to eat just one bite of peach, but Maxwell had been howling since we left Iola, long before Paul finally chose this clearing to pull the car over with a

huff. I tried to lay out the picnic to Paul's liking, but, in the four days
since Max's birth, I had learned one undeniable fact: baby comes first.

Birdcall replaced Max's cries as he nursed. High among the pines,
all across the wide forest, a chorus of screeches, chirps, and warbles
seemed frantic and jubilant and sad and beautiful all at once.

And then, birdcall that was not birdcall.

I listened, unsure. Then, unmistakably, all maternal instincts
aroused: the fragile jagged wail of a newborn.

I tugged Max from his suckling and thrust the disgruntled baby at
his equally disgruntled father, my ear tilted to the breeze. Both father
and son were bemused at my hurried rise. I pulled my blouse closed
and rushed toward the car and the inexplicable sound.

The impossibility of finding what I believed I'd find made my
approach feel dreamlike. But when I peered through the car window,
there he was. A newborn, wailing weakly.

The baby silenced as I swung open the door. He was swathed in a
yellow knit blanket. A soaked knit diaper wrapped his scrawny bottom.
I scooped him to my neck, feeling his feather breath, his feather weight,
and his tiny body, half the mass of Maxwell, like a masterpiece of twigs.

I sat upon the warm leather car seat and instinctively brought him
to my milk. He gasped and spat, nearly drowning, until finally his
suckle patterned with my flow and he drew long, ravenous gulps.

Paul approached with irate footsteps, loosely holding Maxwell with
one thick arm. His face reflected horror, confusion, disgust: before I
had given my inconceivable discovery even one clear emotion, my
husband had assigned three.

Paul looked left then right into the endless forest, thrust Max into
my free arm, turned, and stomped off to find her, the mad mother of
this abandoned, famished infant.

Maxwell shrieked. My breasts ached. My bewildered tears welled.
I was covered in babies.

PEACH

She gave me her baby, and I left her a peach. Small recompense, but
it had been less than a year since my arms were filled with textbooks,
not babies, when I had not wanted one child of my own, let alone two.

I had laid the finally sleeping boys on the back seat and gathered the
remains of our picnic. Then I placed one round peach on the flat top of
a jagged boulder—hoping to say more than "I know you are hungry,"
hoping to say to her, "I have him and will make sure he is safe"—and
waited for Paul to return and declare his verdict.

He appeared a good half hour later, sweaty, defeated.

"Get in the car," he commanded.

I held one sleeping infant in each arm and took a final glance at the
peach I'd left behind as Paul backed the car onto the dirt road, turned
sharply, and sped the way we had come. At the intersection with
Highway 50, he stopped, thinking. Durango left, Iola right.

Without a word, he turned the car left toward home.

We would keep the baby. Even before Paul turned the car, I knew.
Maxwell's birth had not gone well. When blood had trickled from my
womb, the doctor instructed Paul to take me to the hospital in Denver
well before my due date. I lay immobile there for nearly three weeks,
waiting, bleeding, then left barren after the birth. Tubes tied, as they
said, which at least freed me from ever having to suffer through it all
again.

"We'll say you bore twins," Paul said then, and I knew better than
to argue. He had decreed two children on our wedding day, preferably

sons, indifferent to what I wanted. He would not have a miserable only child, as he had been, and he would not have the expense of three.

As ever, Paul would have his way. We had not yet announced Max's birth, but when we did, we'd now announce twins. One born of the forest, half the size and a shade darker than the other. But twins they would be.

Silent miles later, I asked timidly, "Might we name him Lukas?"

Maxwell was Paul's choice, the name of a physicist he admired, one he could flaunt among his colleagues in the math department at the college. My father had been Lukas, a name written on my heart.

Paul grunted disapprovingly but, to my surprise, agreed, insisting, "But we'll call him Luke." He reached into the paper sack between us, pulled out the remaining peach, and took a deep, fragrant bite as he drove.

From then forward, I only called him Lukas, and Paul, it turned out, hardly called him anything at all.

WALKING

Once home, Maxwell wailed night after sleepless night. I cradled him and walked the hall back and forth like a dazed zoo animal, while Lukas mostly slept. Paul made brief attempts to relieve me, and then he'd thrust Max back at me, insulted by the baby's untamable howls.

All I really knew about Paul before we married was that he was a dark-haired, dark-browed, strikingly handsome graduate student willing to talk to me as I stood alone at my first Ohio State social. It was easy to mistake his attention for affection, his arrogance for learnedness and the embodiment of my college dreams. He, no doubt, was more attracted to my naive adoration than the silly freshman girl

I was. I should have walked away that first night when he teased me for studying literature and wanting to be a writer someday. Instead, I drank spiked punch with him and ended up in his arms. After that, I'd often find him pining for me beneath my dormitory window, and, egged on by my giddy roommates and my own misguided crush, I'd leave my books to meet him. When he proposed, I felt dizzy and mistook that for love. Then I, Inga Sabrina Zimmerman—the name so full of my parents' Germany, one I had hoped to see inscribed on book covers someday—became the flat syllables, Mrs. Paul Ray Tate. I had barely adapted to the shock of being a wife when I learned that I would also soon be a mother, the double off switch to all my plans and dreams.

Colorado was not a place I had ever thought about beyond learning its tidy square shape on a map. When Paul announced that he had taken a teaching position out West and we would be leaving Ohio, the name of the town—Durango—seemed more antiquated and lonesome than I could possibly bear.

"But Colorado, Paul . . . it's . . . ," I had tried to reply.

"It's one thing, Inga," he cut me off with fiery eyes. "Colorado is one thing. It's where we are going, and that's all it is."

I realized then—too late—what I was in for, the kind of husband and father he'd be.

But this story is not about Paul. It is about me and my boys. We may have been a reluctant trio, but we were a trio nonetheless. One or the other of my sons, or both, occupied my every moment. Everything I feared about trading my studies for motherhood proved to be true, in double.

My only respite was walking. The minister's wife at the church where Paul insisted on parading us each Sunday pulled an old baby buggy from their shed and offered it to me. That buggy offered far more salvation than any church sermon. Throughout that first year of bewildering mothering, tucking the babies side by side—one large bundle, one small—and walking Durango's sidewalks was my only peace. Around our neighborhood and through downtown, across the wide park and up and down the hill on Seventh Street, Lukas slept or studied the clouds, and even Max was still.

My best days were when the babies let me walk all the way to the Animas River, the River of Souls. It was turbulent and quick compared to the Ohio rivers I had known. I parked the buggy, took a pen and notebook out of the diaper bag, and sat on the riverbank to watch the white water splash and dive over rocks. I thought of marriage and diapers and laundry and all my lost possibilities. I wondered about Lukas's real mother, at what desperation could have possessed her to leave him behind. I thought of the newspaper headlines in the shops I passed, the postwar years so restless and mad, and wondered what kind of world awaited my sons. But just as I'd put pen to paper to try to record my thoughts, a baby would cry, and I would close the notebook, stand, and walk again.

HANDS

Lukas remained smaller, darker, calmer than Max. Yet as the boys grew into toddlers, no one questioned their genetic pairing. Even I tended to forget that Lukas was not of my body and blood, until a certain birdcall or slant of summer light would return me to the day I had discovered him.

Eventually, I gave up the notebooks and novels I pointlessly carried in the diaper bag and stopped longing for the life I might have had.

Instead, I surrendered to motherhood. The choice was motherhood or madness.

In the acquiescence, I learned to love my boys. Max—volatile, moody, too like his father, but also lively, curious, and funny. Lukas—gentle and wise from the start, as if gifted to our family as equilibrium to Maxwell's fire. Whatever the source of his calm, Lukas filled my life with unexpected delight. Paul came and went as he cared to and I tried not to mind. The only real kindness he'd ever done for me was pulling into that forest clearing where baby Lukas needed me to be.

It was not my imagination that Lukas had a charmed touch, an electricity or a heat or just a tenderness of heart. He rescued spiders from sink drains and freed bees from window screens, and if an animal or plant was ill, a caress from Lukas seemed to set it right. Most importantly, he could calm Maxwell when nothing else came close. Even in mid-tirade, Lukas's hands upon his brother could wind Max down to limpness or tears. Then Lukas would return to his play as if it hadn't been interrupted at all.

TREE

The boys grew with the backyard cottonwood tree, which in turn grew with the boys. Limbs delicate as lace the summer they were born stood thick and ready when they were old enough to climb—they scaled it like squirrels, sat like birds, beautiful as blossoms. Until one afternoon when I glanced out the kitchen window to see Maxwell lying motionless on the grass beneath the tree with Lukas crouched at his side. At the slap of my panicked exit from the screen door, Lukas silently raised his hands to show me his brother's blood.

I discovered a mangled arm, not a split skull or cracked spine, a boy broken but not lost. A jagged bone protruded like a snapped stick above Max's elbow. Lukas placed his bloody hand across the wound, trembling, knowing even he could not undo this.

I lifted Max's limp body from the ground while Lukas cradled the injured limb, and we rushed inside. Reaching for the phone, I had to choose: a neighbor, an ambulance, or Paul? The retired teacher who lived three doors down pulled to our curb in his blue sedan within minutes.

Through surgery and recovery and the slow, uncertain return of Max's use of his right hand, Paul blamed me. I had been negligent with my attention and had improperly lifted the injured child, he said; I had been a fool to call the neighbor, such a slow and dim old man. Worse was Paul's fury at the boys, at Max for having climbed too high, for being careless and fragile, and at Lukas—dear innocent Lukas—for pushing Max from the tree, an absurd accusation that Max heartbreakingly corroborated to please his father. It wasn't until Paul stood with axe in hand, poised to attack the beloved tree unless Lukas admitted his crime, that the boy gave false confession. Fat tears rolled from his eyes as he flashed quick sorrowful glances at me. We both knew that Max had leaped.

In time, Max healed. The notion that Lukas pushed Max from the tree remained another family myth, but each time he was accused, Lukas seemed to catch the lie and lay it aside, like a beast too ill to bite.

HALVES

I was hanging laundry in the September sun, my ears tuned to the alley where Max rode one of the new blue Schwinns I'd convinced Paul to purchase as twelfth-birthday gifts. Over and over Max launched the jump the boys rigged with plywood and stacked rocks. I waited for the inevitable crash and wail.

Lukas knelt near me, polishing each spoke of his identical bicycle. His hair shone blue-black in the afternoon light.

"Mama, what's a half-breed?" he asked.

"A what? Where on earth did you hear that, Lukas?" I bent, retrieved more clothes, and pinned them to the line, two pairs of smaller undershorts for each of Paul's large ones.

"Jimmy," Lukas replied, polishing the curved front fender.

"More details," I demanded, accustomed to Lukas's brevity.

"Remember when he caught that fish, the trophy trout?"

I told him I did, and he recounted the trip with Jimmy and his father to the taxidermist south of town. Lukas said the old man had stopped them on his porch and then crossed his arms on his gut and looked them over. The man muttered something gruff to Jimmy's father; then he accepted the cooler with the fish and took it inside his cabin, leaving them standing on the doorstep.

"I didn't want to go in anyway," Lukas said, wiping the bicycle seat. "It smelled. Like dead things. And also like sad things."

I paused from the laundry to look at my son and wonder at his peculiar awareness. A clatter in the alley snatched my attention. I expected a cry from Max but instead heard him curse and kick the bike, then mount it again and take another lap.

"We waited on an old tire in the yard," Lukas continued, adding that's when Jimmy told him what he'd heard the taxidermist say. "Jimmy said the old man didn't want us to come in because we are half-breeds."

My heart skipped a beat. A part of me had always known that Lukas's skin tone could not have come from two white parents, but I assumed Paul's dark hair and distant Italian ancestry sufficiently upheld our facade of Lukas's birth story.

Lukas looked up at me with confusion.

"It's not a nice term," I began. And then I chose the lie. "Your father has Italian blood and my family is German. So you have some of each in you."

"Dad says Germans are Krauts," he said.

"Also not a nice term, Lukas. Don't ever say that about my family. Or anyone, understand?"

He nodded sheepishly. "And Jimmy?" he asked.

Jimmy was blond and blue eyed, clearly not the target of the taxidermist's bigotry.

"I don't know about Jimmy," I said, "but everyone is from somewhere or a mixture of something, half this, half that. Not to worry, love. Just a grumpy old man."

Lukas nodded and asked, "Will you take me to the river? Where I went with Jimmy and his dad?"

I wondered why I hadn't taken him to the Animas myself, like I used to when the boys were babies.

"But let's not catch the fish," he added.

I smiled. "Yes, Lukas. I'll take you to the river."

Satisfied, Lukas's attention returned to his sparkling blue Schwinn. Before he could mount it, Max's crash and howl rang out. We ran to him, pulled him from the wreckage, and helped him inside to clean the wounds as Max blamed Lukas for the flimsy jump.

The next day, the boys and I rode our bikes to the Animas. Lukas immediately began throwing stones into the river. He removed his shoes to tiptoe into the cool water and was soon knee-deep, laughing. Max sulked on the shore, bored and cross to be off his bicycle, asking every *few minutes when we could leave. The more Max whined, the harder Lukas threw his stones, ricocheting them off the larger river rocks until he split a stone in half.*

STONES

Once Lukas knew the route to the Animas, that's where he wanted to be. With the glow of a perfect sunset or full moon, or when Paul or kids at school were cruel, or when Max was selfish or rude, Lukas biked to the river. Only rarely did he invite me along. When he did, I studied him. My boy was changing. A quiet melancholy was slowly nudging out his joy, like he sensed something about himself he could not explain but hoped the river could.

One early winter evening, we both threw stones into the low-flowing water just as the sun set over the white hills. He was quiet and evasive of my questions about school and friends. I let him have his silence. The sadness taking hold in him was too much for me to bear. I decided then that, come May, I would take Lukas to the clearing far over the mountain passes near the Gunnison River— where as a baby he had cried out for me—and I would tell him everything.

That spring—on the long drive north out of Durango, through Dolores and Rico, over Lizard Head Pass toward Iola—I worried I was making a terrible mistake. Lukas bounced excitedly in the passenger seat. Sightseeing trip, I had told him after arranging a playdate for Max. Scout badge, I had told Paul to be allowed his car.

The roads were narrow and winding through endless forests and cliffs. I pulled off to buy gas in Telluride and calm my rattled nerves. Lukas got out to marvel at the cool, thin air, the serrated peaks still topped with snow, the waterfalls spilling into rushing rivers. I encouraged him back into the car, and we pushed on.

The sage-covered hills. The Gunnison River. The rail lines, now abandoned and rusted. Driving into the valley, it all came back to me. A highway sign warned no admittance to the towns up ahead— Cebolla, Sapinero, Iola—but I barely paused to wonder why. I examined each gravel turnoff and chose what I could only hope was the correct one. Up a steep hill, around curves and through the pines, and there it was. The forest clearing where my life had intersected with a stranger's and her baby boy's and everything changed for us all. I parked.

"What is this place?" Lukas asked, leaping from the car into lingering patches of snow and mud.

I didn't answer and he didn't notice as he ran off to investigate.

The clearing was just as I remembered it. The log in the sunshine. The large pine where those nerve-racking jays had cackled overhead. The jagged boulder where I'd left a peach before we drove away. I pictured myself, young and frightened, covered in babies and tears. I could never have known then that this place—this tiny speck on the planet, where we happened to be passing at the precise moment Paul lost all tolerance for Maxwell's newborn wails and yanked the steering wheel to park—would be, for Lukas and for me, a place beyond all other places. I wondered how I could explain this to him when I could barely comprehend it myself.

Lukas and I picnicked in a dry patch next to the log in what felt like strange homage. I was quiet, nervous, calculating the right moment to tell him why we had come. Lukas never stopped talking, smiling, leaping up from the red blanket to run about like a deer freed from a cage, returning to the picnic to take a bite of sandwich then running off again.

He discovered it first and called me over.

"Mama, what is this?" He stood on tiptoes in a slice of shadowed snow, pointing to the jagged boulder's level top.

I approached to see a perfect wreath of flat, round stones.

"I don't know," I said. I truly didn't. Not until Lukas touched each stone with his fingertip, counting.

"Twelve," he announced, beaming. "Like me."

The forest mother. Lukas's mother, I reminded myself. She had come back to this place. Once or twelve times, I could not tell, placing one stone for each year her son was gone from her. It was the only explanation I could believe.

Except he was my son, not hers, and he was not gone. He was right by my side. I pulled Lukas closer, as if a predator lurked. His mother had long been to me more fleeting forest creature than actual woman. I stared at the stone circle and was struck for the first time by the terrifying notion that she might want him back, and that once he knew this, he would surely want her too.

My impulse then was to leave. Never mind that the drive was long and Lukas was happy and the clearing was peaceful in the late-May sunshine. Never mind that I had come all this way to tell him the truth.

"I don't know," I said again, now a lie. "Just don't disturb it."

"Why?" he asked.

"In case it matters to someone," I said.

"To who?"

This was my chance, my opening, but I did not take it. I stared at the stone circle, losing whatever courage I had mustered. I looked into my son's dark, curious eyes and could not expose the lie.

We finished our picnic. I folded the blanket as Lukas begged to stay. I wondered if he somehow felt connected to that ground or if he was simply a child enjoying playing in the woods. He was undeniably lighter there, less burdened by whatever he had lately begun to carry. We stayed until the sun sank away and the sky paled toward dusk. I put my arm across his shoulder and guided him toward the car.

When he suddenly turned and ran back to the boulder, I feared he would refuse to come with me.

He just wanted to add a rock to the circle, he said.

I wanted to say no, to leave without a trace. But I had chosen cowardice once that day. It seemed double cruelty to deny Lukas and his birth mother their one chance at exchange. At my permission, he searched the clearing from end to end to find the perfect stone.

What he finally chose was not at all like the other stones but large and round. He clutched his rock like a baseball, ran it back to the boulder, and stood on his toes to carefully place it in the circle's center. From where I stood at the car, the half-light of evening mixed with memory to make Lukas's rock look very much like the peach I had once placed in the same spot.

GIRLS

Jane was the first. Jillian the second. Max's eagerness for girls started young. Cara, Joan, Kelly, Marguerite, two very similar Kims. A red bow tie at his first junior high dance, then, in a blink, half-nude women papering Max's high school bedroom walls, Playboys hiding beneath his bed. Tall, square-jawed, and green-eyed, Max always got the girl.

I saw so much of Paul in my boy. He was flattering and funny with his girlfriends, until he didn't want to be. Then his affections clamped down like a steel door, the poor girl left in the chill, pitifully groping to *please. More than once I saw Lukas step in, suggesting a soda, checkers, a trip to the movies, anything to throw the abandoned girl a lifeline while Max brooded. Still, Lukas was ignored, and Max, adored.*

Lisa was a tall, auburn-haired beauty with big round eyes and a set of breasts to match. She and Max spilled through the front door one spring afternoon of their sophomore year of high school, loud and giddy. I couldn't tell if they were drunk or high or just happy. Max bulleted her name my way, claimed homework, then pulled her by the hand down the hall to his bedroom. The door slammed. The Byrds blared.

I stood wondering at my next move when Lukas came in. Slump shouldered and grave, he greeted me glumly, dropped his book bag, and hung his jacket on the hook. His eyes widened at the music. He tightened his jaw and asked if Max was alone.

"No," I sighed, "a girl named Lisa."

"That son of a bitch," Lukas snarled, and he took off down the hall.

A broken door. A screaming girl. A toppled shelf. Punches, grunts, and a grating scratch across the turntable. The babies I once held grown monstrous, and I, it seemed, grown small. I yanked and hit and screeched in a futile effort to pull them apart. Lisa clutched a pillow to her chest and fled. Black bra, black eyes, bruised brothers in her wake.

The boys eventually separated, spent and heaving. Lukas lay in tears. Max stumbled to his feet and stormed from the house. I sat against the wall, stunned, surveying the damage.

"I'm sorry, Mama." Lukas reached out his hand, and I took it.

Later, as Lukas and I pieced the room back together, while both Max and Paul were who knows where, I learned that Lisa—like Joan, like Kelly, like one of the Kims—had been Lukas's girl.

"I have to get out of here," he said. I knew he was heading to the river. There, he would do what he had always found a way to do—for

better or for worse—which was to forgive his brother rather than to lose him.

That night, I lay awake in the empty house until I heard the front door open and close. Lukas soon appeared as a dark shadow beside my bed.

"Can we go to the forest? Back to that place with the stones in a circle?" he asked.

I remembered his smile as he had run from tree to tree, placing the peach-shaped rock, having no way of knowing who it was for. This time, I swore to myself, I would tell him the truth.

"I'd imagine it's still snowed in," I replied, "but, yes, we'll go as soon as we can."

I meant it when I said it. But I never took him back, and he never asked again.

BIRTHDAYS

Batman, Bullwinkle, Green Arrow, Flintstones. For years, August 31 meant themed paper plates and a Good Housekeeping *cake for my sons and the neighborhood boys. Then birthdays meant worry. My teenagers out in the night, those same boys inching toward manhood any misguided way they could. Birthdays meant peering under the window shades past midnight, seeing Lukas helping Max up the walk, and Max utterly unable to find his feet.*

On December 1, 1969, birthdays meant destiny. Birthdays meant kill or be killed, flee or fall, families broken or whole.

The draft lottery gathered the four of us for the first time in months. The boys had turned twenty that summer. They shared an apartment with a few friends on the other side of town and had little time for home. Max's half-hearted attempt at college had ended instead with a job selling tires and Paul's humiliation. Lukas apprenticed as an electrician right out of high school. Neither had flat feet or color blindness or a heart murmur or allergies. If their birthday was called in the lottery, they'd go to Vietnam.

All eyes were on the television. Paul sat stoically in his recliner. Max lay on the sofa downing potato chips as if watching Sunday football. Lukas sat on the floor, riveted. I paced.

On the screen, politicians in thick black eyeglasses and thin black ties stood before an American flag and solemnly shook hands. Blue plastic capsules containing rolled slips marked with dates lay in a shiny glass vat. Polished young men in pressed white shirts—feigned symbols of youth's agreement to the old men's war—selected and opened the capsules. September 14, April 24, December 30, February 14. Each date felt to me like a gut punch as it was read aloud and pasted on a numbered board. Each date doomed not my boys but someone's. The list went on. October 18, September 6, October 26, September 7.

November 22, December 6. August 31. August 31. August 31. Blood pumped in my ears. I heard no other numbers. August 31. The day I first became a mother. The date of all those backyard parties with wild little boys. The date I prayed would be curled like a paper slug in the final capsule at the bottom of the horrid glass vat.

Max leapt up with a cheer. Paul frowned but said nothing. Lukas searched my face, panic in his eyes, and I returned a helpless stare. We both knew he was not a boy built for war.

Late that night, I sat alone on the sofa, drinking red wine and already mourning my sons. Vietnam was a death sentence, if not to their lives at least to their innocence. Beneath Max's macho facade, I knew he was as scared as Lukas. I poured another glass and grieved *every child already dead or maimed or broken, every Vietnamese village set aflame. And I mourned for the mothers.*

Plenty drunk, I decided what I had to do. For Lukas was not, to anyone's knowledge, actually born on August 31. I was not, in fact, his mother, nor Paul his father nor Max his brother. Lukas had no birthday of legitimate record. I would go to the Armed Services office and attest that his birth certificate was a fraud. But first, I would have to tell my Lukas that I was a fraud too.

I drained the final drops from the bottle, knowing our family's lie had had its number called.

TRUTH

I should never have told the truth.

Two weeks before the boys were to report for their army medical exams, Lukas came by to do his laundry. Paul disapproved of the boys using our machine instead of the coin-op downtown, so they'd come midmorning to avoid him. I'd never know when one or the other would suddenly walk in the front door, laundry bag in hand, both so striking in their own ways, men no longer boys. Lukas had strong, wide shoulders and sinewy forearms and smooth, tan skin. He had a grin that swelled my heart. On that last day my son would be mine, he wore a white T-shirt and jeans and had just had his black hair trimmed short even though long and shaggy was the style of the day. He was beautiful.

I had retrieved the boys' birth certificates from Paul's files in anticipation of their draft report day. Other than the name, Lukas's birth certificate was indistinguishable from Max's—the same exact time and date and inky newborn footprint. I remembered when Paul had pulled the forged document from his leather briefcase shortly after we'd brought the babies home, commanding I file it and ask no questions. Since then, it had always passed for valid, as I knew it would again.

When Lukas asked for it that day, I handed the certificate to him without a word. He folded it casually and slid it into his back pocket. My mouth felt as dry as old bones.

I asked him to help me in the yard while the washer ran. He obliged in his gentle way, followed me out back, and accepted the rake. We worked side by side, clawing at the dead grass and not talking about war, commenting instead on the sweet spring sun, the return of birdcall.

We began with birdcall, and so, too, did we end.

I suddenly dropped my rake and told him everything. The random choice of pulling off the road into the clearing. The picnic, the gaunt baby on the car's back seat, the decision to raise him as our own, the long drive home. The bewildering chance of it all, the blessedness of our unlikely union, the opening of my heart to claim him. We sat down together on the yard bench beneath the old cottonwood tree, and I held his hands. I told him I loved him. I told him he was mine. But with each word of my confession, his face fell further into confusion and anguish until the cheerful young man who had walked in the front door was replaced with a version in melted wax. He listened intently and asked no questions.

"August 31 is not your birthday, Lukas." I offered this like a pathetic consolation prize at the end of a pummeling.

He looked at me blankly.

"You don't have to go to Vietnam," I explained. "August 31 is not your birthday."

He pulled his hands from mine and thought about this before replying, "Then when is?"

"I don't know," I answered.

"But . . . ." He pulled the birth certificate from his pocket, unfolded it, and smoothed it on his thigh.

"It's a forgery," I said shamefully as we both stared at the paper.

He needed me to meet his bewildered silence with explanations—of when he was born and where he had come from, of why I had permitted such pretense and exactly how I planned to undo it all to save him from war—but I realized then that I had not one of the answers I owed him.

As if in perfectly orchestrated tragedy, the back screen door screeched open then slapped shut, and there was Paul, unexpectedly home from the college for an early lunch. Lukas leapt to his feet, stuffing the paper back into his jeans.

My eyes met Lukas's and silently begged him not to tell his father what I'd revealed. When I received only an empty stare in return, I whispered, "Please, Lukas."

But it had all been too much for my lovely boy. Paul started picking on him as Paul always did—accusing him of freeloading laundry and lunch, distracting his mother from her chores—and Lukas exploded. Two decades of Paul's rule that had balled up inside him discharged as if from a canon. Lukas fought back as I'd never seen him do, meeting insult with insult, until he declared for all the world to hear the previously unutterable truth: Paul was not in fact his father, and he was so damn glad.

"Good," Paul replied cruelly, a malicious smirk spreading where astonishment should have been. "One less burden for me then."

Like a deer suddenly aware of a predator in pursuit, Lukas paused for an instant in stunned stillness, and then he ran. Reaching the yard's edge, he stopped and looked back at me, face flushed, tears welling, and yelled, "What about Max?"

"Max doesn't know," I replied, not understanding his question.

"No," he interrupted, crying now. "How will you save Max?"

He meant from Vietnam. He meant how could I save one son and not the other.

"I can't save Max, Lukas," I choked.

The words hung in the air between us for a terrible moment; then he hopped the fence with ease and grace and was gone.

I fell to my knees in the spring grass while Paul disappeared inside.

I told myself that my son had just gone to the river. But that evening, Max called to report that Lukas's things were missing from their apartment. Truth's blade had stabbed so many wounds that day that I lied and said I hadn't seen him. I transferred his abandoned laundry to the dryer and later cried as I folded each piece, careful to smooth away every wrinkle so the stack would be perfect whenever he returned to retrieve it.

A week later, we received a postcard picturing a clump of skyscrapers in front of white-capped peaks. My hand trembled when I turned the card to read the other side. In my son's precise, familiar script was the date—March 18, 1970—and the verdict: "Inducted in Denver. No longer your burden. Tell Max I'm sorry. Thank you for everything, Lukas."

WAITING

I kept waiting for Max to ask questions. But he appeared no more concerned about Lukas's sudden enlistment than about his own upcoming physical exam and induction day.

"Just two more days, Ma," he boasted over a slice of my apple pie. He had let his hair grow long and it needed a washing. His eyes were bloodshot and dreamy. "Soon I'll be in country with the rest of those bastards, get to waste some commies with Lukas. It's gonna be badass."

War was a comic book adventure to him, the imagined Southeast Asian jungles a profane playground.

"Sorry," he chuckled at my troubled look. "I just can't wait, man."

I sat by the phone the morning he reported. I imagined him standing in line with other eager young men, waiting for their birthday to be called, for the physical exam and crew cut, the green fatigues topped with shiny new dog tags on a silver chain. He was to call me when he finished. I read magazines and waited. I made tuna salad on toast for lunch and waited. I sat the phone next to an open window and busied my hands trimming rose bushes and told myself he had simply forgotten to call. When Paul arrived home from work, I prepared dinner and sat his plate before him. I said I hadn't heard from Max all day.

"He's not a child who has to report to his mommy," Paul derided.

"You're right," I said, as I had learned to do. But something was wrong and I knew it. I'd just have to wait to find out what.

WAR

I fought with my worries all night. The next morning, I boarded the bus to rows of vacant stares and approached an open seat next to a boy in full soldier uniform. He gazed straight ahead as if he hadn't seen me but shifted the green canvas duffel between his black boots to give me space to sit. I said thank you to no reply.

The boy smelled like war. I sat engulfed in his complicated scent of sweat and cigarettes and alcohol and elsewhere.

"Headed home?" I asked.

"Maybe," he said softly, still gazing ahead.

I got off at the Twelfth Street stop. I walked toward Max's
apartment wondering if Lukas, who always smelled so cleanly of Speed
Stick and Listerine, smelled like war now too.

Even before climbing the metal staircase, I could see through the
balcony railing Max's open front door and hear the guitars screaming
from his stereo. I entered when he did not answer my knock. The
apartment was strewn with clutter—pizza boxes, beer cans, wadded
clothes, crusty dishes—and in the midst of it lay a shirtless Max
beneath a lanky girl in cut-off jeans and a yellow bikini top, both of
them motionless on the sofa. I called out a hello. They did not stir. As I
moved closer, I saw the whiskey bottle and pot pipe lying on the carpet.
I stood over them, watching for the rise and fall of their chests, and was
relieved to see it, just like when my babies slept so still and intertwined
in their single crib.

Even passed out, even wearing a drunken girl like a desperate sort
of blanket, I could still see that baby in Max's sleeping face. I wanted
to untangle him from it all—from the girl and the drugs and the mess
and the war—and scoop him in my arms. But all I could do was reach
down to gently smooth the long hair off his forehead.

I rummaged through the debris on the kitchen table, looking for a
pen and scrap of paper to leave a note. Beneath a greasy paper plate, I
found Max's draft papers. A deep red DEFERRED was stamped across
the top.

I read through each page, searching for the error. All seemed in
order, until the section marked "Physical Exam." The page listed
military classifications with an empty black box next to each, a fat red
check on the final line: "IV-F, Registrant not qualified for any military
service." A barely legible physician's note was scrawled below:
"Crooked right arm. Unfit."

I shouted Max's name and rushed to the sofa with the document raised above my head. He slowly looked up through bloodshot slits, entirely unsurprised to see me.

"What happened at the army office yesterday?" I demanded over the music.

"Motherfuckers," he slurred. The girl roused slightly at his voice and started nuzzling his neck. "Nothing happened," he murmured and closed his eyes again.

"Something must have happened. What did the doctor say?"

"Screw the doctor," he said as the girl drowsily snaked her body over his.

She purred something about screwing her instead and they started in on each other, all mouths and hands and hips.

I returned the papers to the table and walked out of the apartment. The sun on the balcony was too hot for April. The music spilling from the apartment, too loud. My son, too confusing. Max would not be joining Lukas in Vietnam. To my surprise, the unexpected reprieve did not soothe me. I feared that Max's own personal war might be war enough to claim him.

NEWS

Five thirty dinner, six o'clock television news. Many evenings Paul did not come home, but when he did, his routine was as predictable as dusk.

I washed dishes instead of watching the news. Nightly footage of popping gunfire and the haggard faces on all those sacrificial sons made me ill. The only news I wanted was to know if my Lukas was safe and when he was coming home, news that never came.

Still, last April, I found myself glued to the television set like everyone else, watching the Apollo 13 drama unfold. The irony did not escape me that the entire country held its breath for just three men while dozens died every day fighting a war no one understood. But I was hooked for those eight long days until the Apollo crew came home, and then I couldn't shake the habit. I watched the dispatches from Vietnam. I watched as American ground troops stormed into Cambodia and, five days later, sat stunned at the footage of people's dead children lying facedown on Kent State's green lawns. On and on the reports unfolded, each tragedy eclipsed by the next, the world I had given my sons even more mad and confounding than I feared it would be. I couldn't look away.

Max came home sporadically. When something at the tire-shop job or on the news set him off, he'd show up at my door with bloodshot eyes. I'd make him a meal and listen to his rants about commies and smacks and narcs and pigs and goons, comprehending only that his anger cast a wide and tattered net. He rarely mentioned Lukas, but I knew we both yearned for him, wished he'd come home and make some sense of the mess.

The last time I saw Max, he was crawling into a van full of hippies in denim and fringe, heading to a summer music festival two thousand miles away at Shea Stadium. He wouldn't have stopped by had he not needed to borrow a cooler, but I'm forever grateful he did.

"Festival for Peace, man. With that fox." He beamed, pointing at the lithe, braless driver, her afro wrapped in a ring of wilted daisies. She smiled and flashed a peace sign, and Max laughed his wonderful, throaty laugh.

I knew Max had no idea whether he was in favor of peace or war, of this girl or another.

"Joplin. Creedence. Steppenwolf. Like goddamn Woodstock," Max said. Then he spread his big arms wide, inviting a goodbye hug.

I dove in. He reeked of pot and gin and sweat, but I inhaled him just the same.

"Have a good time," I said into his shoulder. I wanted to tell him he was a small-town Colorado boy who could easily be eaten alive by New York City. Instead, I said, "I love you."

He tightened our embrace and whispered, "Backatcha."

The van of beautiful, confused children sped down the street, Hendrix screeching from the open windows. They turned the corner and were gone.

I went back into the house and numbly turned on the television. Paul didn't show up for dinner, so I watched ridiculous game shows while waiting for the news.

WORDS

When a pounding on the front door jolts you from sleep; when you can see the blurred outline of two men in uniform waiting stiffly behind the glass; when your heart has already dropped like a cannonball in your gut yet you have to keep moving forward to open the door and receive their news—there are no words.

When your quivering hand manages to turn the knob and the two figures are not army officers but policemen, and relief wrestles with the rise of new fear—there are no words. When you are told that your son, your beautiful baby boy, has been found in a van in Queens, choked by his own vomit, a needle by his side—there is no oxygen, let alone words.

So you utter polite nonsense through your sobs before closing the door, and you say your son's name over and over as if words could *conjure the vanished. You stare at your arms and marvel that you are still flesh when by all right and desire the officers' words should have turned you to ash. You ghostwalk back to your bedroom to find your husband sleeping through your nightmare. You know you must tell him but there are no words. You collapse instead to the floor and weep, gutturally, maniacally, because this is actually all there is to say.*

Max's funeral was yesterday. I could not speak. I had the words prepared, my wholly inadequate attempt at farewell. But as the mourners gathered in the cold stone church, and I watched Max's childhood friends file to their pews, so adult now, so alive, I became stiff as a pillar, stupid with grief and anger and fatigue. Paul sat just as rigidly and dumb at my side. I needed Lukas.

I needed Lukas to honor his brother with words of affection and reverence. I needed him to call me Mama, to help me feel earth beneath my feet. I needed his smile to light up the dim room. I needed him to hold me and remind my blood to flow.

As if an apparition, Lukas appeared, walking up the center aisle, stunningly handsome in formal army dress. It had been nearly six months since my confession had caused him to flee. I had sent word of Max's death to the state Armed Services office, ashamed to say I had no idea where my son was stationed, had only a stack of letters marked "Return to Sender." How shocking then to see him walking toward me up the church aisle, mine yet not mine, his hands in two tight fists at his sides.

Lukas did not stop at our pew on his way to the altar, but he did offer me a quick, sorrowful glance as he passed. It was not the homecoming I longed for, but I clung to it for dear life.

After an introduction and prayer by the minister, Lukas spoke eloquently for our family. He somehow found the perfect words to

eulogize the best parts of his brother and leave out all the rest. He
called Max clever and gutsy and mischievous and his lifelong other
half; he shared stories of their antics that spurred quiet laughter from
the crowd. I sucked in long deep breaths of the stale churchy air so as
not to come undone. Paul shifted restlessly. I offered him my hand and,
for the first time in years, he took it.

FLIGHT

As the last of the black-clad mourners drove from the church lot, I
sat on a wooden bench and watched a bluebird play on the breeze.
The service was already a blur of prayer and song, of hand shaking
and awkward hugging and sentiments now done. I wondered if anyone
would ever again speak of Max or if funerals were mere portals to
erasure.

I anchored my eyes to the bluebird, waiting for Lukas to emerge
from the arched church entrance. When he did, a companion in
identical green military formals accompanied him. They made such a
striking pair that pride momentarily cut through my sorrow. Lukas
slowly approached me as the other young man meandered to the curb
and lit a cigarette.

"Inga."

His greeting stung, but I had, after all, relinquished the right to be
called his mother.

I patted the bench in invitation, and he sat, leaving a wide gap
between us.

"I'm sorry about Max," he said flatly.

"I'm sorry about Max too," I managed. "I'm sorry about
everything."

The silence then was long and agonizing as we both watched the bluebird repeatedly dive and rise and, eventually, float into the gray, unmoving clouds. We both had too much to say to attempt uttering anything.

"I . . . ," he finally attempted, "I should have . . . Maybe he . . . ." He cleared his throat as if choked by a hard ball of sorrow, then went silent.

"No, darling." I turned to him, and he mercifully accepted my extended hand. "You couldn't have helped Max. Not this time."

"I could have tried," he croaked, staring at the concrete. He didn't say it, but I knew he was thinking that I could have tried harder too.

"Not this time," I repeated dumbly. A myriad of story lines sprouted in my mind, the many possible directions my children's lives might have gone in had I not told the truth. Perhaps Lukas was correct. Perhaps he could have saved his brother. But sometimes saying sorry is as absurd as hoping a lone star can explain the universe. Instead, I whispered, "Please come home."

I should have known this would be too much. He dropped my hand and stood.

"I can't," he said, and he glanced at his waiting companion. "I don't belong there anymore."

"You don't belong fighting a war either, Lukas," I quipped truthfully but unskillfully.

"You're right," he said, finally looking at me, his beautiful dark eyes wet with pain and sharp with accusation, "but it's better than nothing. It's better than not having anywhere."

Paul and the minister strolled from the church entry and stopped to converse. Lukas glanced nervously at Paul, then at his friend, who knowingly surveyed the scene and hollered, "Ready, Chief?"

"I have to go . . . Mama." He bent to kiss me lightly on the cheek. I pressed my palm against his soft face, wishing to hold him against me forever but knowing well enough to let go when he pulled away.

Sometimes a woman splits in two. Sometimes a woman is a public self who sits rigid on a bench with proper dignity and acceptance as someone she deeply loves walks away, while simultaneously her private self is shrieking and chasing and grasping and tackling and begging that love to stay.

"Lukas!" yelled the desperate woman. He turned as he reached the curb. "Thank you for coming," said the proper woman.

At least I got to see his perfect grin one last time before he slipped into his friend's car and flew away.

MOTHER

Last night, I drank wine in the dark living room until I succumbed to sleep. Not an hour later, I awoke on the sofa, achy and disoriented. I had dreamed of escaping skyward with the bluebird after the funeral and, in my drowsy haze, I still felt the lightness of flight. In that precious moment before crushing reality obliterated the dream, I was free. Then piece by piece, I remembered: Max, gone. Lukas, gone.

That is when I decided I must try to write it all down. I rose and went to my desk, where I took a pen and this stationery. I turned on the kitchen light and sat at the table, the words uncoiling so feverishly that my pen could barely keep pace.

Only now—as the sun is rising and I'm all these pages in—do I realize: I have not been writing this for myself. I have been writing it all for you, Forest Mother. I do not know how to find you, but I have long been certain that you are the architect of the stone circle Lukas and I discovered when he was twelve. Had I had the courage to tell Lukas the truth that day, had we left you a note instead of a peach-shaped rock, Lukas might have long ago learned where he came from, and, in turn, you and I might both have our son. In my selfishness, I never imagined I could lose him anyway, that one day both of my boys would be gone.

I will place this on the rock where I once left you a peach and pray that you will find it.

I tell you my story because Lukas's story is not mine to tell. For his entire life I told him that he was one thing, and then I broke his heart by admitting to him that he was something else. My precious boy now believes he is nothing from nowhere. Only you have the answers he needs.

Please help us.

PART V

1970–1971

Twenty-Two

I placed Inga Tate's pages on the dry ground beside the log and secured a rock atop the stack to save it from the breeze. I stood. My mind felt too full to think clearly, my heart too swollen and sore. I had to move. I looked up for the reassurance of the blue sky framed by the treetops, and I stepped into the forest.

Inga Tate's story was too much—too surprising, too sad. But it was also too little.

She had revealed so much, but she couldn't tell me where my son was. Now this woman was begging for my help, and I had no idea how to respond.

I was suddenly overcome by the difference between the craving for my son and the actuality of him. He was no longer an abstraction or a wish but a sad young man named Lukas who did not know where he came from, at war with enemies he could not possibly comprehend. And this Inga was not a blurry memory or some sort of savior, but a grieving woman who believed something lost might be found in me.

I paced through the forest, mulling all that I had learned. Returning to the clearing, I imagined them there: Lukas at twelve stepping through the snow patches to discover the circle and place his peach-shaped rock; Inga, years later, returning alone after her other son's funeral and leaving her words beneath a stone with the tenuous hope that I would read them.

At the jagged boulder, I laid both of my unsteady palms upon the circle, hoping the years of longing contained in each carefully placed stone would guide me in what I should do next.

Twenty-Three

Three days later, I was clipping blue flax in my garden when Zelda pulled up the drive in her white Buick and waved from the open window. I arranged the flax stems in a milk bottle and added water from the rain barrel's spigot while she parked. I placed the flowers on the patio table between two glasses of iced lemonade. Cottonwood shadows and fragrant catmint edging the brick patio softened the hot August air, but I was sweaty with nerves.

"What's all this?" she asked as she approached, opening her arms for a hug.

"Just lemonade," I lied, embracing her. I was anxious as a jackrabbit, and she could tell.

She sat and sipped her drink, studying me over the glass rim.

"What's going on, V?" she asked with a piercing stare.

I swallowed and looked her directly in her eyes.

"Well . . . it's high time I tell you a story," I managed to say.

I had decided that if Inga Tate could tell me her story and ask for help, I could do the same.

She looked at me with relief. "A story."

"Yes," I said, fidgeting with the flowers.

"Good." She nodded in a way that confirmed she had known all along that I had secrets. "Please, tell me."

I took a deep breath. She sat expectantly, and I felt I might come out of my skin. I stood.

"Can we walk?" I asked.

We both glanced at Zelda's shoes, which could have been anything from spiked heels to knee boots. The flat strappy sandals that matched her yellow sundress seemed fine for walking.

"Of course," she replied, standing.

We headed into the hot sunshine in silence, skirting the orchard's edge to the gravel path that wound toward my land's back boundary. I wanted to begin but couldn't bring myself to do so. I waited for Zelda to fill the quiet with chatter about something she'd read in the news, but she didn't. At the tall sunflowers lining my back fence, I opened the gate. We crossed the wooden bridge spanning the bog and continued on a shaded path along the ditch that diverted river water to neighboring farms. I wished my story could flow so easily.

"So . . . ," I finally exhaled, feeling the edges of my known universe peel ever so slightly. "I should have told you all of this long ago. Forgive me for not doing so."

"Forgive you?" Zelda shook her head. "Don't be silly. You're just stalling, V."

"Oh, am I?" I laughed. "As my daddy would say, 'Stop lollygagging, Torie, and get on with it.'"

"Torie?" she asked in surprise.

"Oh, everyone called me Torie when I was young."

"I didn't know that," she said. "I do remember that time I asked if I could call you Vicky and you flat out said, 'Absolutely not.'"

We laughed, and it felt good.

"I was so glad you felt that way," she added. "You're not a Vicky. Or a Torie. When did you switch to Victoria?"

A chorus of red-winged blackbirds encouraged me from the cat-tails along the drainage.

"That's part of the story I'd like to tell," I said. I paused, then found a way to begin, saying simply, "There was a boy."

"Aha, I knew it," she teased, but my manner told her this was not an ordinary boy to be joked about.

"Yes, a boy," I sighed. "You'll be the only one I've ever told about him. And everything else that followed. But I'll need to start from the beginning. I'm hoping you can just listen."

"Of course," she replied.

"His name was Wilson Moon," I said.

Wilson Moon. The name had not escaped my lips in over two decades. Just saying it reminded me that the exhilarating rush of first love was still very much in my veins.

BY THE TIME MY story was nearly done, we had walked a mile along the irrigation ditch and back, scrubbed and chopped a bas-ketful of vegetables I had pulled from the kitchen garden that morn-ing, and started a pot of soup for lunch. Reliving it all in detail was more difficult and exhausting and, in many ways, more lovely than I'd anticipated.

Zelda listened attentively to every word. Her face revealed her disbelief that the girl in the story—this Torie—was actually me, and that the whole tale had resided within me like a locked diary these many years. She placed her hand to her heart or her belly several times as I spoke, and, when my tears welled, she wrapped her arms around me. She, too, had known loss, like uncountable women before us. She knew I still felt it all in my body, just as she felt it in hers.

Finally, stirring the soup, astonished at all I had revealed, I said, "I've gone on long enough. Tell me what you're thinking."

My mind spun with the dreadful images I had conjured as I anticipated her response—of Wil's bloody body dumped over the edge of the canyon wall; of me, dirty and gaunt and disoriented from my ordeal in the wilderness, laying my baby on a stranger's car seat and stumbling away.

"You did what you had to do," she said then, with the complete sincerity of a carefully chosen gift. It was the kindest reply she could have given.

"I've never been able to speak about any of this," I said.

"Is this why you've kept this all a secret, out of some sort of shame?"

"I suppose," I quietly confessed.

Zelda reached for me, and we held each other. She reassured me in all the ways I needed to hear. But I was so used to hiding everything about Wil and my son, so seasoned at sharing my sorrow with only the clearing and the river and the orchard, that part of me wanted to escape her arms and run back through the gate and the bog and keep on running.

When she stepped away, she kept one hand on my arm and asked, "What about Seth? Was he ever caught? Accused?"

The last time I saw Seth I had a shotgun pointed at his back as he hung his head and walked away from the home where we had once been a family. Whether he had tried to occupy the farm and got drowned out, or whether he had drunk himself to death or ended up in prison or in paradise, I didn't care to know. Fifteen years ago, when I'd driven Daddy's truck onto this land for the first time, my life had split into Iola and after. Seth was part of my before. He simply did not exist to me anymore. It felt repugnant to talk about him, but I mustered a response.

"Fact was," I said, "in those days, no jury was going to convict Davis or Seth of murdering Wil, especially after he was portrayed as a thief." Seth's name in my mouth felt as sour as Wil's felt sweet. Davis's name felt like pure poison. "Lyle, the sheriff . . . he was a good man," I managed to continue. "He knew justice needed serving even if few others believed Wil's death really . . . mattered. But he didn't pursue the case. There certainly were no civil rights laws back then, not for Indian people, no concern for all they'd endured. There barely are now. You know this."

"I do." Zelda nodded, placing both palms on her heart. "But I only know it as history or some faraway news story. The actuality of it is so appalling. A travesty. If only he had returned home when you told him to go."

Wil had given me just one small hint about where that home might be, once pointing southwest, saying, "You call it Four Corners." I had heard of it—the point where Colorado, New Mexico, Arizona, and Utah converged, where tourists stood on the crisscrossed lines of a brass marker to touch all four states at once—but *I* had never called the area anything and was too naive to understand what he meant by *you*. When I asked him if he missed it, he only replied, "No land has corners," as if that told me all I needed to know.

"He couldn't go back," I said to Zelda. "I don't know why. I was just a girl. I had no idea how to make sense of it or to make any of it right."

I stirred the soup in absentminded circles, still bewildered by the bigotry and horror that had been unleashed on that innocent young man.

"Then everyone in Iola scattered, off to new lives," I said through what felt like a stone in my throat. "It was all erased."

I raised my eyes to hers and silently implored her to drop the topic of Seth and of Wil's murder, and she did, as a kindness, though I suspected she was thinking of what she had learned about Emmett Till and of Dr. King and how I had failed to accuse Wil's murderers, how fiercely she would have fought for justice if Wil had been hers. I chopped another carrot and added it to the soup, stalling to give my voice a chance to steady.

Zelda allowed the long pause before asking the inevitable question that I both dreaded and needed to hear.

"Have you ever tried to find your son?"

I shook my head. "No."

She winced. Of course, my answer was inconceivable to her. "Can I ask why?"

"It was a different era," I said. "It would have been impossible to track him down."

She nodded.

"And even if I had found him, what then?" I continued. "I couldn't steal him away from his new family. I made choices. I had to trust they were the right ones, that moving on, creating all of this," I gestured toward my acreage, "would be enough."

"And is it? Enough?" she asked gently but unafraid to push me.

I didn't answer. I had so desperately wanted it to be enough: caring for Daddy, for Ruby-Alice, for my family's trees, saving all I could and regrowing my life with the blessing of the land. But, finally, I could admit to myself that, no, it was not enough. I could not save enough to make up for all I had lost.

"He's your son," Zelda said. "Out there somewhere. I'm sure you still wonder where he is, what he's like."

I nodded, for not a day had passed in twenty-one years without my wondering about my son.

"V, we have to find him," she said.

I looked away. Part of me wanted to take it all back, tuck my story deep into the solid earth where it had rested like a fossil all these years.

But the time had come to face the past, to admit that as long as my son was missing, I could never be truly home, and, as Inga Tate's story helped me understand, neither could he. I remembered the day I led Abel from his stall and headed into the mountains knowing I was setting in motion forces and outcomes that could never be undone. Facing Zelda's questions and deciding on my next step felt similar. I just needed to muster the same resolve.

I walked from the kitchen to the dining table, where I had placed Inga Tate's story. I returned to Zelda, holding the pale-blue pages out to her. Her big eyes grew wider.

"I found this, with a note," I said. "A few days ago, after you were here for breakfast. I went to the clearing that day. This was left on my circle of stones."

She accepted the pages, her mouth agape.

I returned to stirring as she began to read. The soup's aroma suddenly soured my belly.

"It's from . . . ," she began.

"Her," I confirmed.

"Oh, Jesus," Zelda exhaled, frantically scanning through the pages. "So you've talked to her?" she asked.

"No," I admitted.

"Why not?"

It was the question I had been asking myself for three restless days and three sleepless nights. No midnight walks in the orchard or queries to the waxing moon had given me an answer. Every decision from the day I'd first felt my baby boy flutter in my womb had required my untapped bravery. I had risked and overcome so much, but Inga Tate's story had reminded me that even hard-won courage is not bottomless.

"He's grown now," I ventured. "I can't imagine he'd accept a woman appearing out of nowhere, claiming to be his mother. I have no right."

"You have every right," Zelda countered.

"I can't upend his life. It wouldn't be fair." My words were all wrong, but I had to say them aloud, let them ricochet back at me in the dumbfounded face of my friend.

"What's not fair is allowing him to go through life never knowing why he changed hands," she said, unable to restrain her exasperation.

"He didn't *change hands*, Zelda. He wasn't livestock," I bit back.

She was unfazed by my defensiveness and threw her arms out in dismay. I was testing my resolve on her—someone capable of receiving full honesty and tossing full honesty right back—and she knew it.

"And what about what you need, V? This is about you just as much as him."

I shook my head. "It's not. Women endure. That's what we do."

"That's nonsense," she replied more harshly than I expected. "A woman is more than a vessel meant to carry babies and grief."

"Meaning what, Zelda?"

"Meaning you deserve to have your son."

"No more than you deserve to have your children."

"Oh, I deserve to have my babies. Let's be clear on that. Every one of them," she argued. "Loss has nothing to do with what you deserve or don't deserve, for God's sake."

I had no idea how to be certain that I deserved better. Endurance was all I knew.

"You're afraid," Zelda said pointedly, and I felt caught in a trap I'd set for myself.

"Of course I'm afraid," I said, my eyes burning with stifled tears. "I don't know how not to be."

"If you believe that, then you weren't listening as carefully as I was to the story that you told me today," she said.

ZELDA LEFT, AFTER ASSURING me she would help me move forward whenever I was ready. I needed to lie down. I took Inga's story upstairs to my bedroom intending to read it again. Instead, I put it aside and lay my head on the pillows. The windows next to the bed were open wide, but the air was hot and still. The heat and decisions and next steps weighed so heavily. I closed my eyes and escaped into sleep.

When I woke hours later, a blessed breeze fluttered the bedroom curtains, wafting cool air across my body. The breeze blew in from the east, over the peaks and foothills, bringing with it scents of wildness, of pine and sage and soil and the slightest hint of rain. I inhaled deeply and rose. Inga Tate's story sat on my dresser. I still didn't know how to respond. All I knew for sure was that the forest was calling.

I drove the new truck toward Mount Lamborn. The road smoothed out on the mesa's broad top, winding past a dozen dispersed houses and farms and pastures, then dipping down before curving up a steep hill. At the top, where blue spruce and Douglas fir engulfed the road in shade, I parked and stepped into the silence. Stretching, inhaling, exhaling, long and slow, my mind began to untangle.

I walked a familiar deer trail through the scrub oak and yellow rabbitbrush to a favorite meadow, lush and lively with summer. White butterflies danced among the frilly corn lilies and tall grasses. Bees and swallowtails probed the sunny centers of tansy asters. Grasshoppers launched away from my footsteps. I sat at the edge of the narrow creek running like a vein down the meadow's center and admired the little trumpets of purple gentians clustered in the moisture. I cupped my hands in the cool water and splashed my face, again and again. I wanted to feel this place on my skin, to wake up and listen. When I stood to continue walking, I felt lighter, as if something I had been carrying did not rise along with me.

I followed the creek to where it dove into the forest as a mossy waterfall. I descended the hill alongside the waterfall's music and misty rocks, my steps quick and sure as a deer's. I wondered when it had happened—when I had learned to walk in the wilderness more forest creature than clumsy human, when the ground had ceased being for me too rocky or slippery or steep and had become instead essential earth.

I sat down in the cool darkness cast by the pines. Reaching to my sides, I scooped two handfuls: black dirt, pine needles, pebbles, twigs, leaves, one tiny snail shell, one white downy feather. I looked around me at the birth and growth and death piled atop one another, at the open bellies of downed trees feeding new sprouts, all the life pushing through every crook and crevice and possibility for light. It was an ancient intelligence far too rich and complex to fully grasp but exactly what I needed to remind myself that it is in these layers of time that everything becomes itself.

Yes, Zelda was right that I, like my orchard, had been resilient in new soil, uprooted by circumstance yet able to get on with things anyway. But I had also faltered and fallen, lost my resolve, and curled into fear more times than I could count. Strength, I had learned, was like this littered forest floor, built of small triumphs and infinite blunders, sunny hours followed by sudden storms that tore it all down. We are one and all alike if for no other reason than the excruciating and beautiful way we grow piece by unpredictable piece, falling, pushing from the debris, rising again, and hoping for the best.

I decided then that this was what I would reply to Inga Tate, and what I would tell my son if I was ever fortunate enough to know him: that I had lived my life willing to face what came to me, and that I'd always tried to do the next right thing. I would explain that what I had learned most about becoming is that it takes time. I would say I had tried, as Wil taught me, to go as a river, but it had taken me a long while to understand what that meant. Flowing forward against obstacle was not my whole story. For, like the river, I had also gathered along the way all the tiny pieces connecting me to everything else, and doing this had delivered me here, with two fists of forest soil in my palms and a heart still learning to be unafraid of itself. I had been shaped by my kindred—my lost family and lost love; my found friendships, though few; my trees that kept on living and every tree that gave me shelter; every creature I met along the way, every raindrop and snowflake choosing my shoulder, and every breeze that shifted the air; every winding path beneath my feet, every place I laid my hands and head, and every creek like the one before me, rolling off the hillside, gaining strength in gravity, spinning through the next eddy, pushing around the next bend, taking and giving in quiet agreement with every living thing.

I would tell them that this and the land that sustains me is what I had to offer my son. If he was anything like his father—and my deepest hope for him was that he was—he would feel the fragile courage in who I had become, and he would find a place in his own frightened heart to give me the chance to love him.

Twenty-Four

Heat rose from the black parking lot as Zelda and I exited the hotel lobby. I wanted to turn around and retreat back to the air-conditioned room.

I had chosen to come to Durango after I found the courage to send Inga Tate a note in which I'd first attempted to explain everything but ended up simply writing, "I'm ready." It was Zelda who'd pushed us to come so soon, just days after Inga had replied with an invitation. Sliding into Zelda's hot Buick on our way to meet Inga, I'd repeated to myself, *I'm ready for this. I'm ready.*

"Excited?" Zelda asked as she turned the ignition.

"Nervous," I replied, and I patted her leg to thank her for sticking with me.

Cool air slowly suffused the heat as she drove. I pressed my forehead against the window to watch Durango's arid landscape speed by. I found it beautiful in a stark and unrepentant sort of way. It seemed a brutal land to get lost in, the blond sandstone cliffs and gnarled pinyons more like a warning than a summons to wander. I wondered if my son had grown up thinking this landscape was inhospitable, or if it delighted and enticed him, or if it was mere background to his upbringing and he barely noticed it at all.

We crossed the river where it was wide and rushing, tumbling in fits of white water and spinning eddies even in early September, rimmed with yellow rocks and willows and ragged cottonwood groves. The sign on the bridge read, "Animas River," and, in smaller letters beneath, "Rio de las Animas." The River of Souls, as I recalled from Inga Tate's story, where my son had sought solace.

"Zelda, pull over," I said.

At her first chance, she left the road and parked.

I walked across the hot silt to the river's edge. The water's roar obscured the sound of birds and nearby traffic; the tall cottonwoods eclipsed the arid land all around. It was just the Animas and me and my mental image of a boy throwing stones into the current. I had never seen a river so similar to the one I had lost, the once wild-and-free stretch of the Gunnison that had nourished Iola's fields and my childhood in equal measure. I removed my shoes, rolled my trousers, and stepped into the cold flow to just stand there, where my son might have stood, rapt by the clear waters. I wondered if he had listened to what those waters had to say about love and time just as I had, and, if so, perhaps I might not be such a surprise to him after all.

WHEN WE PULLED UP to a small brick house with a manicured front lawn, a woman with short dark hair was sitting in a wicker chair on the front porch. I fumbled with my purse as Zelda reached over with a gentle caress to my shoulder.

"Ready?" she asked.

"Okay," I replied. *Okay*, I thought, reminding myself that this was true.

I opened the door into the rush of heat. Zelda scurried around the car to help me stand.

Behind her, the woman had risen and was descending the porch steps.

I wanted to say something, but the woman was coming nearer, her face bubbling up through the mud of memory. Then Inga Tate was greeting us from the opened gate, and Zelda was tenderly coaxing me, and I was walking unsteadily forward.

Our eyes locked and Inga lurched toward me. She clutched my hands between both of hers, pulling them to her chin and holding them there as if in prayer. Her brimming tears told me she had held me in her heart these many years, just as I had held her, in such an odd but certain way, two mothers of the same beautiful boy. I freed a hand to wrap my arm around her shoulder, and this stranger who was not a stranger collapsed into the embrace. For a long moment we both disappeared into the brutal ache of all we had given and lost, clinging to each other as if we might be torn apart by a sudden gust of wind.

I whispered into her sweetly scented hair the words I had for two decades been longing to say: "Thank you, thank you, thank you, thank you."

She shook her head against my shoulder and, when she eventually pulled away, she looked at me with sad eyes and spoke the words I least expected.

"I'm sorry," she whispered.

"Inga, no," I replied.

She held up a flat palm to halt my protest, and I realized that she, too, had been holding what she needed to say for far too long.

"I'm sorry I kept him from you," she said. "And I'm even more sorry that I lost him."

Twenty-Five

I nga and I sat for over an hour in her tidy yellow kitchen after Zelda drove away. We said all we could stand to say, each gracing the other with details and sympathy, until Inga rose to go freshen her face, allowing us both some silence after our shared stories and tears.

I pictured Lukas and his brother Max at the Formica kitchen table, where they had grown from toddlers to men. Lukas most loved spaghetti with meatballs, Inga had told me, and the German apple cake her mother had taught her to bake. I considered how every meal Inga served Lukas at that table, she had served for me. Every bath time and homework hour and comforting hug and laundry basket with double the dirty little boy's clothes, she had done for me. When she perceived in Lukas a sense of severed belonging, she had driven him to the clearing to at least try to tell him the truth. It was for her, for him, but also for me. Every day of her loving him was her love in place of mine.

I had finally held the other mother's hands and spilled my story and given her my thanks. But I would never be able to explain the true depth of my gratitude. The details of their family life that Inga had shared left me believing that they were like many families, their lives together a weave of sad and complex and happy and sweet and tragic all at once. They were far from perfect, but, for my son, they had at least been there, and I had not.

I gazed out the window at the massive forked cottonwood in the center of the backyard and recalled the story of Max's broken arm and the false accusations against Lukas. I stared at the yard bench beneath the tree, picturing Inga there by Lukas's side, revealing to him the awful truth before he leapt up and ran, jumping the fence and disappearing. I felt the strangeness of knowing their family's private details. And I marveled at how so much of their lives, in the bizarre and twisted way of the world, had been put into motion by my walk to town on an October day when I was seventeen years old. It had even played a peculiar role in Inga finally asking her cruel husband for a divorce, emboldened, she told me, by the courage she found in making the decision to find me, in finally writing her story and delivering the pages that had brought me to her.

"Victoria?" Inga stood at the kitchen doorway. "Please, come look."

I followed her to the living room, where she had spread photographs across the glass-topped coffee table.

"I thought you'd like to see these," she said.

My heart pounded. My family had never bothered to own a camera. I had no photographs of my past, of the people and land I had loved and lost. And yet, there, right before me, was a square Koda-chrome of Wil.

I lifted the photo with a shaky hand. The muscular teen in white T-shirt and jeans posed in a rose garden, his gentle dark-brown eyes and generous smile hurling me through time. I studied the image, unable to stop my stare.

"Lukas on his seventeenth birthday," Inga said.

"He's . . . lovely," I said, reminding myself to breathe.

Inga handed me another photo—a black and white of two swad-dled infants in a double stroller, one of them my Baby Blue, exactly as I remembered his precious face. I eased myself unsteadily onto the flowered sofa. She handed me more: a diapered baby with a toothless grin crawling across a braided rug; a proud toddler astride a tricycle; gap-toothed brothers wearing pointed birthday-party hats; two skinny preteens riding matching bicycles. I ached for all I had lost by not being the mother on the other side of the camera, never knowing my child's voice or the subtle ways he had grown and changed each day.

"I took this one just a couple of weeks before he left," said Inga, handing me a Polaroid of Lukas laughing, seated at the kitchen table where Inga and I had just bared our souls. "Oh, his smile," she said. "So easy and sweet . . . ." Her voice caught and we were quiet.

"Victoria," she said when she could go on, tracing his face with her fingertip. "Look. The arch of his eyes, his nose and chin. There's so much of you in him."

I saw only Wil. "I suppose," I said anyway. "His skin . . . ."

Inga smiled and nodded. "It darkened as he aged," she said.

"Yes," I said. I stared at the photograph and felt suddenly un-settled.

If, as Wil once told me, there were more folks like Seth than stars in the night sky, Lukas had surely endured the venom of Seth's kind all his life. Inga's story of the bigoted taxidermist calling him a half-breed was most likely only the beginning. I longed to tell him all I knew and didn't know about his father, but what if learning of his parents' forbidden love and Wil's brutal death proved far worse for Lukas than his not knowing?

For the first time since I'd left him, I felt he was my son to protect.

"What if everything I have to tell him hurts too much?" I asked. "We have no idea what it is like to be Lukas. To understand what he is running from, or running to. Maybe we're not the ones to help him."

Inga nodded thoughtfully.

"You're right. We're not. Lukas's life is up to him. We can only let him know where he comes from, and that he's always been loved," she said. "That's all he needs from you now, Victoria. Then he can choose the rest."

I thought of my farm and the orchard and the North Fork River, of forests and meadows and every perfect thing I had waited so many years to show him. I took another long look at the young man in the photograph. I nodded, agreeing with fate and mystery and all the wild, unpredictable forces sculpting our lives, and vowed to myself to finally invite my baby home.

"How do we tell him that I am ready?" I asked with a quivering voice.

Inga smiled and placed her hand on mine.

"I'll find a way," she said.

Twenty-Six

1971

I stood at the edge of Blue Mesa Reservoir under a hazy spring sky and imagined the remains of my childhood home—collapsed and sodden, perhaps mere nails and doorknobs now—at the bottom of the lake.

Zelda and Inga tossed stones into the water as I paced the shore-line. To the east, I could see the upper Gunnison meandering down the valley until it was absorbed into the reservoir near a new con-crete bridge. So much had changed, but history still clung to me like stabbing, stubborn burs. This seemed to me the proper place for a reunion, a reckoning with the past before turning to the future, but looking at the restless blue water where Iola once stood, I was no longer sure.

The nearby parking area held only pale gravel and Zelda's car, but I couldn't stop glancing in its direction. Inga had sent a letter, and Lukas had replied. I had waited the long and worrisome winter for him to agree to meet and then for his tour of duty to end.

My son would arrive at noon.

Above the reservoir hovered the snowcapped mountains of the Big Blue wilderness, where my baby was born. My eyes traced the route where I had once followed Wil into those hills and to the hut. My heart still ached for all he and I had discovered there about love, and for everything he had risked and lost because of it. The wilderness had since been renamed the Uncompahgre, in homage to the displaced Utes, and I wondered what Wil would think about that, if he'd find it an ironic and insufficient attempt at redemption, or if he'd simply say, "As you like."

I glanced again at the parking area, then at my two anxious companions. I reached into the pocket of my barn coat and removed the twig of pink peach blossoms I had clipped that morning for my son. I inhaled the sweetness and twirled the twig between my fingers to watch the delicate flowers spin; then I gazed at the reservoir, picturing the orchard and the town and the wild river I once knew. I checked my watch. It was almost noon.

I eyed the length of empty highway on the other side of the bridge. I could not deny that I feared my son's disappointment—at his scandalous conception, at his father's cruel death and lack of justice, at my leaving him behind and starting my life over. Part of me questioned if he would come at all, or if he would take the opportunity to rebuke me, and Inga, by failing to show. And yet I felt optimistic too. I had chosen to meet on these shores because my rising wisdom understood that I must carry my whole past alongside the new space I had created in myself for hope.

As the thin clouds parted and the water sparkled with sunlight, I wondered at the sense of it all—this journey I have called my life, so like this drowned river that keeps being a river even as it is forced to be a lake, moving forward against obstacle and dam, continuing to flow with all it has gathered because it knows no other way.

A dusty silver pickup truck turned off Highway 50, crossed the bridge, and pulled slowly into the parking lot. Zelda and Inga sprang to attention. Zelda's face lit with triumph, as if helping me to find my son had soothed her own pained heart, as if reclaiming him was a small victory for mourning mothers everywhere.

Inga came to my side and searched my eyes for solidarity. I returned the peach blossoms to my pocket. I reached for Inga's hand, and then I reached for Zelda's. We stood there, three women, waiting for what came next.

A young man in a white T-shirt and jeans stepped from the truck and, for an unsettling instant, rewrote history. I wondered if I had been terribly, tragically mistaken—if, in fact, Wil had lived, and the bloody body found dumped over the steep edge of the Black Canyon was another boy after all.

"It's Lukas," Inga whispered as if intuiting my need for confirmation, a shaky jumble of awe and relief in her voice. She tightened her grip on my hand, and I squeezed in reply.

He looked out across the water and then turned to us with a nervous grin. I saw him then not as a likeness of Wil or of me, but as himself, his solid soldier's stance and surprisingly angular jawline, not a boy at all but a man who had known loss and loneliness and war yet had summoned the courage to arrive here to meet me. He plunged his hands into his pockets and tilted his head, squinting at me uncertainly, and in that instant, I also recognized him, my memory flooding with the moment he first opened his newborn eyes and gazed at me in a similar way, when I somehow felt I already knew my child, just as I knew him still.

Though I could not feel my legs beneath me, I took a step forward on pure faith. Zelda and Inga let go of my hands and nudged me ahead on my own.

My son walked toward me, as I walked toward him, each trusting that the earth would hold us as we made our way along the pebbled shore.

Acknowledgments

My appreciation must first go to my agent extraordinaire, Sandra Bond. Sandra, thank you for seeing something special in this novel even when it had not yet fully become itself, and for working tirelessly to find its perfect home. Your encouragement and friendship throughout this journey have meant the world to me.

My enormous gratitude also goes to Cindy Spiegel for taking a chance on me. Cindy, your editing expertise, patience, deep heart, good humor, and faith brought this book to life. I can never thank you enough. It is a joy and an honor to work with Cindy, Julie Grau, and the entire Spiegel & Grau team. Thanks to Nicole Dewey, Liza Wachter, Amy Metsch, Andy Tan-Delli Cicchi, Jackie Fischetti, Stephan Moore, Shaya D'Ornano, and Nora Tomas, as well as to Jeff Farr, Meighan Cavanaugh, Barrett Briske, and Charlotte Strick and Claire Williams of Strick & Williams. My gratitude and downright awe also go to Susanna Lea and her colleagues Mark Kessler, Susie Finlay, and Lauren Wendelken for so determinedly introducing *Go as a River* to the world, and to Jane Lawson, Larry Finlay, Alison Barrow, and Vicky Palmer for their enthusiasm and expertise. To all, I could never have expected such a perfect mix of kindness and professionalism at every turn of this process, and I thank you.

Heartfelt thanks to my incredibly supportive family, friends, community, and colleagues, who have encouraged and celebrated me at every stage of writing this book. I hope you know who you are and how much I cherish you. Special thanks to my earliest readers and steadfast cheerleaders—above all, my husband, my daughter, my mom, and my beloved friends Alison Catmur and Jackie Burt, as well as my dear ones Jason Burns, Sean Madsen, Jennifer Read, Jeremy Burns, Mark Bosso, Kiplynn Dickson, Kay Forsythe, Kathy Burns, Jenny Pankratz, Emma Burt, Lynn Sikkink, and Deb Reid. My aunt Joanne Hall and friend Marie Vargas would most certainly have been early readers if they were here, but are still, no doubt, supporting me from beyond. Thank you to Dawn Ehlers and Bill Depper for decades of bedrock friendship, and to Virginia Catmur for her hospitality, generosity, and keen editorial eye; and to my CB ladies and all of our remarkable kids. I'm also grateful for the support of local arts champions Crested Butte Arts Center, Gunnison Center for the Arts, Vita Institute, and Townie Books.

Thank you to my teachers, who believe words and stories matter— William Wiser, Bin Ramke, Donald Revell, Eric Gould, Jan Whitt, Susan Stewart, Alan Singer, Toby Olsen, William Van Wert—and to my students at Western Colorado University and Orsch, who have inspired me beyond measure. My understanding of Gunnison County history is deeply enriched by local treasures and storykeepers: my colleagues and polka buddies Duane Vandenbusch and George Sibley, the venerable Glo Cunningham, Crested Butte Mountain Heritage Museum, and Gunnison Pioneer Museum. Any historical errors or fictional imaginings are entirely my own. I am also deeply honored and humbled to have learned from Isabelle Walker and Louise Benali of the Diné Nation at Big Mountain, many generous members of the Lakota Nation at Pine Ridge and Cheyenne River, the good folks at Re-Member, and University of Colorado scholar Charles F. Wilkinson. Lee Bradley of Orchard Valley Farms in Paonia and Doug Mattice of Mattice's Fruits & Vegetables in Hotchkiss were kind enough to help me learn about peaches. The teachings of

Thich Nhat Hanh and Anam Thubten have inspired my best life as well as my novel's title. And I'm grateful to my grandfather Ferman Burns for teaching me history and our family's stories, and to the Burns clan and Read clan and my long line of tenacious, humble, Colorado-loving ancestors.

My deepest gratitude and love go to my mom and dad, Kathryn and Richard, whose unwavering love and support in everything I do has made all the difference; to my brother and friend, Chris, kind and true man of the mountains; to my brother, Scott, animal whisperer, so deeply missed; to my grandmother Maxine Read, best person I'll ever know; to our loyal rescue pup and friend, Beanie O'Sullivan, forever by my side; to my beautiful, beautiful children, Avery and Owen, who romp in the woods and skip river stones with me and bring such light to my life and to this world; and to my brilliant husband, Erik, my biggest fan, who cried every time he read this novel (which, bless him, was many, many times) and encouraged me to never give up.

Finally, thank you to the mountains and rivers of the Gunnison Valley for nurturing me and my children, and to the resilient, wild, weird, and wonderful valley residents, who, past and present, have shared and cared for this place. May we cherish the land and one another in homage to all who came before and will come after.

About the Author

SHELLEY READ is a fifth-generation Coloradoan who lives with her family in the Elk Mountains of the Western Slope and is most at home on a mountaintop. She was a senior lecturer at Western Colorado University for nearly three decades, where she taught writing, literature, environmental studies, and Honors, and was a founder of the Environment & Sustainability major and a support program for first-generation and at-risk students. Shelley holds degrees in writing and literary studies from the University of Denver and Temple University's Graduate Program in Creative Writing. She is a regular contributor to *Crested Butte Magazine* and *Gunnison Valley Journal*, and is a board member for the Vita Institute for the Arts.